THE ARMITAGE LEGACY

Book One

The Armitage Family Saga

Jane James

THIS BOOK IS DEDICATED TO THE MEMORY OF NANCY ADAMS WHO WAS A SOURCE OF CONSTANT INSPIRATION TO ME AND A MUCH LOVED NAN.

THE ARMITAGE LEGACY

Jane James was raised in Derbyshire in a small market town on the edge of the Peak District. She studied at St David's University College, Lampeter, gaining a degree in History and Theology. She then went on to work for the National Trust. After meeting her husband, Roy, she spent many years in Stoke-on-Trent raising four children and working in various primary schools in the area. In 2006 she returned to her roots and now concentrates on writing, gardening, hiking in the countryside and looking after her large family. This is her first novel and was inspired by memories of her family and a love of the county she lives in.

Acknowledgements.

For Roy, David, Richard, Jenny and Beth. You make it all worthwhile.

PROLOGUE

February 1901

On a bitterly cold day on 2nd February 1901, the crowds stood silently as Queen Victoria's coffin made its way to St George's Chapel where a state funeral was held. Two days later, Queen Victoria was taken to Frogmore Mausoleum to rest beside her husband, Prince Albert.
On the same afternoon, 130 miles north, an eleven-year-old girl with tousled mousy brown hair stood in St Peters Churchyard in Derby with her coat wrapped tightly around her. The wind howled through the trees, and the crows spiralled upwards into a stormy sky. The dustbins of the countryside whirled like dervishes as Betty Armitage was laid to rest.
Only a handful of people were gathered at the graveside as the vicar's rich baritone voice filled the silent space around him. Agnes Massey watched the simple pine coffin, holding her former neighbour, descend into the bowels of the earth. Another one gone, she reflected. Soon there would be nobody left she knew of her generation. Growing old had its compensations, but loneliness wasn't one of them.
Agnes glanced around at the other "mourners." One middle-aged, slightly rotund lady caught her eye and gave an almost imperceptible nod as if she might recognise Agnes. Agnes certainly didn't remember the other two women and the solitary man scattered around the grave. They also didn't seem to know one another and seemed strangely

disconnected from the scene that was being played out in front of them.

Maybe, Agnes thought, they had turned out to add a bit of interest to an otherwise dismal morning. She'd been guilty of it herself – seeing the obituary in the paper of someone she vaguely knew and convincing herself that it was only right that she should go and say her goodbyes. If truth be told, it was more of an excuse to get dressed up and an opportunity to break the monotony of the daily routine.

Agnes had known Betty more when they had both been young women just starting out. However, though they had shared the usual daily banter as neighbours would Agnes had never really connected with Betty, finding her at times a little abrasive and hard to get to know. Jack, Betty's husband, on the other hand, always had time for a laugh and joke and was well-liked in Alfreton.

Agnes had felt a momentary sadness when she heard of his death about ten years previously. However, it was curiosity that had mainly come to the fore. After all, once she'd left Alfreton and moved to the town centre, she'd rarely seen either of them. It was said that he'd killed himself by falling downstairs. An accident, so it was believed. However, there had been rumours in Peel Street that he'd had one or two more whiskeys than might have been prudent. There'd also been an ugly rumour that Betty had spied her chance and pushed him. Most people had dismissed this as idle gossip though Betty had been known to have a temper. Agnes had seen her on several occasions thump one of the children when they wouldn't do as they were told. She'd also been known to bolt the door against Jack if he came back from the local a bit worse for wear on payday.

Still, Agnes thought, there was nothing wrong in keeping your children under control and teaching them right from wrong, and a woman was bound to get worried if she thought her husband was drinking away the money intended to put food on the table for the next week. It was all water off a duck's back, anyway, now. Betty and Jack lay side by side for an eternity, as did Victoria and Albert, and God would judge them as he thought fit.

Anyway, there were more pressing matters to consider now that she had done her duty. Was it to be fish or mutton for tea, and could she afford to buy either? Her mind now preoccupied; Agnes didn't notice the young girl standing about twenty yards away. She was partially concealed by the trunks of the massive elm trees that towered above the south end of the churchyard.

Lily's piercing blue eyes followed Agnes's progress and then she turned in the opposite direction. Unnoticed she made her way onto the high street. Visitors to the church would probably have considered her of no significance to the primary business of the day. Just another passer-by come to pay her respects to the dearly departed.

CHAPTER ONE

February 1901

And where have you been up to now? Our tea isn't going to grow itself in our backyard now is it?" Ethel pushed her hair out of her rosy face as she bent over the gas stove. "I hope you bartered with Mr Jackson and got a bit off those spuds this time around. His last lot weren't fit to give to the pigs."
"In case you hadn't noticed, we haven't got any pigs, love," Bert spoke calmly from his usual position in the battered wing armchair that stood on one side of the empty grate. Most of the rest of the kitchen was dominated by the stove and a large wooden trestle table surrounded by a clutter of pots, pans, kettles, pastry cutters, jelly moulds, and other antiquated objects that Ethel had inherited on her mother's death. Most of them had come from the farmhouse where Ethel had grown up until her father was killed in a freak farm accident and her mother, sister, and herself moved to the city.
Lily envied the freedom that her mother had seemed to have when she was a child. The owner of the farm had been away a lot living it up, mainly in the South of France, and Ethel's family had pretty much had the run of the place. Ethel had spent many happy hours roaming the countryside and lanes of Kirk Langley with her sister, Dorothy. Lily wondered that if "Big Jim" had not been killed whether she might have been born where the air was fresher and skies larger instead of being incarcerated in this hovel with these people.

She loved her mum; of course, she did. Everybody loved their mothers, didn't they? However, Lily didn't want to grow up to be like her mother. Ethel was always out of bed before first light and seemed to spend her whole day cooking, cleaning, washing and scrimping for goods on the high street so that she could knock together a half-decent meal. When Lily was older, she was going to be someone, and she knew exactly how she was going to achieve it.
"What else have you got in there, Lil?" Bert smiled across at his daughter as she unceremoniously dumped the string bag with the vegetables onto the table saving an onion as it made an escape bid for the floor.
"Oh, just a few bits and bobs from the market," Lily answered directing her words towards Ethel. "You'll probably be able to make a tasty stew out of them anyway. Mr Jackson was in a good mood today and gave me a bit of scrag end as well. Said it had probably got another day in it."
"That's grand, love. Go and sit and take the weight off your feet and chat with your dad for a few minutes while I get these peeled and into the pot." Ethel busied herself getting the vegetables out of the bag.
What Lily wanted to do was go upstairs and immerse herself in "Alice's Adventures in Wonderland" for half an hour. Mr Poynton had called round with it last week and given it to Ethel telling her Lily could borrow it for as long as she wanted.
"You can read it as well, Mrs Armitage, if the mood takes you, "he had joked with Ethel. Lily had been able to tell that her mum had been pleased, as Ethel went off into her slightly shrill "posh" voice that she reserved for special occasions. Everybody liked young Mr Poynton even though he hadn't been teaching at the school long.
His grey-green eyes had glinted in the early evening sunlight as he had looked towards Lily who had been busy hot

starching her father's shirt for next day. She didn't see the point of it as he rarely went anywhere, but since leaving the school, she had been expected to pull her weight around the house.

Lily had felt vaguely embarrassed at Mr Poynton seeing her with her sleeves rolled up, hair in her face, and sweat running down her cheeks from the steam in the kitchen. She wanted him to see her as a sophisticated, well-read young lady rather than a drudge. Lily always dreamt of being transported to the worlds she read about and would have given anything to live in the upmarket end of town where a girl's main problem seemed to be what dress to wear to the next social event she was invited to attend. The only downside of that would be that Mr Poynton wouldn't visit and to Lily that was unthinkable.

Maggie, Lily's best friend, had laughed at her when she talked about his visits and the books. She said Lily had a crush on him. Lily wasn't quite sure what that meant. Maggie was a year older than her and sometimes came out with things that Lily didn't understand. However, if what Maggie said meant that Lily would marry Mr Poynton one day, then she guessed that Maggie must be right.

"And what else have you been up to this afternoon while your mother's been slaving away?" Bert said half-jokingly, bringing Lily back down to planet Earth with a jolt. Bert gestured to the simple wooden chair that stood on the other side of the hearth and Lily reluctantly went to sit down.

"Nothing much," Lily mumbled as she wondered what both would have said if she blurted out that she had been to her grandmother's funeral. The devil in her tempted her, but she had vague memories of when she was about six or seven years old. She'd decided that somewhere in the world, her mother and father must have a mother and father of their own. After all, they hadn't been found under a gooseberry bush as Maggie was fond of telling her as well as other things that Lily couldn't make any sense of at the time and knew couldn't possibly be true. Ethel had gently told her that her own parents were both dead. It was the first time she had heard of "Big Jim" and his accident or of Ethel's mum dying of TB shortly after they had moved back to the city. Her father, Lily remembered, hadn't said anything and just stared stony-faced into the fire. When Lily had tentatively questioned her mother again, Ethel had guided her away and quietly said, "Your dad's mum and dad are dead to him as well."

At the time Lily had thought, "well that's that," so when about three years later, she had heard about her grandmother's death through overhearing a neighbour, it had made no sense at all to her. Maybe that's what made her turn left to the church and not right to the shops when she had set off after dinner. Even at just eleven years old, Lily knew that it wasn't always a good idea to tell the whole truth. She'd heard her mother talk about "white lies," and she gauged that this might just be the time to tell one.

"I went up first to have a look in the window of that toy shop on the corner. You know the one just before you turn down into Marygate."

"What did you want to waste your time doing that for when you know your mother's waiting on her tatties?" Bert tapped his pipe on the side of the hearth in a staccato motion that set Lily's nerves on edge.

"Well, first, I thought if I got to the market a bit later there would be some bargains, and it's James's birthday soon. Maggie told me they'd got plasticine for sale up there. You know how he's always interested in something a bit different and I just wanted to see how much it cost."

"What's plasticine? Never heard of it," Ethel shouted above the sound of chopping vegetables.

"It's some new-fangled modelling clay. Been around for a year or two now, but I don't see the point in wasting good money on it," Bert replied from the depths of his armchair.
"Perhaps not," Lily sighed, not being surprised at her father's attitude. "I'll get him a book instead."
"You and your books," Ethel chided. "Anyway, it's not for weeks yet, and he's too young for books."
Lily didn't agree but decided to hold her tongue.
"Anyway," Ethel carried on, "have you heard about all the fuss up at the school?"
Bert leaned forward in his chair, fixing Lily with his watery hazel eyes. "It appears that your nice Mr Poynton isn't quite so nice after all. It's a good job you're out of that place else it could have been you."
"What are you on about? What's Alex done?" Lily almost shouted at Bert and then bit down hard on her lip as she saw the glowering look on her father's face.
"Oh, Alex is it now? Pardon me, but I didn't know that you were on quite such friendly terms with our local ex-schoolmaster." Bert's veins seemed to almost pop out of his neck as he stared at Lily across the hearth.
"Calm down Bert." Ethel put her hand gently on his shoulder." You know our Lily's a good girl, and he only lent her a couple of books. You know that's all, love."
"Well, none of that will be going on anymore anyway. Your precious Mr Poynton will probably end up in prison." Bert said in a slightly calmer voice.
Lily felt her heart beating faster. "You're talking rubbish, you are."
"No, I am not, my lady, and mind your manners. You want to know the truth about your precious Mr Poynton. He's been interfering with Maisy Dawkins – the dirty swine."
"Mind your language, Bert. She doesn't know what you're talking about." Ethel scolded.

"I'm not a child. I know exactly what he's on about, but it's all a load of nonsense and lies. Mr Poynton isn't like that. You know that mum." Lily pleaded.

"I'm afraid it is true love," Ethel replied gently, seeing the stricken look on Lily's face. "Bill Hawkins says he got their Maisy in a room on her own after school and well..."

Lily felt herself trembling and sweat dripping down her face. She moved over to the small window that looked out onto the yard so that she couldn't see either of their faces. The kitchen felt even more claustrophobic than it usually did. Ever since she had left school last year, Lily had felt her horizon narrowing and every day felt much like the one before. Today, however, ravaged by the day's events, she didn't feel that would necessarily be a bad thing.

"Anyway, you won't have any time to worry about things that don't concern you soon. Come Monday you're starting a new job." Bert's voice came to Lily as though from the end of a long tunnel- audible but distant until his words filtered through and she understood what he was talking about.

"It's at Royal Crown Derby on Osmaston Road. Just making tea for the lads, writing a few letters, keeping the place tidy. It'll help towards the bills, love," Ethel interceded.

"And where have you managed to find me this little number from?" Lily retaliated. She knew she was being unreasonable but couldn't help it. If she didn't get angry, she would cry, and she wasn't going to give her father any more ammunition today.

"Jack Mellor's daughter's ill and is going away for a bit, so it's come open, at least for a few months," Bert answered.

"Why don't you just say it, dad. Amy's pregnant. She's going to have a baby, so she's being shipped off – out of sight, out of mind."

"There's no need to be coarse, Lily," Ethel said sharply. "You should be grateful for the work and be proud that you've only got it because you're educated and know your letters and things."

"You can't make me go. When am I going to get the time to...?"

"To do what, my girl?" Bert spat out." You sit in your room most of the day and fill your head with fairy stories. You're lucky. Maggie's ended up at the hall like most of the girls around here. Half a day off every other Sunday and you're moaning about a job on the doorstep where you'll come home every night."

"Maggie's happy with it though, so don't worry about that," Ethel said, trying to smooth the waters. "She says they're good to her, so that's something in today's day and age."

"Good to her!" Lily spluttered. "She's not a poor whipped puppy dragged in from the cold to do their bidding. Maybe she's not as bright as me, but that doesn't mean she should be treated like a slave."

"Just hark at you, Lady Muck." Bert was almost purple with rage. "It's about time you realised which side your bread is buttered on."

"Just leave it, dad. You wouldn't know what aspiration was if it flew up and hit you in the face."

"You can use all the fancy words you like, but the fact remains you're going," Bert replied.

"And you can stop talking to your father like that, "Ethel interrupted, wiping her hands on her apron. "It's because of him you've never had to go to bed hungry or cold."

"And so, I have to be grateful for that for the rest of my life and never try to be anything other than what you are trying to mould me into? What about James? You've got him earmarked for Oxford before he's barely out of nappies."

"One day James will have a wife and family, and he needs to be the very best he can be for them," Bert answered.

"What, like you've been for us, Dad -the very best?"

Bert sighed, and all the fight seemed to disappear from him. "I can't talk to you anymore, Lily. There's nothing else to say. At least nothing that you will listen to."

Bert had always seemed a grey character of a man to Lily, and she had been momentarily surprised by his passionate outburst. She had to admit that a part of her was disappointed that he had once again shrunk back into his shell.

"Go on up, love, and have a lie down before tea. You look tired." Ethel lightly touched Bert's shoulder. "I'll give you a shout when tea's ready."

Lily couldn't understand her mother at times. How could she care for a man who just sat there staring into space for vast portions of the day while she worked her fingers to the bone to make life easier for him?

"Do you want me to help you with that?" Lily muttered to her mother's back as Ethel got busy filling up the kettle. At first, Lily thought she wasn't going to answer at all until Ethel said with a sigh, "No, go up to your room, Lily. You've said enough for one day, but you will be at Crown Derby at eight sharp on Monday, and then you will be there every working day after that until God shines on you more favourably."

Lily noticed a catch in her mother's voice and wondered if she was crying but then dismissed it as one of her "flights of fantasy," as her father would have called it.

"Well, call me if you need me," Lily said softly as she turned to make her way upstairs. Deep down she knew that it wasn't wrong to want to better herself in life, so didn't understand why she felt warm tears trickling down her cheeks as she made her way up the narrow staircase to her attic room.

CHAPTER TWO

February 1901

The bitter wind that swept across a grey barely awake Derby town centre seemed fitting to the mood that Lily found herself in. She trudged head down against the driving rain pulling her shawl more tightly around her as she hurried to catch the bus that would drop her off at the end of Osmaston Road.

A couple of young women on bicycles whizzed past. Despite the early hour and the inclement weather, they were chatting animatedly and obviously looking forward to their day ahead. Lily envied them their apparent freedom and confidence. One of them was even brave enough to sport the emerging fashion of cycling trousers. Much less encumbering Lily thought as she hitched up her skirt above her boots to avoid another puddle knowing that her place in hell might as well be booked, as far as her mother was concerned, if she came home wearing a pair of them.

"Cheer up love. It might never happen," a young man going in the opposite direction lifted his cap to her. Lily gave the man a half smile to set him up for the day. Deep down she knew she was irrational. Young girls of her class after leaving school were expected to help support their families, and it wasn't James's fault he had been born the correct sex to stand a chance of achieving some of his ambitions. She wasn't jealous of James – not really. How could she be when he was barely a babe out of arms? It was just when she thought of her father sitting by the fire all day long not doing a tap and her mum working from dawn to dusk to keep the house going it made her blood boil. It seemed that keeping a family going unless you had wealth and privilege, was an all-consuming process. Surely her mum had some days where she wanted to walk out and never look back leaving them all to it.

It had been a horrible weekend. Lily hadn't intended to hurt her mother, but she knew that she had, even though she wasn't entirely clear on the reasons why. Ethel, unusually, hadn't been up when Lily had crept out of the house that morning for which she was grateful. Lily had heard her getting up at least a couple of times in the night, so maybe she had overslept, or perhaps just hadn't wanted to face Lily. Over the past couple of days, you could have cut the atmosphere with a knife, and for once she had been pleased to hear James's tantrums splitting the silence. Hearing about Alex had about put the top on it though she still couldn't quite believe what her father said was true but then what reason would he have to make it up. And then there had been her grandmother's funeral.

She smiled wistfully as she remembered Alex telling her what a bright girl, he thought that Lily was and that she would go far. Alex had come from the right side of the tracks though and remained eternally optimistic about the world in general. Well, I'm sorry to disappoint you Mr Poynton she thought to herself, but I don't feel that I've come very far up to now and bright or not I can't understand why grandma has been shuffled out of sight as though she never existed. Lily vaguely wondered if anyone would pay for a headstone or lay flowers on the grave, but she only considered it in a remote unattached way. She'd never been allowed to know her grandmother so felt no secure emotional attachment to her. It had been curiosity more than anything that had told her mind to say to her feet to walk towards the churchyard last week.

It all seemed a bit surreal anyway now, Lily mused as she boarded the bus. She took a deep breath as she squashed onto a seat beside a lady wearing one of the incredibly large hats that seemed to be creeping into fashion amongst the higher echelons. Lily scowled as she narrowly missed having her eye taken out by the sharp end of one of the hat pins that secured the hat to the lady's pompadour hairstyle. The bus driver must have been half asleep as well as Lily knew that women were not allowed to wear unprotected hat pins on the buses. She felt the lady shift her position slightly to avoid contacting the "unwashed." Lily wondered why she was even on the bus in the first place as she looked the type who should have had her own personal chauffeur attending to her every need at the very least.

Lily adjusted the navy ribbon that held her long tresses together at the nape of her neck and then flicked her wet ponytail clear of her shawl narrowly missing the "posh" lady's face. Lily stifled a giggle as she heard the lady's sharp intake of breath as Lily continued to study the passing world through the opposite window. The most fun she had had all week, she thought as she settled in for the short bus ride.

By the time she had alighted and walked about halfway along Osmaston Road, a weak sun had managed to break through the gloom of the morning. The red brick buildings of the factory had now come into view on the other side of the road. The central part of the building had tall rectangular windows that stood almost as tall as the factory itself. The rest of the building seemed to consist of two stories which seemed only slightly less imposing. Lily felt her heart banging uncommonly fast as she wiped her sweaty palms on her navy skirt, which was a little bedraggled from the damp.

She knew that the building had originally been one of the workhouses and had been sold to Royal Crown Derby about a quarter of a century ago. Her father had filled in the historical details for her during a slight lull in the tension of the weekend. A small part of Lily had been begrudgingly impressed by his knowledge though she justified it with the reasoning that he had to do something with all the spare time he spent idling around the house.

Lily straightened her shawl, brushed down her hair with her hands and took a few moments for her panic attack to subside. After all, she thought she was far better off than many of the sick children and mothers who had been forced to darken the door of the workhouse for want of anywhere else to go. Stepping into the entrance hall, her fear subsided a little more. It felt airy and clean. There were a couple of gangly foreign looking plants in large earthenware containers that gave the area a sense of the exotic. Lily thought they looked a little like something Robinson Crusoe may have come across – another book that Alex had persuaded her to read. Not that Lily had enjoyed it very much. She'd always thought Robinson to be a bit of a tramp. To be fair though, as Alex had pointed out, if you had to spend thirty years on a remote desert island, encountering cannibals and mutineers before being rescued, your personal hygiene might have slipped a little.

"Yes, young woman, may I help you?" A rather formidable middle-aged lady with a huge bun situated on the crown of her head and delicate pink rose tucked behind her left ear rose from behind a Remington typewriter to peruse Lily. Lily wasn't sure if she was more overawed by the lady or the typewriter. It was the first one she'd ever seen though she had heard the clacking of the keys of the one behind the doors of the hallowed school office.

Her eyes drifted towards the pink rose that looked a little incongruous in such a sombre setting though she supposed the lady must have a reason for it.

"Well! Do I pass muster, child?" The lady fixed Lily with a beady stare though if Lily had been a little less petrified, she might have noticed the slight give away quirk of the lady's lip.

"I'm here for the job!" Lily stuttered feeling a blush beginning to creep through her body making her feel a little faint.

"Oh, the job! Well, there's the Deputy Manager's job coming up shortly or maybe the caretakers. I think he's leaving us soon. He was over the hill ten years ago, if the truth is told, so you might stand a chance there or..."

A rush of cold air entered the room.

"That's enough, Miss Hardcastle. You've had your fun for the day."

"Yes, Mr Anthony. Of course." Miss Hardcastle said turning to the smartly dressed slightly balding middle-aged man who had just come in. Lily suspected that Miss Hardcastle would have had plenty more to say if it wasn't for the interruption, but the man who had entered the conversation didn't look cross, just amused. Maybe the stories Lily had heard about women being treated like second-class citizens by the men who employed them was a myth. The thought was ripped away before it had barely had time to formulate.

"This is our latest dogs' body, Miss Hardcastle. Come to keep us all on the straight and narrow and more importantly make us copious amounts of tea on demand.

"Let's hope she lasts longer than Amy Mellor anyway, Mr Anthony."

"I think she's a bit too young to get up the duff, my dear but then again none of them nowadays seem to be able to keep their knickers on until they're married. Well come along then, Miss Armitage isn't it? We'll get you started. Time is money and all that."

The obnoxious man turned his back on Lily, gave Miss Hardcastle a wink and proceeded to make his way to the door that Lily presumed led to the central part of the factory. Lily felt herself getting hotter by the minute, but her nerves had evaporated in the wake of her anger. Nobody was so crucial that they could talk to people as though they were something nasty, they had stepped on in the street.

"You can't talk to..." Lily began but didn't get the chance to continue as Miss Hardcastle touched her lightly on the shoulder and shook her head furiously.

"Hold your tongue girl...at least for now," Miss Hardcastle whispered fiercely as Mr Anthony continued his journey along the corridor like a warship fully equipped for battle. If he wanted a confrontation, Lily knew that she could be the one to give it to him but for some reason, she trusted this woman and would do what she asked – at least for now. Lily gave a quick nod and screwed her hands into two tight balls like she often did when she was trying to bite back her words. She wasn't always successful, but this time sensed that it would be in her best interests to bide her time.

"I'm right behind you, Mr Anthony, Sir," Lily called down the corridor and quickened her pace to catch up with the receding figure. What a day, Lily thought, though it certainly hadn't been lacking in interest. She was also beginning to realise that, as the Bible taught them in Sunday school, it was maybe time to start to put away childish things and play the adults at their own game.

CHAPTER THREE

January 1903

"You shouldn't be in here, Lil. You'll get us both in trouble if his nibs walks in."
"Don't worry, Timmy. Sir is out for the day. Gone to Birmingham on important business. At least that's what Miss Hardcastle says." Lily handed a mug of tea to the tousled hair wiry young lad and then plonked herself onto the stool across from the bench where he was working. The lad smiled.
"I give up with you. You'll lose me my job one day."
"While the cats away..." Lily laughed "and anyway we both know what kind of business Mr Anthony is finishing off in the big wicked city."
"If I weren't a man of the world, you'd make me blush, Miss Armitage. Seriously though, Lil, your mouth will get you into hot water one day if you don't zip it."
"Not if I don't let it, Mr Lewis. I know when to keep it shut. Don't you worry about that."
Timothy Lewis thought that she was probably right. She'd always been a bit different to the other girls on the street. Quite often of a night when he was making his way home after a shift at the factory, he'd see her sitting there on her doorstep with her head in her book or leading the other kids up and down the cobbled street inciting them to save the princess from the dragon or some such like.

Not that he'd had that much to do with her before she turned up at the factory – her being a few years younger than him and a girl of course. It was comforting now to have a familiar face a bit closer to his age around than most of the blokes that worked his shift. It wasn't that they excluded him but that they had more in common with each other than him. Also, though Timmy was not a prude – growing up in a small two up and two down with three brothers and two sisters the luxury wasn't available – he found some of their language a bit offensive. Not the words they used but more how they talked about their wives and girlfriends.

"Had to give her a bit of a backhander the other night. Keep her in line you know!"

"Quite right too. It's us that are out all day long slaving our fingers to the bone. They need to be made to appreciate us from time to time."

Timmy knew his own mother wouldn't have stood for any of that talk from his father and besides which he thought a lot of the men in the factory were whiners. There were a lot worse dirty and dangerous jobs out there they could be doing. Two of his brothers worked in the pits. They got paid more than he did but came home at the end of their shift filthy and exhausted. He knew that Bob, the younger one cried himself to sleep every night at the thought of being catapulted back into "the bowels of hell" next day.

Timmy glanced across at Lily swinging her legs from side to side as she drained the last dregs of tea from her mug. Her blue eyes studied him from over the rim. She had a disconcerting habit of staring at most people without realising it most of the time. She was pretty, no doubt about it but he didn't think of her like that at all. She reminded him a bit of his kid sister – funny but wilful, and both prepared to stick their heels in at the slightest provocation. Anyway, he knew that Lily was usually more interested in what he was working on than himself personally.

"You're so lucky you know, Timmy," she said almost as if she had just read his thoughts. "You get to spend your days in here creating works of art while I sit in that pokey back room all day sifting through papers that don't seem very important and occasionally escaping to bring you a much-deserved mug of tea."

"I don't create them, Lil. I just paint them, but you're right some of them are beautiful."

"That looks more like something you would find in a doll's house," Lily remarked watching Timmy apply a striking blue colour to a small coffee pot.

"In a way you're right. This is going to be part of a miniature tea set, and this colour I'm putting on now is called cobalt blue. It makes a charming contrast with the gold and derby red."

"I can't imagine anybody around here buying something like that though. It looks as though it should be produced in a foreign country rather than dismal Derby."

"You're wrong, and you're right." Timmy replied washing his brush off. "First of all, you're wrong about Derby. It's a great town if you look around you a bit and you'd be surprised who will buy this stuff. The managers know exactly which markets to target so at least they have got some uses. You're on the right lines with the design though. It's called Imari and is influenced by the fibres and porcelain that are imported from Japan."

"You certainly know your stuff, Timmy. I'm well impressed."

Timmy was also impressed at how intently Lily seemed to listen to him. Timmy found the whole process fascinating though the only reason he'd got this job in the first place was that he had shown a bit of a flair for art at school and that had somehow got back to one of the bosses. He occasionally tried to talk about his work at home, but his family were too caught up in surviving from day to day to show much interest in which design was selling well or what new painter had come to join the factory that week. It made a change for him to have a captive audience.

Lily was fascinated by the fruit, flowers and foliage that were hand painted onto the bone china. Not that she thought she could do it as she watched Timmy's steady hand as he applied the gold gilt to the rim of the coffee pot lid.

If Lily had married Alex, circumstances might have been different. He'd always encouraged her to expand her horizons, and she knew that he wouldn't have laughed at her dreams to become a famous writer as she travelled the world gathering material. However, since entering the world of work Lily had begun to see how naive her ideas must have seemed to other people around her. She assumed that Alex was in prison now, probably for a very long time and she now saw no reason why he would have been interested in her as anything more than a bright student. Lily wasn't in any rush to marry at all now. Like Timmy, she heard the men at work talking about their spouses as though they were second-class citizens. Lily supposed she had to give her father his due. She had never heard him speak about her mother with anything but respect, but then again, she did virtually everything for him. Lily saw the grey exhaustion on her mother's face at the end of every day. Why would she aspire to that?

She could hardly believe that she had been working here for almost two years now. She wouldn't have said that the time had flown by but at least it had got her out of that depressing house where nobody seemed to have any drive or ambition left in them. With a sigh, Lily dropped down from the stool and gathered up Timmy's mug.

"I'd better get back to it I suppose then."
Timmy made some muttered reply, but it was apparent he was reabsorbed entirely in whatever he was creating. Lily pushed away the small pangs of jealousy and trudged back towards her cell pausing to collect Miss Hardcastle's mug on the way through.

"Thank you, my dear." Miss Hardcastle sat in her usual position, back ramrod straight as she tapped frantically away on the keys of her precious Remington. Miss Hardcastle remained a bit of a dichotomy to Lily. She'd never seen her leave or come to work, and Lily really couldn't imagine her in any other setting. The prominent pink rose was always in situ and fresh though, so she must get them from somewhere. Maybe an amorous suitor crept in, in the dead of night to present her with a new bloom. Lily had noticed that Miss Hardcastle was the only employee in the factory who seemed to get away with much at all from the hierarchy, especially Mr Anthony. Maybe they were having an affair Lily pondered. She supposed it took all sorts, but she just couldn't picture Mr Anthony's fat sausage-like fingers tearing Miss Hardcastle's clothes off and making passionate love to her in the foyer. It seemed to Lily the lady had better taste. She suppressed a laugh as she thought how soft she was sometimes.

"Something amusing, dear?" Miss Hardcastle enquired with her left eyebrow slightly raised and a small smile on her face. Lily always suspected that there was a deep belly laugh, rumbling away somewhere in Miss Hardcastle's physiology, just waiting to escape. Now that would be a sight to behold. Lily shook her head and gave Miss Hardcastle a genuine smile though what she would say if she knew what Lily was thinking. Mostly they only passed the time of the day, and Miss Hardcastle let Lily know what was expected of her each morning, but Lily would always be grateful to her for warning her to keep her mouth shut that first morning she had arrived. She now knew if she had opened her mouth that morning she would have been out of a job by midday. For whatever the reason Lily found Miss Hardcastle far and beyond the most interesting person in the factory.

"Why don't you go half an hour early tonight, dear? Mr Anthony won't be back today, and if you finish up what's on your desk, I haven't got anything else for you either. I won't be long myself."

Lily must have let the surprise show on her face.

"Don't worry girl. St Peter will still grant us both access through the pearly gates when our time comes. It's a lovely afternoon out there so go and enjoy it for once."

Lily had learnt not to ask twice when good fortune came her way and by 4 o'clock she was lifting her face to the sunshine. Having time to herself was luxury. Since starting work her days had developed a routine that varied very little. Saturdays were taken up with helping her mother and Sunday was reserved for administering to her soul at St Peters Church. Not that Lily was sure that she believed in an omnipotent presence, but it seemed to be expected, and she didn't feel passionately enough about it to question it one way or another.

Lily gratefully breathed in the fresh air and decided she would make a small detour and walk home via the Wardwick. She'd always loved this area of Derby with its museum, art gallery and library. It was full of vitality and enthusiasm, and she thought back about what Timmy had said about Derby not being a dismal place and at that moment she couldn't disagree. Lily sat on a bench by one of the vividly coloured raised flower beds and drank in the atmosphere.

She envied the men and women who looked so carefree and relaxed as they went about their late afternoon business. Some were carrying piles of books or huge canvases under their arms, and they all looked purposeful as though they had somewhere important to be or something essential to do. What Lily envied almost as much though was that they had the time to indulge in what her mother and father would have called frivolous activity. She'd seen her father dip into the "Derbyshire Times and Chesterfield Herald "when he managed to pick up a free copy, but she couldn't recall ever seeing her mother with a book. She thought back to how embarrassed she had seemed when Alex came around with books for Lily, at even the suggestion that she might like to try one. Thinking about it when had her mother ever helped her with schoolwork unless it was finishing off a piece of needlework or embroidering a sample? Activities that Lily found arduous and repetitive. An awful thought crossed her mind – suppose her mother couldn't read. Lily knew that many people couldn't but what if her mother was one of them and she hadn't even realised?

"A penny for them. Miss Armitage."

She jumped as a shadow fell across where she was sitting and momentarily blotted out the sun. She looked up into the face of a tall slightly plump well-dressed gentleman. Lily had a vague recollection of seeing him somewhere before but couldn't just place it.

"I'm afraid you have me at a disadvantage, Sir." Lily rose straightening her skirt down and adjusting her navy-blue shawl across her shoulders. The afternoon was now turning a little chilly.

"Please don't rise on my account. It's been a lovely afternoon, and it would be a shame not to enjoy the last few rays. Knowing this country, it could be snowing tomorrow."

Lily smiled and sat down again though this time on the edge of her seat. She wasn't the type to go around having conversations with random gentlemen, and it made her feel a little uncomfortable.

"I apologise, Miss Armitage. I feel that I have got you somewhat flustered and it was never my intention. Henry... Henry Ingram." The gentleman offered his hand to Lily who tentatively shook it briefly.

"I'm one of the main shareholders at Crown Derby, and I have to pop in from time to time just to make sure the wheels of my investment are still in motion."

Lily remembered where she had seen him. It had been about a month ago, and he and Mr Anthony had stopped briefly at Timmy's bench to ask him a couple of questions. She had been doing her usual gathering of mugs duty. At the time she thought he was quite a good-looking man for his age though as she whispered to Timmy, he could maybe cut down on one or two of his Sunday roasts. Timmy had told her not to be so rude but that hadn't stopped him from having to stuff his fist in his mouth to keep from laughing. Now Lily had to admit she felt a little flattered that he had apparently noticed her enough that day to find out her name.

"Mr Anthony tells me that you spend quite a lot of time in the paint room. Miss Armitage. Perhaps more than you ought to, do you think?"

"That's probably true Sir, and I'm sorry Sir. It's just when I bring in the tea and the like and see all the work that's going on in there, I can't always drag myself away as quickly as perhaps I should."

"Curiosity is not a bad quality, Miss Armitage, especially if channelled in the correct direction. I've never known it to kill a cat anyway."

"No Sir. Thank you, Sir, but I think I should be getting away home now. There'll be wondering where I've got to." Lily was beginning to feel a little out of her depth. Kind though the gentleman appeared to be she didn't want it getting back to Mr Anthony that she had been fraternising with her "betters." She needed her job for the moment though one day she planned for the screw to turn but when she was ready.

"Of course, my dear. Off you run then, but I hope that we will see each other again very soon." With a flourish of his top hat, the gentleman turned his back and made his way along the street in the opposite direction to Lily.

What a strange afternoon Lily thought as she quickened her pace. By the time she'd got to the corner of Peel Street though she reasoned that she would probably never set eyes on him again and that would be that.

CHAPTER FOUR

New Year's Day 1906

"Well, what time is this young man of yours going to grace us with his presence?" Ethel called through to Lily who was busy sweeping and sprucing up the backyard for the New Year.
"I'm sorry, Mum. I know he was supposed to come yesterday and anyway he's not that young and more of a friend really."
"Hm. Whatever you say but don't think you can pull the wool over my eyes even though you've spent years trying."
Lily came back into the kitchen pushing back a lock of dark hair that had almost fallen over her right eye.
"Sit down mum, before you fall down."
Ethel looked exhausted, and Lily was worried that the strain of the last few weeks was catching up with her. At the beginning of December Bert's back seemed to take a turn for the worse.
"Lying flat on a wooden board is the trick." Dr Parfitt had postulated after a cursory examination of his patient. Lily knew that it was unfair, but she didn't really trust doctors. Maybe it was because of Maggie's father. One minute he was right as rain with just a slight cough and a week later he was dead. Mitigating circumstances, Maggie, on one of her rare days off, had told Lily. Well, mitigating circumstances or not Bert had been on his back for the best part of three

weeks with either Lily or Ethel going up to him at least a dozen times a day.

Not to be outdone James had developed measles and had been incarcerated in the other bedroom which he usually shared with Lily. Lily had ended up sleeping on a shake me down in the kitchen which hadn't improved her mood. The curtains in James's room had remained tightly closed so that not a chink of light penetrated the room for fear that it could influence his eyesight.

"He'll have to remain there for at least a fortnight...plenty of fluids and rest." Dr Parfitt ordered. James had emerged the day before Christmas Eve. Though weak he was still irrepressible with his mischievous grin and unruly mop of brown hair.

Lily and Ethel had been too tired to really get into the Christmas spirit though Lily was delighted with a copy of "The Hound of the Baskervilles" by Sherlock Holmes.

"You can thank your dad for that, "Ethel said, "because if it had been left to me, you would have got something a bit more practical." Lily found it hard to conceal her surprise as she remembered how her father had blown up when Alex had lent her books in the past, but she supposed that had been five years ago now.

She'd been equally pleased with the birthday present that she had received yesterday – a Kodak Brownie camera. She'd seen them selling in Derby for five shillings and had been tempted to save up for one herself. As always though her birthday had to be shared with the shenanigans of seeing in the New Year.

New Year's Day had dawned with all of them feeling a bit worse for wear though very little drink had passed their lips. Even James was curled up on his bed reading "The Tale of Peter Rabbit." Lily was almost beginning to wish that she hadn't said yes when Henry invited himself around for tea for her birthday.

"Time, I met the parents and all that. Anyway, I couldn't miss out on your sweet sixteenth, could I?"

Well, he had missed out. Some excuse for having to work late at work. Lily didn't see what on earth needed to be done at the factory on New Year's Eve that couldn't wait. Not that she had been sorry really. Birthdays were generally family days, and Henry was a stranger to the rest of them, and maybe a family celebration wouldn't have been the best way to break the ice.

One worry Lily had was how Henry would react to her father. What would he think about a man who never seemed to raise a finger when he was always so busy? She had no worries about her mother. Lily knew that she would conduct herself with good manners and grace as she always did do in company. Lily had always thought her mother could have done better for herself. At times she felt almost ashamed of considering it, but at least it had made her confident she wouldn't be settling for second best.

Since that first meeting at the Wardwick Lily began to see Henry, as she quickly came to think of him, most days. Maybe he'd always been there, and she just became more aware of him. Lily had always thought that she would be at the factory a couple of years at the most and then move on. Meeting Henry had turned those plans on their head.

At first, she'd been flattered and then excited at the attention he gave her. She enjoyed seeing Mr Anthony's strained expression as Henry would greet her with, "And how's the beautiful Miss Armitage this fine morning? "It didn't seem to matter to Henry that she was just the tea girl. They'd begun to meet after work for a quick coffee in the cafe across the road from the factory. Henry seemed genuinely interested in Lily's plans and dreams.

"When there's an opening we'll train you up to move out into the factory."

"You've got rocks in your head suddenly, Lil," Timmy said one morning when Lily came in with his usual cuppa. Lily was momentarily taken aback. She'd always regarded Timmy as her mate – indeed the only real mate she had made at the factory.

"Henry...Mr Ingram to you Timmy is the perfect gentleman."

"Huh, for now maybe but you watch your step, Lil. Anyway, he's old enough to be your dad. I just don't know what you see in him."

Lily couldn't deny that she felt hurt by Timmy's lack of understanding. They'd never really had any disagreement up to now. Surely, he could see how much harder it was for women to break down doors and that having Henry's support could make all the difference and of course, she really liked Henry. He made her feel that there were possibilities where before there had been only barriers.

"Lily, are you dreaming? For the second time, what time is he coming? "Ethel demanded as she took Lily's advice and sunk down onto the chair opposite Bert's.

"Goodness, girl," she continued, "you're all over the place. We won't shame you; you know."

"Of course not." Lily glanced towards the grandfather clock in the corner that was the only piece of authentic furniture in the room though she still wasn't sure where it had come from.

"He'll be here at 3.30 sharp. Anyway, he's only popping in for a bit of tea. There's no need to make too much of a fuss."

"Just enough fuss, eh Lily?" Bert chimed in. Lily knew that he was trying to be funny so gave him a half smile for her mother's sake.

A couple of hours later a screech of brakes and a cloud of dust heralded Henry's arrival.
"You didn't tell us that he's got a car." James ran to the window his eyes alight with excitement. Lily smiled. Well, at least she'd got one member of the family on side.
Henry had scrubbed up well for the occasion. Even though he was seventeen years older than Lily, he didn't look his age, and Lily felt the familiar flicker of excitement as she opened the door to him.
"Cigars for the gentleman and ..." Henry took a step back, and for a moment Lily thought that he was going to faint. His face had lost all colour, and a slight sheen of sweat was beginning to form on his forehead. Lily instinctively went over to take his arm.
"Henry! What's wrong?" However, even as she was saying it, some colour began to come back into his cheeks.
"My fault entirely, my dear," Henry said regaining most of his composure. Too late a night working and maybe one or two more whiskeys than I should."
"Tell me about it." Bert sympathised as he gestured to the chair opposite to his own by the fireplace. "Come and take the weight off your feet and Ethel will make you a nice cup of tea. That'll set you right."
Ethel slowly emerged from the shadows that the late afternoon was casting on the floor.
"I do apologise, Mrs Armitage. Flowers for the lady of the house and of course a gift for you dear." Henry handed Lily a long slim white envelope.
"What about me?" James interrupted not seeming very concerned that a stranger had nearly collapsed in their home.
"James, don't be so rude." Lily chided.
"Don't worry young sir. Last but certainly not least. How about if you, me and your sister go out for a spin later?" James looked as though he had died and gone to heaven.

"It'll be too late for him." Ethel's curt tone slightly shocked Lily. She knew her mother was tired, but that didn't mean she couldn't try. She knew how important this was to Lily.
"Of course, Mrs Armitage. I should have thought more before I spoke. Your mother's right, James. All young boys need their beauty sleep but perhaps next time." Henry said seeing James's disappointed expression.
"I'll get that tea then. I don't suppose you've got time to stay long being such an important man and all that."
"Thank you, Mrs Armitage. I wouldn't want to outstay my welcome and the beginning of the year is always a busy time for us."
It was the first Lily had heard of it as she had always been under the impression that January was a slow month, and nobody had spare cash, especially for plates and cups regardless of how pretty they were. She also couldn't believe how her mother was acting.
"Mum! What's the matter with you? Do you feel ill?" Lily could think of no other explanation.
"Why don't you open your gift, Lily?" Henry interrupted. Glad of the distraction Lily ripped the envelope open with trembling fingers and took out the two tickets it contained.
"I can't believe it. Peter Pan! How did you get these? They're still like gold dust, aren't they?"
"Not so much now and I have to admit I've been a bit selfish as well. I've never seen it myself even though I've always seen myself as a bit of a lost boy. I do hope you will be able to accompany me to London next weekend and we will enjoy it together."
Lily heard her mother muttering in the background but couldn't listen to what she was saying above the clatter of the cups and saucers she was violently arranging.

"Take no notice," Bert said as he glanced towards Ethel with a worried look on his face. "She's just tired. Had a lot on recently."

Lily spent the next half an hour feeling a little deflated. Her father and Henry were engaged in conversation. She heard the name, Desire Leroy mentioned and travelling to the factory in a cab dressed in a silk hat and carrying a cane. Though Lily couldn't make head or tail about it, it had apparently amused her father. She hadn't heard him laugh like that for years, if ever. Her mother was at the sink doing nothing that Lily could see. Just making a lot of unnecessary noise. When Lily stepped outside to escape the tense atmosphere, she nearly tripped over James who was sitting on the front step gazing adoringly at Henry's car.

"An Albion 16HP Wagonette. It must have cost him a bomb" Lily automatically nodded though she didn't really enjoy cars – noisy, smelly things – not that she'd seen a lot of them around these parts. She felt tears pricking at the back of her eyes and then felt angry at herself for being so weak. It was just that the afternoon was supposed to have been about her and Henry and celebrating becoming sixteen. "Damn them all," she murmured under her breath and then felt guilty for including James in her thoughts. He had the excuse of being young. Being self-centred and naively enthusiastic about life came with the territory. But as for the rest of them, she wondered what more they all wanted from her. She'd swallowed her pride and got on with her job and a pretty pickle they would be in as well without her earnings. As for Henry, well she hadn't asked him to literally stalk her after their initial meeting, and she certainly hadn't led him on. Not like some of the girls on the street who seemed as though they would do anything for an extra pack of fags. Maybe that was it. She hadn't given in to him enough. There still hadn't been a glimpse of any of the training that he had talked about when they'd first started meeting, but she wasn't going to be another Amy Mellor for anyone.

Pushing her shoulders back and flicking her hair over her shoulders she set off towards one of her favourite places to go to when she was feeling upset or needed space to think. By the banks of the River Derwent, the air always seemed to feel a little fresher, and there was usually something interesting to look at. Today a cob and a pen sailed serenely on their way. Lily thought that they were beautiful birds and was pleased that it was illegal to kill them. She stuffed her hands into her pockets and followed them downstream.

Time ran away with her as she let the babbling of the river soothe her nerves and when she finally arrived back at home Henry had gone.

"A fascinating chap you've got yourself there, Lily," her father smiled "and a clever one...he knows all there is to know about the factory and the history of Derby."

"Don't you think that might be because he's got the time and not running around all day to keep the likes of you lot clothed and fed?" Ethel challenged Bert.

Bert looked a little hurt but got up from his chair and put a tentative arm around Ethel's shoulder.

"I was only just saying, love. Lily make your mum a cup of tea. She's run off her feet."

"Don't bother yourself. I'm going up for a bit of a lie-down." Ethel replied while at the same time jabbing her finger towards Lily. "As for you and your fancy Mr Ingram. Can't you see that he's nothing but trouble? I can't stop you seeing him, but it'll be over my dead body before he steps foot in this house again." As Ethel turned her back on them both, Bert drew in a deep breath and rolled his eyes to the ceiling.

"Well, I thought that he was a nice chap anyway."

Lily felt pathetically grateful for her father's remark, and for once Bert and Lily were united in their feelings of complete bewilderment.

CHAPTER FIVE

September 1906

The room felt warm and uncomfortable, and the September sun was shining right into Lily's eyes, so she couldn't entirely focus on Mr Anthony who was sitting on the other side of the desk.
"So, Miss Armitage. I hear that you wish to leave us. Are we not good enough for you anymore?"
Lily could feel the sweat accumulating on her brow, and the stuffiness of the room was making her feel a little nauseous.
"Come on my dear." Mr Anthony pointedly looked at his heavy gold watch chain which hung from the pocket of his waistcoat. "You might not wish to have a job anymore, but some of us haven't got that luxury."
Lily was desperate to voice what she thought of the pompous snob. She might feel hot, but he was sweating cobs and fingering his high necked stiff collar as though it would strangle him if he had to wear it a minute longer. Maybe if she sat there long enough, he might just keel over from a heart attack eventually.
"Remember, Lily that you need a good reference." Miss Hardcastle had lectured her before she had entered the inner sanctum of Mr Anthony's office. Sometimes she felt that Miss Hardcastle knew her better than her parents. Funny how even though the two of them had never had what Lily would call an in-depth conversation she'd always had the feeling that Miss Hardcastle had her back.

She bit her lip as she now stared back at her boss.

"Not at all, Mr Anthony. I just thought its time I moved on. Try new things, you know?"

"Nothing to do with a certain Mr Ingram then?"

Lily willed herself not to blush or get angry – either course of action would have provided fuel for Mr Anthony's flames.

"Mr Ingram has been a good friend to me, Sir. Nothing more."

Lily didn't feel particularly guilty about telling a little white lie. There'd only really been a couple of occasions when Henry had got a little carried away, and Lily had soon nipped that in the bud. She was acutely aware of what happened to ordinary girls who got themselves into trouble. Not so apparently in high society, Lily had read. Many husbands and wives regularly overlooked extramarital affairs if their spouse did their duty and in the case of women provided heirs. However, in all classes, a single woman was supposed to remain a virgin until marriage and Lily had no problem with that. From what Amy had told her when she came back from her "holiday" it all sounded a very messy business indeed.

Lily heaved a sigh of relief as she shut the office door behind her clutching the all-important piece of paper with her reference.

"Miss Armitage has an enquiring mind, works hard and should go far." She quickly scanned Mr Anthony's fancy handwriting. She couldn't find a single negative comment. Hand on her heart she couldn't pretend that she had ever liked Mr Anthony, but after working at the factory for a few months, she had come to realise he was no better or worse than most bosses. It was just the way things were.

"What you're leaving for?" Timmy had moaned when she'd told him. "You're my mate and who's going to bring me my mug of tea now?"

"I've got to go Timmy. You know me now, so you know that's true. "Lily pleaded. "I'll go loopy if I stay here any longer."

"Is it because of him...has he upset you? I'll sort him out for you."

Lily stifled a laugh at Timmy's indignant stance. She didn't want to hurt his male pride, and she had to admit she was touched. If only Lily could fall in love with Timmy how much simpler life would be? He made her laugh more than anyone she'd ever known, and she felt more comfortable with him than any member of her family, but the spark wasn't there for either of them.

"Don't worry. It's got nothing to do with Henry. To be honest, Timmy, since our disastrous New Year tea party things have cooled off quite a bit between us."

"Has your mum said anything about why she acted so funny around him?"

Lily shook her head.

"Not a word. Maybe Mum was just having a bad day, but it was so out of character. Anyway, it's beside the point now really. She's made it clear that she doesn't think Henry is good enough for me, whatever the reasons."

"And you're ok with that?"

"You know what? I think I am. Henry's an interesting man but our relationship if you can even call it that, wasn't going anywhere. Maybe I expected too much of him."

"Time to move on then, Lil."

"Indeed, it is, Mr Lewis but don't you worry you'll still see plenty of me. After all, we do live on the same street."

"Don't remind me." Timmy grinned giving Lily a soft punch to her shoulder.

Ethel had made no protest at all when Lily announced that she was handing in her notice.

"Probably for the best." Ethel had continued chopping vegetables for the stew as though as far as she was concerned, the topic was closed.

"How can you say that, love?" Bert had challenged his wife. "She hasn't got anything else to go to you know?"

"Oh, stop fussing, Bert. She'll find something. She hasn't got cotton wool between her ears."

"Well, I can't understand your attitude." Bert then turned his attention to Lily.

"And why has that grand gentleman friend of yours not come to revisit us? Your bread was buttered on the right side there, girl."

"It's not all about..." Lily was cut off by the sound of the back-door slamming. The stew bubbled merrily away on the stove as its creator stalked along the street until she turned the corner and was out of sight."

"Perhaps it's the change." Bert reflected and went back to resume his position by the fire.

It had been a strange few days Lily thought as a week later she trudged along Derby's streets that were dark with rain though the day sort of suited Lily's mood. She'd began to think, reluctantly, that maybe her father did have a point. Perhaps she had been too quick off the mark assuming she'd get another job just like that. It wasn't even just about the money. The family had done well out of her, and she'd also managed to put back a little for herself. Lily now found she felt even more hemmed in at home than before she worked. Crown Derby hadn't been all gloom and doom. She'd found a good friend in Timmy and Henry for a while. Lily somehow earned the respect of Miss Hardcastle and from time to time had even felt useful. She'd enjoyed the routine up to a point and when the weekend came around thought she'd earned the right to disappear to her room with her books for an hour or so.

Lily thought that she probably could get work in domestic service. There seemed to be long columns of "help wanted" in the paper, but she didn't see herself as a house or parlour maid and anyway knew that the pay was minimal and far less than she'd been getting in the factory. Also, the hours were long and work hard and if nothing else Lily was at least honest about her shortcomings, at least the ones she saw. She wasn't exactly frail but didn't want to spend her life laying fires and tending to grates at the whim of some upper-class mistress who would spend most of her day looking down on "the girl."

Lily smiled, despite the driving rain. It was a good job people couldn't see inside her head sometimes. Such irreverent thoughts, way above her station!" However, Lily didn't see the problem in aiming high even if she never got there.

"And what are you finding so amusing on such a grey day as this one, young lady? "Lily had her head down against the rain, so the first thing she saw was a pair of brown button boots and black woollen stockings though she didn't need to look up to put a face to the voice. Miss Hardcastle had a particularly distinctive voice – a cross between a broad local accent and the cut glass tones of "those in society." How that could be Lily never had worked out, but it always made her jump to attention and today was no exception.

Lily's first thought, however, was how peculiar it was to see Miss Hardcastle's legs which made her laugh out loud at how absurd she was being. Miss Hardcastle had been known to explore beyond her Remington occasionally.

"Miss Hardcastle! It's lovely to see you." Lily genuinely meant it.

"And you, child. They do let me out sometimes for good behaviour you know but what are you doing roaming the streets in the middle of the day?"

"Still looking for meaningful employment. You know maybe I shouldn't have left so hastily, Miss Hardcastle. Even my father thinks so, but it just seemed the right time."

"Agreeing with your father now, are we? Amazing how much can change in a week." Lily sensed that she was being teased though Miss Hardcastle's expression had hardly changed as she continued. "It was the right time Lily, and you knew it. If you had stayed any longer, you would have lost the will to look."

Again, Lily was surprised at how much this formidable, but kind woman seemed to understand. It made her feel even more disappointed in her parents and then she immediately felt guilty for harbouring the thought.

"I suppose you're right Miss Hardcastle, but I'm not sure my father yet sees it that way."

"I wouldn't be too sure, Lily. He's just worried about you. Most fathers I've known have been immensely proud of their daughters even though they might at times find it difficult to show their feelings. Anyway..." Miss Hardcastle continued seemingly ignoring Lily's doubtful expression "this meeting may have been very fortuitous for both of us. I happen to have a friend who is in the process of establishing a small bookshop in Sadler Gate."

Lily felt a stirring of interest as she did when anybody mentioned anything to do with the literary world.

"That sounds such a satisfying thing to do. I've never noticed it. I

don't get up that way much but I'll go and have a gander when I've got a minute."

"I do indeed think that you should go up and have a gander as you put it as my friend is looking for an assistant. Now don't get too fixed on the idea..." she said taking note of the growing excitement in Lily's eyes. "Philip is a bit like me- a bit of a perfectionist. He's sent two girls packing now in as many weeks, but I've just got a feeling you might be able to stand up to the old bully."

"Well it's the best lead I've had so far, and I've dealt with a few awkward men in my time."

"And you'll deal with plenty more my dear I'm sure. Anyway, tell Philip Elizabeth sent you. It just might get your foot in the door."

She was a strange one Lily thought as she watched Miss Hardcastle stride purposefully into the distance, but she was proper nice. A real lady not like some of those stuck up snobs that lived up Allestree way and the like. She smoothed down her hair and adjusted her shawl. After all, she had nothing to lose, and it would give her an excuse to look at the place anyway.

As Lily wandered along Sadler Gate, keeping her eyes peeled for the shop Miss Hardcastle had described she couldn't help staring at some of the young people who often frequented the area. Many of them she knew were students from Derby Art College and came to drink in the bohemian atmosphere. There were almost as many young women as men, and they seemed entirely at ease with each other laughing and joking as equals. Lily had never really felt like that with any man apart from maybe Timmy, but he still had had a better job with more pay than Lily.

Lily had heard about Emmeline Pankhurst and her daughters, Christabel and Sybil. She couldn't disagree with their belief that women had the right to vote, but she didn't agree with how violent they seemed to have become of late. Henry used to talk of them occasionally after one of his big

London meetings though here in Derby such goings on almost seemed to belong to another world.

Lost in thought, Lily almost missed the bookshop which was slightly set back from the shops either side of it. Lily stepped tentatively inside to be greeted by more shelves of books than she had ever seen in her life. From outside she would have thought it impossible to fit so many volumes in such a small space. Shelves towered above her, at least half her height again and every spare foot of floor space was piled with books and magazines. There was just about enough room between the shelves to sidle along the aisles though it was one way only.

There didn't appear to be anybody in the shop, or if there was, they were probably very good at hide and seek.

"Hello, is there anybody there?" Lily rang the hand bell that stood on the small wooden counter to the right-hand side as you walked through the door. The ringing sounded impossibly loud, and Lily immediately felt foolish. Of course, there wasn't anybody else here, but the door had been open, so she didn't see any harm in having a look around.

The shop was a veritable treasure trove though there didn't seem to be any order in the chaos as H.G. Wells rubbed spines with P.G. Wodehouse and "Alice in Wonderland" was mixed in with military history. She picked up P.G. Wodehouse's latest offering, "Love among the chickens" surprised that there was a copy as it had only come out three months before. She smiled at the title. Even if it was rubbish, the title at least made you want to pick it up and find out for yourself.

"Put that down, girl! Put it down now!"

Lily hadn't heard the shop door open as she had been so engrossed in browsing and nearly dropped the volume. Lily looked up at the incredibly tall gentleman who was

addressing her. She imagined that his natural complexion would have been quite pale, but now his cheeks were flushed. His grey-green eyes reminded her of a fish as they looked as though they were about to pop out of his head.
"Well, Sir. I did ring the bell, and I was only browsing. That's what a bookshop is for surely, and I wasn't hurting anything."
Lily could feel her mettle rising and willed herself to be polite to the gentleman who continued to admonish her.
"That copy..." he continued pointing with a trembling finger to the book Lily still somehow held in her hand, "was only given to me this morning."
"Well, maybe it should be looked after better then instead of being shoved under a pile of magazines that look as though they've been here for years...Sir." Lily added as an afterthought.
"You respect books then do you...hm... Well, at least that's something. What are you doing here anyway apart from trying to sabotage my business?"
The gentleman pushed his shoulder-length silvery white hair back off his face as he seemed to calm down taking on a more regular countenance of which Lily quickly took advantage.
"Miss Hardcastle sent me about the job. She said you might..."
"Lizzy sent you. Well, why didn't you say so before girl and save us all this trouble?"
The gentleman's demeanour completely changed, and a broad grin lit up his face.
"Philip...Philip Devine. Very pleased to meet you, my dear." He stuck out his right hand and vigorously shook her left. Lily thought once again of what a dark horse Miss Hardcastle was. Lizzy indeed! Lily took a deep breath to hold her laughter in.

"You'd better get started then. I've meant to tidy this place up ever since I moved in but as you can see, I haven't got very far. See what you can do with it girl."
Mr Devine opened his arms wide and then turned and went striding to the bottom of the shop with the pile of offending magazines under his arm leaving Lily at a loss for words which was indeed a significant accomplishment.

CHAPTER SIX

October 1906

"Well, I think that it will suit you down to the ground, love but I'm not sure about you moving out."
"What are you worried about Ethel. Lil not being there to help with the chores?" Bert called across from his usual spot by the hearth and gave a wink to Lily who was getting ready to head out.
She busied herself lacing her boots as always unsure how to respond to her father. She had to admit that when she'd told them about a couple of rooms above the shop, that Mr Devine had said Lily could have if she wanted them, her father had been more supportive than her mother.
"I'm not going at all until next week, Mum and then I'll be popping round most days. I'll not see you short. Mr Devine's taking a bit out of my wages for bills, but he's paying me more than the factory did in the first place, so we should be in clover."
Ethel handed Lily her lunch bag.
"I'm glad you're shut of that factory anyway, love. All clouds have a silver lining, or so they say."
Lily had never been quite sure who "they" were, but they indeed seemed to be the fountain of all knowledge.
"I'll be off anyway. See you about five." Lily closed the door and stepped out into the street feeling more carefree than she'd felt in years. The couple of rooms that were over the shop might not exactly be the "Ritz", but they were modestly

furnished and there for Lily to put her stamp on. She had a new job that she enjoyed, and already she could see the difference her ideas were making to the book shop. What was perhaps even more exciting was that Mr Devine had told her she could borrow any of the books she wanted if they were not on order for a customer.

Mr Devine could be a bit of an odd character at times. His worst problem was that he would insist he had told Lily to complete a task, but five minutes later would have forgotten what he'd said in the first place so maybe it didn't matter. Most of the time he seemed to trust that Lily would know the right thing to do and that was a novel experience. For most of her young life, Lily had been under the impression that everyone else always thought that they knew best. Now maybe the tide was turning. She thought perhaps she had Miss Hardcastle to thank for most of her good fortune though she still hadn't got to the bottom of the relationship between her and Mr Devine. All she knew was that when Miss Hardcastle was mentioned Mr Devine seemed to go off into more of a dream world than usual.

Immersed in her thoughts about what she would need to beg, borrow or buy for her move she only caught a glimpse of the figure retreating from the bookshop. Her first thought was what an early bird. Mr Devine opened the shop at seven though he didn't expect Lily till eight. He was convinced that he would catch the custom from the early morning workers though Lily was trying to convince him that most people were only interested in getting to work on time and the rich would still be in bed. They would be better staying open later in the day, especially in the summer months.

Her second thought came crashing in like a freak wave on a beach entirely obliterating the first. She dismissed it almost immediately as fanciful thinking. It was still early, and she'd skipped breakfast as she'd stayed up late reading "In the

Days of the Comet" by H.G. Wells. She'd felt that Mr Wells might be a little beyond her, but she would persevere. It wasn't possible anyway she reasoned going back to the figure she'd seen emerging from the bookshop. That relaxed gangling gait had been achingly familiar for a few moments, but there were lots of people in Derby, and Lily was sure some walked the same. Fantasy was getting a grip on her again and since she'd been working, she'd tried to adopt a more logical and practical approach to life. Lily pushed open the shop door smiling a little as she reflected on how that might go.

"How's my little miracle worker this fine morning?" Mr Devine handed Lily a steaming mug of tea before she'd even had the chance to take her shawl off. Mr Devine must be in a good mood she thought as although it was a warm morning the clouds outside with their darker bases were well on the way to becoming thunderclouds and the wind was increasing at a steady pace.

Today Mr Devine was dressed in a thick, slightly tatty navy jumper that would have looked more at home on a Cornish quay and a pair of scarlet trousers that should have come with a health warning so early in the day.

"It's going to be a good day, my dear. I can feel it in my water. We've already had a decent order from the chap you nearly bumped into at the door."

Lily could hear her heart thumping in almost every part of her body and was sure that Mr Devine would hear the crack in her voice when she spoke.

"And who has been mad enough to give us that then, Mr Devine?"

"A grand chap. He works at Repton High. It isn't the first time he's come in ordering bits and pieces for his students though usually, he's even earlier than today. I can't quite

recall the name even though it's only five minutes since I wrote it down. That's what I've got you here for my dear."
Lily didn't have to look in the order book. Her mouth felt dry, and she had to force the words out.
"Mr Poynton. Alex Poynton," she croaked.
"Yes, I think you're right dear. Know him, do you? Not surprised. Got an idea he used to work in your neck of the woods a few years back. There was something...on the tip of my tongue...but can't quite remember. Anyway, no matter. A fine young man. Said he'd be back early tomorrow morning to pick his order up."
Lily felt distracted all morning though Philip Devine didn't seem to notice as it was a common occurrence for himself. She didn't know what to think. Alex had never entirely left her mind but with work and domestic responsibilities he'd been put to the back of it. She'd also changed from a naive schoolgirl who had blushed every time he approached their door into an independent woman – well almost. The last she'd heard of him he was banged up in Vernon Street prison and likely to remain there for a long time. Everybody knew that the judge who had presided over his case had decided to make an example of him. Quite rightly so, Lily thought, if he'd done what he was alleged to have done. All the evidence had been there apparently though facts tended to get distorted and changed as they travelled along the Derby grapevine. Lily had struggled with the verdict not able to join the image of the monster that the case had created with the gentle schoolmaster who lent her books. Yet Mr Devine had said Alex now held a respectable position at Repton. How could that be, Lily thought, if they knew of the crime he had been convicted of and how was he out of prison in the first place? By the end of the day Lily felt exhausted with trying to fathom it out and unusually was glad to get out of the shop at the end of the afternoon.

"You alright, love?" Ethel asked when Lily came down to tea that evening. "You look worried. Everything at the shop is alright, and your moving plans are coming on, aren't they?"

Lily smiled at her mother. Ethel could fuss sometimes, but she began to think that she might miss that – just a little bit. "Fine, mum. It's been a long day that's all." That was no lie Lily thought, and she had no intention of mentioning Alex Poynton in this house at least for the moment. Too many other subjects seemed to be taboo such as Henry and even her grandmother. Best to keep stum. Lily wasn't sure she was going to confront Alex at all. She didn't have to, and it would maybe look odd if she were at work for seven. Lily eventually drifted off to sleep and dreamt of Henry in prison and an Alsatian dog with the face of her mother dashing itself against the bars of Henry's cell. She woke feeling still tired though she couldn't quite bring the images of the night to mind in the light of day.

An hour later Lily was the first person in the shop. Mr Devine had lent her the spare key in case she wanted to begin to move any of her things into the rooms above. The morning was beautiful – sunny with blue skies – and it looked as though it could stay that way. The walk to work had refreshed Lily, and she felt readier to face whatever the day might bring.

"Coffee, Mr Devine. Black and strong. Just as you like it."

"Good heavens girl. What are you trying to do? Give me a heart attack." Philip Devine said as he strode purposefully through the door at seven sharp.

"Too beautiful a morning to let sleeping dogs lie, Mr Devine."

"Maybe so but perhaps you could have let them sleep a little longer. I can't cope with this much bonhomie before my first coffee of the day."

"Exactly, Mr Devine." Lily placed a huge mug into his hands. "Now, don't you worry about a thing. I'll sort out the customers, seeing as I'm here, while you get yourself together."

"That's my girl." Philip Devine said as he sauntered towards the small back room sipping his coffee as he went. "Don't think you'll be rushed off your feet. Just the schoolmaster's order, remember!"

"As if I could forget." Lily's heart fluttered like a bird trapped in a cage beating its wings, desperate to be free. She took a couple of deep breaths willing herself to be calm. Alex probably wouldn't remember her. She was probably just another snotty nosed schoolgirl to him, and he perhaps lent books to all his students.

At ten past seven Lily felt the familiar cold draught of air that signalled the opening of the shop door. Fixing a smile on her face and screwing her hands into fists to stop them shaking Lily turned to stare into those grey-green eyes that seemed to change colour with the light. They widened in surprise as Alex obviously recognised Lily.

"My dear Miss Armitage. You're the last person I expected to see. "He laughed, and Lily noticed there were a few extra lines, especially around his eyes that hadn't been there before. "No, I take that back," he continued as he threw open his arms to encompass the volumes and manuscripts around in very much the manner Mr Devine had on Lily's first day. "This is exactly the kind of place I would expect you to be, but you know what I mean."

"Mr Poynton...your order, Sir." Lily had rehearsed everything that she was going to say, but it had all been forgotten the moment Alex had walked into the shop. She handed the package that Mr Devine had packed the previous evening, over the counter to Alex.

"My dear. Are you alright? You look as though you have seen a ghost."

Lily struggled to find her voice.

"Good Lord. Nobody thought to tell you."

"Tell me what, Mr Poynton? I was just a child remember. Perhaps they thought they'd said too much anyway."

Alex didn't speak for a moment and then let out a long weary sigh.

"Look have you got twenty minutes? We can grab a cup of coffee in the cafe opposite. I'm free first lesson so don't have to be at school until nine."

"I can't. I'm working."

"Yes, she can." Philip Devine's head appeared above a mountain of books heading towards them. "She was here far too early for my liking this morning. Doesn't give a man time to think. Take her away young man as long as you return her at eight on the dot in one piece."

"With pleasure, Sir. Thank you, Sir" Alex opened the door and gestured to the cafe opposite

"Shall we, Miss Armitage?"

Flanked by a man either side in agreement with each other Lily felt that she didn't have much choice.

Lily had to admit that the coffee tasted good and was helping to settle her nerves slightly though she still found the whole situation surreal. Alex looked almost the same as the last time she had seen him, but he wasn't the same, and neither was she.

"You look well, Lily," Alex said as he smiled at her over the rim of his cup. Lily jumped slightly at the mention of her Christian name though why she should have done, she didn't know. He'd always called her Lily before apart from when he was having a joke with her or the like.

"So, do you," Lily replied. They were acting as though they were two acquaintances at a tea party.

"This is ridiculous." Lily blurted out without thinking." You didn't do it did you?"

"There's the Lily I know." Alex laughed." Never holding anything back."

"I have improved somewhat." Lily smiled back at him as she viewed his sceptical expression.

"I don't doubt it, and no I didn't." Alex's face took on a graver complexion." But for many months most people thought that I had."

Lily sensed that Alex had been to many dark places since they had last met despite his attempt to make light of the situation.

"They locked me away for six months though I was lucky. It was supposed to have been for ten years."

"But I don't understand. How can you be here if you were sentenced to ten years and what's more a pillar of the community if Mr Devine is to be believed."

"If it weren't for Maisy's brother, I would still be rotting in a cell somewhere."

Lily vaguely remembered Ronnie – a bit of a rogue but a good lad at heart and very protective of his sister.

"What's Ronnie got to do with it?" Lily was conscious of the minutes ticking inexorably towards eight o' clock but was determined to wrest the whole story from Alex now they had come this far.

"Well, you know how close the two of them were?"

Lily remembered. There was only fourteen months between the two of them and as far as she knew they hardly ever argued. Lily had always enjoyed listening to them chatter to each other as they seemed to have proper conversations unlike many of her contemporaries at the time.

"Well, Ronnie thought from the beginning of the whole affair there was something a bit off kilter about it all. To cut a long story short, Maisy eventually told Ronnie that she had made it all up."

"But why Alex?" Lily could feel herself getting hot and bothered as she realised how easy it had been to revert from "Mr Poynton" to "Alex."

"I always thought that she was one of the girls who had a bit of something about her. I never saw her as someone to jump at the first person she saw and go off and have babies when she was old enough, and she never came across as mean-spirited."

"You're exactly right in your observation Lily, and that's why the whole situation got out of hand. Maisy came to me one day after class and admitted she eventually wanted to become a teacher but didn't' think that she was confident or knowledgeable enough. I saw a spark in her though much like I saw in you. Something that most of the other children didn't have and I didn't want it to go to waste, so I started giving her a few extra lessons after school."

"And what was wrong with that?" Lily replied, up to that point feeling an affinity with Maisy.

"Nothing in itself." Alex sighed. "However, what she failed to mention was that as far as her father was concerned, she was going into domestic service straight after school and could forget about getting any ideas above her station."

Lily still felt bewildered.

"But it still doesn't make sense."

Alex gave a bitter laugh- the kind of which Lily had never heard from him before.

"It does when you get to the part where her father comes charging to the school after hours, finds me in the back room with his daughter and assumes the worst."

"But Maisy put him, right?"

"No, she was terrified of her father finding out that she had been acting against his wishes and so she went along with his accusations."

Lily was horrified.

"How could she Alex? And then to see you go to prison and still not say anything!"

"It wasn't her fault, Lily. Well not exactly..." Alex amended taking note of Lily's sceptical expression.

"She was afraid and then got in too deep and by the time I'd been tried and convicted it was easier for her to bury her head in the sand and hope it would all go away. Which I did of course!"

"Alex, how can you even begin to make light of it? Was its Ronnie who told the police then?"

"They went together. Imagine how hard that must have been for Maisy, Lily and how ashamed she would have felt. She is basically a decent person, and the upshot, of course, was that my sentence was completely quashed."

Lily also felt ashamed that she had had any doubts at all about Alex's innocence. Even after everything that he had been through he was still worried about how the experience had affected Maisy.

"It all worked out for the best really. I was lucky enough to find a head teacher who could see beyond the "mud sticks" philosophy, and I've got a super job now. Also, a little out of the town where I've always felt happiest. It's five years ago, Lily. I've let it go."

Lily nodded but could hear the pain in Alex's voice as he recounted the incident and she guessed there was a lot more that he hadn't said, especially about his experiences inside.

"Anyway..." Alex said getting up from the table. "We're both fortunate to have jobs to go to so perhaps we'd better think about making tracks."

"It's been the strangest beginning to a morning I think I've ever had," Lily replied wrapping her shawl around her shoulders.

"Not entirely unpleasant I hope." Alex smiled.

"Not at all. Well, at least not in the way you mean."

They stepped out into a day that had seemed to become even brighter.

"I would be very honoured if I could maybe have the pleasure of your company again, Miss Armitage. Next time to talk more about you I hope." Alex tipped his trilby at Lily as she turned back towards the shop.

"It would be my pleasure, Mr Poynton," Lily replied in the same manner.

"Oh dear. I'd better go." Lily laughed as they both saw Mr Devine emerge from the bookshop with a watch in hand.

"I think you'd better but let's not leave it for five years next time."

Lily heard Alex's voice drifting across the cobbled street and felt an inexplicable sense of "joie de vivre."

CHAPTER SEVEN

December 1907

Another term done and dusted. Alex shut the last of the exercise books he had been marking. The school might have seemed a bit like a mausoleum now that all the students had departed for the Christmas holidays, but Alex found the silence soothing.
He'd been a bit of a loner growing up. His mother had died when he was a couple of days short of his sixth birthday. She'd always had a weak constitution, and a particularly severe bout of influenza finished her. His father who was the local parson tried his best, but he didn't really understand what his young son needed from him, and he was also dealing with his own grief. Besides, that people seemed to see him as community property and called at all hours of the day and night with their own problems expecting him to solve them at the drop of a hat. The truth was that Jenny had been the guiding force behind both Alex and her husband and without her, they both became a little lost in their different ways.
Alex didn't really realise this at the time. He spent long days roaming the countryside usually with a book under his arm, and he thrived at school excelling in English in particular. Many of his teachers had him earmarked for Cambridge though none of them thought to tell him that. He would have revelled in the atmosphere at the time as in 1897 a proposal

had been put forward that women should be granted full degrees the same as men. "No Gowns for Girtonites" and "Varsity for Men" banners fluttered above Cambridge's imposing colleges. Alex would have been in the minority being firmly on the side of the women. From a young boy, he had always believed everyone should have the opportunity of an equal chance in life.

When the Cambridge option was eventually presented to Alex, he turned it down. In part, this was because he didn't feel knowledgeable enough or confident enough to enter such a revered national institution and in part thought that he couldn't leave his father rambling around an enormous vicarage on his own. Twelve months later and Alex's father was dead. From the moment he'd lost Jenny, he disconnected from life, and though he'd gone through the motions, Alex couldn't remember him ever laughing out loud or even smiling very much again.

The vultures, otherwise known as the well-meaning relatives, swept in and took charge. For a week Alex was surrounded by a sea of faces he barely recognised. One of their demands was that he go and view his father "as a good son should." Even now Alex remembered the shock he had felt at the open-mouthed white figure that seemed to bear little resemblance to the man who had stood in Quarndon church pulpit every Sunday putting the world to rights. The hordes eventually left leaving Alex with less furniture and few memories.

"You'll be fine, lad. School teachers have got it made." A rotund man calling himself Uncle Bill shouted along the vicarage path as he struggled towards his car arms laden with boxes. Alex felt more confused than anything as he watched "Uncle Bill" – he was sure that neither his mother nor father had siblings - lead the entourage in their procession towards Ashbourne. Alex felt that by the end of the week Ashbourne's auction shops would have acquired several new possessions.

The following morning Alex calmly stood on the same path and handed the vicarage keys over to the young parson who was taking over. By nightfall, Alex was installed in modest but comfortable lodgings about ten minutes' walk from where he worked.

For once Alex was looking forward to Christmas. He'd been walking out with Lily for about a year now, and it was only since then he had begun to realise precisely how lonely he'd been before. Not that Alex was ever going to be the life and soul of the party and didn't want to be. He still enjoyed the quiet life with his reading and love of the outdoors and anyway Lily more than made up for him with her chatter and boundless energy. Alex thought of them a bit like Yin and Yang – each complementing the other to make a whole.

It was going to be a cold one he thought as he stepped outside buttoning his calf-length overcoat as a few flakes of sleet fell onto his upturned face. Alex relished the contact though. He still vividly remembered the confines of prison life and the fetid air of the cell he had shared with two other inmates.

"Have a good one, Sir." One of his students shouted across the yard.

"You too Ted but keep going with that algebra in your spare time. You're nearly there you know."

Ted laughed.

"If wishes were horses, Sir but I'll keep trying."

Alex smiled raising his hand in farewell as he quickened his pace as he was running late for meeting Lily. He realised that he felt almost complete again – a girl he adored and a job he loved. It was over six years now since he'd been expelled out of Vernon Street and even the nightmares were gradually lessening. He'd made a vow that the brutality he had experienced inside wouldn't break him and neither would he burden anybody else with his memories.

Lily felt exasperated and couldn't quite point her finger as to why. Even Philip had noticed so she must have appeared tetchy as usually, his head was in the clouds somewhere.

"Don't worry, my dear. Your beau will be here to pick you up shortly I'm sure, and then we will have the whole week to do with exactly as we please."

"I still don't see why we're closing for seven days, Philip. We're going to miss the late Christmas shoppers, and we won't get them back again you know?"

Both knew this wasn't likely. Last six months they had worked all the hours God had sent to secure "Bookends" as the top booksellers in the district. The shop had been completely transformed from the higgledy-piggledy mess it had been in when Lily had first set foot on the premises. The store was now airy and spacious with all the books arranged into sections according to interest and author. With the floor space cleared of clutter, they'd managed to install two small seating areas where customers could browse in comfort and Lily had been known to put the kettle on for customers who looked as though they might be there for the duration.

"We're closing because we both deserve it. You're going to have a peaceful family Christmas, and I'm going to have a completely riotous Christmas in London. It's what we both need."

Lily had to laugh. Philip was shameless and didn't care who knew it. She also suspected that he might be going to London with Miss Hardcastle as the lady herself had been spotted hanging around in the shadows of the shop's environs the previous evening. Lily suspected that they would both be having a very decadent Christmas and enjoying every moment of it. She should have felt shocked but to be honest, she didn't see the harm. They had nobody to answer to, and there was a great deal more insincerity in many conventional marriages. She also had to admit she felt a little jealous and immediately chided herself for being so selfish.

Her own life was infinitely better in so many ways than it had been eighteen months previously.

Lily's wages at the bookshop and Philip's generous Christmas bonus meant that for maybe the first time in their lives they had money to spare. Ethel took this to heart, and even Lily had to admit that the house looked wonderfully inviting. The usual evergreens decked the walls and windows, but there were also more elaborate synthetic decorations that Ethel had made herself, and there were more presents under the tree than Lily had ever remembered seeing.

Bert smiled across at Ethel as she busied herself with basting the turkey. They had been going to break with tradition and have pork, but they'd taken a bit of a risk and waited until Christmas Eve. That was when the butchers became desperate to sell what meat they had at rock bottom prices merely to get rid of it and stop it from going off over Christmas. They'd been known to stay open as late as eleven and Lily had secured their turkey at ten minutes to that hour.

"Just because we've got a bit more money than usual this year it doesn't mean we have to be wasteful." Ethel had told Lily on Christmas Eve morning. The downside was that they had spent until about one in the morning plucking the doomed creature.

"You've done us proud, love." Bert came to stand by his wife and gently put his arm around her.

"Indeed, you have, Mrs Armitage." Alex's face shone with contentment and maybe a drop of wine.

"Get away with you both and let me get on," Ethel said shooing everyone away from where she was working but gave Alex a smile. She still felt ashamed about how she and Bert presumed him guilty even before his trial. They weren't generally a family who jumped on the bandwagon at the drop of a hat, but this time they had been swept along in the tide of idle gossip and the testimony of an impressionable schoolgirl. But then again so had the police Bert had reminded Ethel.

"Leave those alone James." Lily admonished as he went to pick up one of the mince pies that had come straight out of the oven.

"Ouch, they're hot," James said nearly dropping one on the floor but managing to find his mouth in the nick of time.

"Of course, they are! What did you say mum about our James going to Oxford?"

"Well, he's got a few years to improve yet haven't you lad?" Ethel gently cuffed him around the head.

"I'm hungry. When's dinner ready? James easily dodged Ethel with a mischievous grin.

"Just about now young man, I think." Alex interrupted as Ethel brought the remaining vegetables over to the table which they had all just about managed to squeeze around.

"Are you going to carve, Bert?" Ethel asked her husband. Bert came across to the table and took the carving knife only to give it to Alex.

"Let Alex do the honours. After all, he is almost a member of the family."

"Well, if you're sure, Mr Armitage. I would be delighted. After we say grace of course."

Alex didn't seem to notice the uncertain look that passed between Bert and Ethel. It wasn't that they didn't believe in God, but in the past, they'd just got on with it before the meal went cold.

"Of course, lad. Of course." Bert replied. "Grace away."
"Dear God. Bless this food and this family..."
The slightly awkward silence that followed Alex's blessing was thankfully shattered by James's clattering of knife and fork. He'd surreptitiously been feeding next door's cat that had crept in somehow while the rest of them had their eyes closed.
"Now can we eat?"
Lily heaved a sigh of relief. Little brothers had their uses sometimes, and she smiled across the table at Alex to give him encouragement, but he seemed well settled.
Christmas afternoon passed precisely as it should do. The family had opened each other's gifts that morning, but Alex gave his out after Christmas lunch had been digested. He'd been particularly generous. Ethel received a beautiful print scarf from Liberty's in London. Bert was plied with Cuban cigars, and James was delighted with a box of magic tricks that he then continued to annoy them all with. To Lily, he gave the most delicate heart-shaped locket that he proceeded to tenderly fasten around her neck while the others watched.
"Thank you, Alex, but you needn't have done." Lily knew that he probably earned less than her now.
"Nonsense. I wanted to treat you all. You've made this Christmas the happiest of my life, and that's the greatest gift you could have given me."
The food and drink continued well into the evening as Ethel served up her salt beef, brawn and pickles for supper while the adults sipped port wine and James slurped Stones ginger wine.
By the time the clock struck nine James was in bed, and Bert was snoring in his usual place. Even Ethel was relaxing for once, and more refined snores were heard coming from the opposite chair to Bert's.

"It's been perfect, Lily. Thank you." Alex said as the two of them made their way to the door to say goodnight. Alex was heading home, but Lily was staying the night to help tidy up in the morning and prepare for a slightly smaller celebration on Boxing Day.

"I'm glad you've enjoyed it and thanks for all the beautiful gifts."

Alex gently took Lily's hand and kissed her softly on the mouth.

"Goodnight Lily. Sleep well, and I'll see you tomorrow."

Lily watched until Alex was safely on his way and then closed the door quietly. She sighed as she looked at the mess surrounding her and gently covered Ethel with a blanket. Her mother seemed so peaceful for once. It will all have to wait until tomorrow Lily thought.

As she wearily climbed the stairs to her old room, she knew that she should feel happy. She was pleased for her mother that it had all gone well. She deserved it for all the effort she had put in. Even her father had been more entertaining than usual and what nine-year-old boy didn't love Christmas? However, Lily felt disappointed, but in what she couldn't rightly say. Maybe the emptiness she felt would disappear after a good night's sleep. Of course, it would.

CHAPTER EIGHT

June 1908.

"Do you think these Suffragette women are going about their business in the right way, Alex?" Lily enquired as she packed a small bag. Ethel had been a little under the weather and the warm days weren't suiting her this year, so Lily was going over to help for a couple of days.
"I certainly think their passion is there. There's going to be a rally in London tomorrow, or so I hear. Don't know what good it will do. Our country is a bit backward sometimes in its thinking. New Zealand is about fifteen years ahead of us."
Lily smiled at Alex. She enjoyed his company immensely when he was caught up in explaining some philosophical or political point. At times he made her feel quite naive still even though she was very well read for a young woman of her age and social status. She realised though she had hardly been anywhere outside the environs of Derby, apart from that one time with Henry. Not that many of the other women she knew had either. She guessed the exception was probably Miss Hardcastle. Only last Easter she had come back from a trip to Paris with Philip though perhaps the less Lily knew about Miss Hardcastle's jaunts, the better.
"How long are you staying with your mother?" Alex continued.

"I'm not really sure. I've got the week off, but it will probably only be a couple of days."

"We'll do something special at the weekend then."

"Can't wait," Lily replied though she thought that probably meant going and getting some fried fish and chips. She knew that they were supposed to be highly nutritious and last time she guessed it had been fun eating them in the twilight on a bench by the Derwent. It wasn't precisely Paris in the springtime though. She was surprised that Alex wasn't put off by the smell of the shop like many of the middle class seemed to be. On the other hand, Lily supposed she would always be working class and however high Alex rose in his profession she doubted he would ever look down his nose at anyone or anything.

Lily got off the bus a couple of stops early as it was such a lovely afternoon and her bag wasn't unusually heavy. It was a day to be out in the countryside in an open top car though they were still far and few between. Lily couldn't help thinking back to her trip with Henry to see "Peter Pan" in London not long after her 16th birthday. It had taken them hours to get there in the car that James had been so impressed with though Lily had forgotten the name of it almost as quickly as he'd said it. The whole day had been magical, and Henry had treated her like a lady.

Undoubtedly, life with Henry was exciting but not very enduring. Once back in Derby Lily wouldn't sometimes see him for days. In the end, they hadn't exactly fallen out but drifted apart. Lily wondered what would have happened if her mother hadn't been so rude towards Henry. Probably much the same thing though Lily still hadn't got to the bottom of it. Finally, she had tried to put it to the back of her mind.

Anyway, what did it matter now? She was with Alex, and everybody assumed that they would get married eventually.

That had been her dream growing up, and now it was almost a reality.

She was startled to see that somehow; she had ended up just around the corner from the factory. She must have been daydreaming and had gone a long way around. Lily turned to retrace her steps. If she cut through the street just behind and to the right of her, she was sure she wouldn't be far off from where she wanted to be.

"Lily! Hold up a minute. What you doing down here? Changed your mind and come back to join us commoners." Timmy screeched to a halt in front of her and clambered off the safety bike that was now one of his proudest possessions.

"Have you escaped for the day, Timmy? On a joy ride, are we?" Lily teased slipping effortlessly back into their banter of old.

"Just been out to get a spot of late lunch."

As Timmy held up a paper bag full of sandwiches Lily realised that lunch had somehow passed her by and that she was ravenous.

"Come on in for ten minutes. You can share a sandwich with me." Timmy said seeing Lily eyeing up the bag he had in his hand.

Lily wasn't sure. She felt a bit as though she was trespassing already despite still being on a public highway.

"I don't know, Timmy. I don't want to get you into trouble."

"Don't worry, Lil. You won't. All the big nobs are in the city for the day. Some important meeting. Blowing a lot of hot air if you ask me. Miss Hardcastle's there of course, but you've always had her wrapped around your little finger."

"I'm not so sure about that, but I'll perhaps come in for ten minutes then. Where's the harm? I am starving, and I'd love to see what you're working on at the minute."

Nothing much had changed in the factory though Lily had forgotten how many people worked there. She welcomed the hustle and bustle as though she enjoyed her work at "Bookends" it could get a little isolated at times. They got a steady stream of loyal customers through the door but were never really rushed off their feet. Lily perched on her old stool and gratefully took the cheese and pickle sandwich that Timmy offered her.

"Thanks, Timmy. I could eat a horse. What are you working on at the minute?" Lily asked before she took a massive bite out of the sandwich.

Timmy smiled and produced a blue pattern teacup and saucer from underneath his workbench. Lily was impressed by the richness of the colours. Maybe if Henry had kept his promise, she would be working as one of the painters now. Whether that would have been a good move was irrelevant now though, Lily thought.

"It's the new range. The Wilmot Blue Pattern. Only just come out. It is striking though isn't it?" Timmy said taking note of Lily's admiring glance. Lily was so lost in admiring that and the other pieces on the bench she didn't notice him come up behind her.

"Well, Miss Armitage, I didn't think that you would be likely to grace us with your presence again."

Lily was so startled that she almost dropped the delicate teacup that she was holding. She realised how keyed up she'd been since entering the workshop and knew that she shouldn't really be there.

"Mr Ingram...Henry! I didn't expect you to be..." Lily could feel herself blushing and suddenly it seemed to have got very warm in the room.

"No need to get flustered, Lily. I won't tell if you don't especially if you let me buy you a drink for old times' sake." Lily hadn't set eyes on Henry for the best part of a year, and a great deal had happened since then. She had no intention of going for a coffee or whatever he had in mind.

"I'm afraid I can't, Henry. I've got to ..."
"Nonsense, my dear. I'm sure half an hour isn't going to make much difference to your busy life. I'll just go and get my coat."
Timmy shrugged his shoulders as they both watched Henry's back as it receded down the factory floor.
"I'm sorry, Lil. I assumed he'd gone with the rest of them to London. You know I wouldn't want to make it awkward for you."
"Don't worry, Timmy. I know it's not your fault." Lily gave him a wry smile." After all its only coffee and we didn't really break up on bad terms. We just sort of stopped seeing each other as much. It'll be alright."
"Well, be careful, but it's been great to see you again. You always were the only one who seemed remotely interested in what I do."
"See you around, Timmy," Lily said as she watched Henry rapidly approach them.
Before Lily could make any more protest, they were ensconced in a cafe about ten minutes' walk from the factory. Little was said between them until they were seated.
"Well, Lily. Just like old times, eh?" Henry was downing his third Gibsons while Lily sipped half-heartedly at her coffee. The atmosphere had been tense since they'd left the factory and Henry seemed much changed from how he'd been the last time Lily had seen him. She felt increasingly uncomfortable in his company
"I really must be going, Henry. It's been lovely to see you but..."
"I'm glad, Lily. Glad you're finding this a lovely experience. Thought since you'd been walking out with that schoolteacher, you'd forgotten what a real man was."
Lily's discomfort escalated, but she couldn't really leave without creating a scene. She couldn't even remember seeing

Henry drink this much when they had been together. It had been a mistake to come here with him, but he hadn't really given her much choice.

"Henry, please. I think we both need some fresh air. It's still a beautiful afternoon out there."

"You're right, my dear. Your wish is my command. Perhaps it is time we were leaving."

Lily felt relieved as Henry got to his feet if a little unsteadily. At least he was up and moving in the right direction. She'd just see him on his way. He deserved that much from her she supposed.

Lily had felt so claustrophobic in the cafe, but out on the street, she breathed in the air with relief and unbuttoned the top button of her blouse to help her cool off.

"Oh, I see. That's the way you want to play it is it? Henry lurched towards her. The fresh air had apparently hit him hard, and he was weaving quite seriously from side to side. Lily's sense of unease increased. It was now late afternoon, and the side street the cafe was on was deserted.

"Henry, you're drunk. You need to get home and sleep it off, and I need to be on my way."

Henry was now close enough to Lily that she could smell the alcohol coming from his breath in waves. He leant with one hand on the wall of the alley efficiently blocking Lily's exit to the main street.

"Come on now, Lily. You know you want it. You're a little tease. That's what you are."

Henry reached out with his other hand and placed his fingers just inside the neckline of Lily's blouse. Lily felt her heart beating nineteen to the dozen. He was a solid man, and she knew that she could never hope to push him off her. Henry placed his blubbery lips on hers, and his body weight pressed her further back into the hard-stone wall of the alley.

"A little prick teaser aren't you our Lily? Come here. I'll show you what it's like to be with a real man."

At the same time as feeling horrified Lily was also fixed in a state of fascination. She'd never been this close physically to a man before. She and Alex kissed and held hands and indulged in a few cuddles and hugs, but this was the first time she'd been privy to brute male sexuality. Amazingly, despite the alcohol, Lily could feel Henry's hardness pressing against her as his right hand groped under her blouse and found her left breast. Lily felt suspended in a world of unreality and could hardly believe that this was respectable Henry Ingram as she had known him. Far from feeling embarrassed Lily felt a surge of anger flood her body.

"Get your hands off me, you filthy creature." Thoughts of Amy Mellor swamped Lily's mind, and she kicked Henry's shin as hard as she could. She then dug the nails of her left hand into the skin on Henry's face. He staggered back clutching his cheek. Sweat was running down his forehead. "I'll give you what for now you bugger," Henry shouted as he momentarily let Lily go. She saw her chance and legged it towards the alley gap that led out onto the main street. All the while Lily could hear Henry cursing and shambling after her. She threw herself into a door recess and pressed herself as flat as she could against the wall.

"I'm coming to get you bitch. You Armitage women are all the bloody same. Think you're too good for anybody but at least your mother opened her legs for me. She begged me for it. Can you hear me, Lily? Begged me for it."

Lily shrank further back and took a few deep breaths to try and quell her shaking. Henry's voice was getting more distant. He hadn't seen her. Slowly, her breathing returned to a more regular rate. Thank God, Lily thought. She felt sick to the stomach from the tussle she had had and from what she had just heard. Lily tried to push the unwelcome thoughts out of her head as her breathing steadied. She smoothed down her skirt. She was alright apart from a bruise or two that would form where Henry had grabbed her.

But what had all that talk about her mother been about? Was it the manic ramblings of a drunk? She desperately wanted it to be. Her mother was a pillar of morality and loyal wife to Bert who she clearly loved. This was what made sense. However, yet another voice that became insistently stronger was niggling Lily. Something had upset Henry and why would he have said all those dirty things if there was no substance to them? She then immediately felt disloyal to her mother. By the time Lily had made her weary way home, she had convinced herself that Henry's outburst had all been caused by the demon drink. Lily was also determined that she would keep the encounter all to herself.

CHAPTER NINE

July 1908

Lily spent three days with her parents, and by then Ethel was feeling a lot better.
"Thanks love. You've been a big help, but you've been a bit quiet. Everything alright with Alex?"
"As far as I know, Mum. I'll be catching up with him at the weekend."
Lily had no idea what she was going to say or do when she did. She'd spent the first day after her sordid encounter with Henry playing the scene repeatedly in her mind. It wasn't that she was utterly traumatised by the experience. She was resilient and had suffered little physical damage in the attack. She was more confused than anything as Henry had acted so out of character. Lily felt that he would have come to his senses before he went all the way and if he hadn't Lily would have fought tooth and nail to get away from him. Previously he had behaved like the perfect gentleman and Lily had to admit that she had enjoyed being seen with him. It had been as though some of his affluence rubbed off onto her and for a brief time, she could imagine she was someone else. Even now she was struggling to equate that image of him with that of the filthy drunk who had tried to force himself on her a few days ago.
Part of her also debated whether any of it was her fault. Yes, he had been persistent, but he hadn't physically dragged her to the cafe. Before Henry had started downing Gibsons as

though there were no tomorrow, Lily had felt a rush of familiar excitement at being seen with "a man of means." She knew that she had never been in love with Henry, but maybe she had led him on. Lily knew that men's needs had to be met. She'd heard them in the factory boasting about their conquests though she suspected that many of them lay in the realms of fantasy rather than fact. But what if Lily had encouraged Henry to believe that she was willing to give more out than she was? When Lily thought of Alex, she felt a little guilty. She supposed he wouldn't have approved of her meeting up with Henry.

Lily's greatest dilemma though was the vile things Henry had said about her mother. It was hard enough for a child to think about their parents having sexual relations let alone her mother having a wild affair with a prominent local businessman. While helping Ethel out, Lily had tried to view her mother with an objective eye. She supposed that she must have been pretty once. Lily had seen old photos of her with "Big Jim" on the farm. She'd been an athletic, healthy looking girl with her long brown hair scooped up into a ponytail most of the time. Lily's mother still retained the long hair though it was now streaked with tinges of grey and she wore it up in a bun most of the time. Her blue eyes were still beautiful though and often reflected her moods. But it again didn't make any sense. Lily was honest enough to realise that she had issues with her father, but it was clear that her parents still had a great love for each other. Lily had to admit that she was a little jealous as she wasn't sure that she had found that with Alex. Maybe it came with time she mused.

Lily was completely perplexed. Why would her mother risk her marriage by having an affair? Everything she knew of her and the way she lived her life made it seem incongruous. But then again what cause would Henry have for saying what he did? Even in his drunken ramblings, it seemed likely there was an element of truth. Also, it would explain her mother's inexplicable attitude to Henry when he'd come to the house. Lily had kept her relationship with him previously very private mainly because of the age gap. It didn't take much to get tongues wagging down their way, and Henry was a pretty standard name. Lily felt as though her head was about to explode. Maybe it would be best if she went back to the shop tomorrow and pretend none of it had happened.

"What's the matter with you, love? You've been like a cat on a hot tin roof for the last day or so."

Lily jumped as Bert came through the back door.

"I'm sure I've got something to do with it. I usually have."

Lily was surprised, firstly that Bert had been out walking anyway and secondly by his attempt at humour. She felt a wave of rare sympathy for her father as if what she suspected was true it would break his heart.

"It's not you, dad. I've just got a few things on my mind. Don't worry I'll sort it out. I think I'll go and get a breath of fresh air. It might clear my head."

"Why don't you take your mother with you? It's warmer than I thought, and it will do her good. Get a few of those roses back in her cheeks."

"Thanks, dad. That's a kind idea." Lily could hear the catch in her voice as she turned away to go and root her mother out.

Lily and Ethel sat down to rest on a bench just outside Markeaton Hall and grounds.

"We've walked quite a way. I must be feeling better."

Ethel's face had more colour in it than Lily had seen for a while.

"How the other half live, eh!" Ethel exclaimed to Lily looking over towards the hall's extensive parkland and grounds.
"Those Mundys have always been in the money though."
"Money's not everything though is it, Mum?" Lily smiled.
"Not everything, love, no. It won't bring back my mum, dad or sister but it could buy you a place like that. Give you room to breathe."
Lily knew that her mother missed the open spaces of the countryside that she had been brought up in. She was sometimes guilty of forgetting that her parents may have had dreams once – so caught up as she was at times in working out what she wanted from her own life. Observing her mum's sad expression, Lily felt an intense pang of sorrow for what her mother had lost and the way she lived now. Though nine times out of ten she knew that if she'd been asked Ethel would have said that she was happy with her lot. Lily smiled at Ethel and took her hand. She knew that her mum could see the unanswered questions in Lily's eyes.
"You know I love you mum and wouldn't hurt you for the world?"
"My goodness, Lily. Nobody's dying as far as I know. Of course, I know that. You've got a good heart even though..."
"I get a bit carried away at times. You don't have to spell it out, Mum." Lily laughed.
"What's really bothering you, Lily. I know there's something. You'll feel better for getting it off your chest. Spit it out. It can't be that bad."
"I'm not sure, Mum and I could be so wrong." Lily felt panic rising. What she was about to say could blow her whole family apart. I won't let it though, Lily thought. Even if it's true, I won't breathe a word of it to anyone, but Lily knew that she had to ask.

"Henry..." Lily began but didn't have to go on. She could see the anguish in her mother's eyes and realised that it was true.

"Ever since that day I have dreaded this one coming, but I knew that it would. You're too intelligent and Henry too arrogant for it not to rear its ugly head."

Lily realised that she wasn't as shocked as she could have been. Instead, she almost felt relieved that it was out in the open and the confusion she'd felt for the last couple of years might finally be resolved. Also, she hadn't had to accuse her mother of anything. Ethel had guessed. Lily was still afraid her mother might break down or feel that she had been betrayed, but Ethel sat perfectly calmly though Lily could feel her hand shaking slightly as she still held it.

"I think that I would have told you one day, you know. Maybe in a few years when you were settled with children of your own and maybe understood a little more about what life can throw your way."

Lily felt a new bond with her mother. Over the last couple of years, Lily had begun to see that the world far from being black and white was painted in myriad shades of grey.

Ethel briefly touched Lily's cheek.

"It was never meant to happen. Please don't think I planned it, Lily."

"Of course, I don't think that Mum and anyway its none of my business really, but you know me."

Ethel gently laughed.

"Curiosity killed the cat when you were born. Come on let's walk. It's a beautiful day, and I think I'll find it easier to talk if we walk."

"You don't have to tell me anything, Mum." Lily got up and straightened her skirt, and the two of them set off towards the lake.

"I do have to tell you, Lily. I owe it to you, your dad and James."

Lily increasingly had the feeling that she'd opened more than a can of worms, but the ball had started rolling, and she intuitively knew that all it could do was gain impetus.

"I know your dad annoys you, Lily. No, you don't have to deny it." Lily opened her mouth and then blushing slightly closed it again. "I can see it in your eyes every day. I wish you'd known him before his accident. He was so like you. Ideas flying around inside his head and never enough time in the day to bring them to fruition."

"I'm sorry, Mum. I know that you're not lying, but I find it impossible to see him like that."

"I know, love." Ethel pulled Lily down onto another bench overlooking the lake and took Lily's hands in her own. For a moment they were both silent drinking in the serenity of the spot as they watched a mute swan sailing majestically over the top of the water.

"It was the boy who died that did it. He can take the pain but not the guilt."

Lily shook her head.

"I'm sorry, Mum. You've lost me. What boy?"

"He saved two of them, Lily. When the tunnel caved in, he physically dragged two of the boys to safety." Ethel put her head in her hands, and when she moved them again, Lily could see her eyes glistening. "He must have been in so much pain. One of the doctors was convinced he'd never walk again, but he went back again. There'd been another rock fall, and although he could hear the boy crying out for his mum, your dad couldn't get to him."

"What happened to him? The boy?" Lily whispered.

"He's still down there and will be for all eternity. The blokes did all they could, but I'll always remember it. When the women got to the shaft entrance, we saw grown men crying without shame. I can still remember the sight of the coal dust mixed with the blood as the men scrabbled with their bare hands to try to get to Billy, but God wasn't on their side that day."

"But they couldn't just leave him!" Lily looked incredulous.
"In the end, they had to. The men tried for days underground and from above, but each time they tried more rubble fell amongst them. Enough lives were lost that day, and Billy would have been gone long before they gave up. Despite their grief, it was Billy's parents who stopped it."

Lily had known about the accident of course but had never heard the details until now.

"But why does Dad feel guilty? He saved two lives. They did survive, didn't they?"

"Oh yes. Both boys have got their own families now. As to why your dad feels so guilty, I don't know, but once he came out of the hospital, he shut down. Just sat there barely functioning. He's faced worse but..."

Ethel coloured slightly as she saw Lily's puzzled expression. "What do you mean, worse? You mean when he found out that you were having an affair?" Lily could hear her voice rising as it did when she got stressed or wanted to get a point across.

"He never did find out. He wasn't capable at the time of processing that sort of information."

Lily could feel her mum's silent sobs as they still sat side by side.

"I gave in, Lily. I gave in to temptation because I found someone who made me feel alive again and I conveniently forgot I was your mum and your dad's wife." Tears ran down Ethel's face, and Lily had never seen her so ravaged.

"Please, Mum. Calm down. You'll make yourself ill again." Lily put her arm around her mum's shaking shoulders.

"Whatever happens to me I will deserve it, Lily. I ignored my husband's pain, and I cheated on him because I felt flattered and I wanted to feel like a woman again. I was selfish and..."

"Mum, stop please." Lily could feel herself almost on the brink of tears. "I've never known anyone less selfish. You bend over backwards for us all, and I get it. I really do."

"But at least you had the sense not to sleep with him. You know what I see when I look in the mirror? I see a withered middle-aged woman who is no better than the prostitutes that frequent the corner of Pear Street. At least they're honest about what they do. There's only one good thing that came out of the whole sorry situation."

Lily's mind felt like it was in overdrive. She felt uncomfortable about her mother's revelations though pleased her mum thought she could take her into her confidence, but she was confused about what possible good could have come out of any of it.

Ethel got up briskly from the bench, wiped her eyes on her hankie and took a deep breath.

"Let's not talk about it anymore. Enough's been said, and you know what I feel better than I have done for a long time. It's been pent up for too long, but it's time to get back to normal.

Lily remained seated as she watched her mum stride purposefully towards the park gates. A cold coil of certainty began to form in her gut. As her mum said she didn't lack in brains and now she knew it all seemed so obvious.

"James. You mean James?" Lily's words split the silence of the evening. Ethel stopped dead. Lily was glad she was still seated as she'd suddenly come over all faint.

Ethel turned slowly, and she didn't have to speak. Her face told the truth.

"Yes, James but he doesn't know, and neither does your dad, and that's the way it's going to stay. Now let's get back. They'll be waiting for their tea."

CHAPTER TEN

July 1908

"You seem a bit quiet since you've come back from your mums. I thought she was doing better now."
Lily regarded Alex from the recess of the shabby but comfortable chair he kept in his study. Alex was doing well at Repton and had bought himself a modest house on the outskirts of the city. Lily loved spending time there. The front of the property opened onto a moderately busy road but the rear, where the study was situated, looked out onto open fields. In winter the room was cosy and warm with the books that adorned three sides of the walls enveloping Lily in a cocoon of wellbeing. In the summer the windows could be flung open, and the skylarks could be heard singing their hearts out, soaring high above the grass luring potential predators away from their nests.
Today even though it was the middle of summer the fire was lit as it had been an unseasonably cold dull day. Its flickering flames were dancing and making odd shadows on the brick wall opposite. Lily wriggled her toes deeper into the Persian rug and smiled up at Alex who was standing warming his back against the fire.
"She's much better. It's really not that important so don't worry about it, Alex."
"But I do worry, Lily. I always want what's best for you, and when we're married, it will be my duty to take care of you."

To Lily, it seemed strange to hear him talking about marriage though she knew that it had always been assumed by her family it was inevitably going to happen. Alex was such a kind, sweet man who made her feel even worse when she allowed herself to think about Henry. She'd decided that the incident between them was going to remain a secret. If Henry was going to say anything, she reasoned that it would already be out there travelling the grapevine. It was of no benefit to him to have people regard him as a potential rapist though Lily thought that Henry at his most suave could probably talk himself out of that one as well.

She had thought of telling Alex about her mother but worried about what he would think. He'd always held Ethel in proper esteem, and Lily smiled as she thought back to how he would gently tease her mum when he came around lending Lily books. On the other hand, if he was the man Lily was destined to marry, she shouldn't hide things from him, at least not the things she felt she might be able to speak to him about without hurting him. Lily patted the stool beside her.

"Come and sit with me. There's something I need to tell you."

After what seemed a long time later, though really wasn't, Lily flopped back into the comfortable chair. She rested her head on its back feeling flustered and a little apprehensive but also relieved. At least she wouldn't have the burden of keeping it to herself, and if there was one thing she had learned about Alex, it was that he could be trusted.

The ticking of the wooden ornate Japanese wall clock filled the room. It was one of the few pieces that Lily disliked though she knew that it was important to Alex as it was one of the few objects he'd inherited on his father's death. Alex had never really opened up about his relationship with his

father though Lily picked up that it had been difficult with Alex's mother dying shortly after giving birth to him.
Alex stood looking out at the rapidly receding daylight. Lily wondered what was going through his mind and couldn't help being a little afraid. Maybe it had been too much information to give out all at once. She was even surer that it had been the right decision not to speak of Henry.
"I think I knew." Alex slowly turned to face Lily who was beginning to feel a little dizzy from the heat and tension in the room.
"But how could you and why didn't you say something?" Lily could hear her high-pitched voice inside her own head. She wanted to appear measured and calm to prove to Alex what a mature young woman he kept company with. Yet to her own ears she sounded like some maniacal harridan.
"How could I, Lily?" When we first met, you were a child and besides which I didn't have my suspicions confirmed until a couple of years ago. Would you really have wanted to start walking out with me if I'd told you that your mother had had an affair behind her husband's back and that your brother was your half-brother? Would you have even believed me back then?"
"Probably not," Lily muttered looking faintly embarrassed. "But you could at least have given me a chance."
"I couldn't risk losing you my dearest, Lily. I was amazed when I realised that this intelligent, interesting and beautiful girl I'd had my eye on for ages might just have some vague interest in me."
Lily was slightly taken aback by the passion she could hear in Alex's voice. She'd always admired his intellect and sincerity though at times got a little frustrated with how level-headed he could be. Even when he'd been unjustly incarcerated, he didn't seem to harbour any bitterness towards Maisy. He'd been through a lot, and Lily realised

that she couldn't be too hard on him. If she'd been in his shoes, she might well have done the same. She glanced up at him and tried to keep any reproach out of her voice.

"It makes no real difference anyway I suppose. Me knowing a few days ago or years ago wouldn't alter the facts but how did you find out?"

"In the pub I'm afraid. Many a tortured soul heads for the whisky bottle, and after I came out of prison, I wasn't exempt."

Alex smiled wistfully at Lily's slightly shocked expression. "I'm no saint Lily but a real man made of flesh and blood. Pinch me, and you'll see."

Alex laughed softly as Lily, not so gently, did just that.

"So, you are, Mr Poynton. Well, fancy that. Pray continue I'm all ears.

Lily tried to repress her smile but couldn't keep it from creating a twinkle in her piercing blue eyes.

"Bert, your dad, was in there downing pints like there was no tomorrow."

Lily knew that on the odd occasion her dad had been known to declare he was fed up with the claustrophobic atmosphere of the house and would go on a blinder. Lily could understand the feeling but felt he should have been out looking for work rather than knocking back the booze.

"He was belting out "Everybody works but Father" and getting more maudlin by the minute." Alex continued. "I tried to get him outside Lily, but he was having none of it. The best I could do was manoeuvre him into the snug where he bought me a drink and proceeded to tell me how he'd known that James could never be his."

"Too intelligent that boy. Going to Oxford you know, Alex. Takes after his mum and that bastard she hooked up with. Keeps all his brains in his pants though bloody Henry Ingram does."

Lily winced as she pictured the scene and could almost feel her father's humiliation.

"I did the best I could, Lily to stop him from rambling. If it's any consolation most of the men in there were too far in their cups to even know what day it was."

"But he's always loved James, Alex. Sometimes I've thought he loves him more than me, so I don't understand."

Alex knelt and took Lily's hands in his touching them lightly with his lips.

"He loves James like his own, Lily, because to all intents and purposes he is. Whatever you may think of your dad his family means everything to him. He would never intentionally hurt Ethel for the world, and he's always been a far better father to James than Henry ever could have been. And I also got the impression that Bert thought he was to blame in some way

Lily snatched her hands away from Alex and started to pace the room. She felt that she would go mad if she didn't do something. Any longer spent in this place with the revelations that kept coming and she would no longer be able to breathe. She felt far more mixed up than she had ever done. Alex's passionate outburst had surprised her, and he seemed almost in sympathy with her father.

"Does my father remember what he said that night?" Lily almost spat the words at Alex and immediately felt ashamed.

"If he does, he has never let on, so I've always left it that way. Don't be so harsh on him, Lily. He loves you very much."

"He's weak, Alex. He should have stood up for himself. It's as though he offered my mother to Henry on a plate. He had no intention of fighting for her." Lily swallowed hard to keep her tears at bay.

"He's been fighting all his life, Lily. Bert was protecting his family in the only way he knew how. Can't you see the strength it has taken him to forgive Ethel and raise James as his own? Sometimes life is more than just about you. It's not all black and white with neat lines painted so that you know where to tread."

Lily was shocked. Alex had never raised his voice to her in all the years she'd known him, and he was now practically shaking.

"What are you saying then, Alex? That I'm a bitch. Why not chuck "whore" in for good measure along with "pathetic" daughter." I probably deserve it. I don't know how such a respectable member of the community can stand to be seen with me."

Lily was now almost choking with emotion and undisclosed feelings. Alex immediately stepped forward as tears began to run down her face.

"I'm so sorry, Lily. The last thing I wanted to do was upset you, and I don't know why you are talking like that. You're spirited, proud and yes, sometimes a little stubborn. An Armitage, all the way through, I would say."

Alex opened his arms, and Lily walked into the haven of his love. For now, maybe this was the only place she wanted to be, and the future would have to sort itself out."

CHAPTER ELEVEN

June 1910

After the turbulent summer of 1908 Lily began to think that maybe her destiny was mapped out for her and in some ways, she found this a relief. The excitement she'd craved hadn't turned out to be nearly as satisfying as she'd hoped. The main feeling it had brought Lily was one of vague disquiet.

She'd seen Henry in passing a few times since "the incident", and he'd behaved impeccably. Sometimes Lily felt as though it hadn't happened. She still couldn't square the image of the prosperous business gentleman with that of the maniac almost beside himself with lust and rage. It was a similar feeling to the one Lily experienced after witnessing her grandmother's funeral. Of course, she knew that both events had happened, but she felt disconnected from them, almost as though they had happened to another person and she'd merely been a bystander. Lily surmised that perhaps she had been in her grandma's case.

She also now felt a little awkward around James though thankfully he seemed oblivious to it. Even when he caught her staring at him trying to work out if she could see any of Henry in him James just gave her one of his mischievous smiles and carried on with what he was doing. He was going to be a heartbreaker one day Lily mused as she watched him flick his dark brown hair away from his eyes as he pored over yet another book about cars.

"I thought Mum and Dad wanted you to be a famous doctor or something equally highbrow. I don't think car salesman was on their itinerary." Lily teased him one evening as she sat by the fire darning her father's socks.

"You know, Lily, sometimes you talk so posh I don't know what you're on about. What's an itinerary?"

"It means what are you going to do with your life?" Lily laughed.

"Why didn't you say that then? Anyway, I've plenty of time to think about all that. What do you think of this Vauxhall?" James held the book in front of Lily at the relevant page and beamed up at her with hazel eyes remarkably like her father's.

Alex remained Lily's one constant and the person she trusted the most in the world. It was a safe, comfortable feeling to know that somebody had her back come what may though Alex still insisted that they wait a few more years before they got married.

"I want you to be sure, Lily. I'm older than you and maybe lived a little more. I don't want to hold you back from doing anything, and when we become husband and wife, I don't want you to have any regrets." Lily knew how lucky she was to have a man whose first thought wasn't about getting " a bit of your father" as the workers in the factory had been so fond of saying.

Consequently, a couple of years passed with life going on in a similar vein. Lily saw very little of Henry, and he faded into the background. She realised that James was the brother she'd always known despite the circumstances of his birth. The shop was ticking over, and Lily felt content until the summer of 1910 when Lily's world was turned upside down.

"What's the matter? Calm down. I'll be with you in a minute." Lily shouted from across the room as she struggled to put on the boots she'd discarded earlier. The rapping on the door increased, and Lily began to worry that her landlord would throw her out if it carried on. Probably not though Lily smiled. She and Mr Jennings had hit it off from the start. As soon as he'd found out that Lily worked in a bookshop and there were generous discounts for friends, he'd not put a foot wrong.

Lily had left the rooms above "Bookends" six months ago as though she loved the work, she'd had enough of living on top of it. She planned to eventually get a small place of her own with her savings, and she wasn't far short of being able to do that. The flat she was in now though was tastefully furnished and cosy and it suited her fine for now.

"Who is it? What on earth is the matter? Don't you know I've got work tomorrow."? Lily flung the door open while still trying to lace one of her boots properly and then stopped in her tracks. The first thing that Lily noticed was that Miss Hardcastle was wearing no hat. Later she would reflect how absurd that had been but maybe a little understandable. In the last couple of years, Miss Hardcastle had become a milliner's dream and purchased several large hats with wide brims in differing colours and sported them whenever she was out and about.

"We have got to do our best to keep up with our dear Bertie," Miss Hardcastle would announce as though impressing our current King of England was a matter of national honour. Lily thought it unlikely that Edward VII had visited or was ever likely to visit Derby soon but didn't like to dash her former colleague's hopes.

Without waiting to be invited in Miss Hardcastle pushed past Lily and proceeded to agitatedly pace up and down the relatively small room. Eventually, she paused by the slightly open window from where Lily was lucky enough to get a view of the river. In the dimming light, Lily could just about make out a heron swooping in to secure his supper.

"Miss Hardcastle! What is the matter?" Though the two women had become close Lily would never dream of calling Miss Hardcastle by her Christian name and to Miss Hardcastle she was usually "child."

"Lily..." Miss Hardcastle turned from the window, and Lily felt she had never seen anyone age so much in a matter of days. Her skin was pale while at the same time rivulets of sweat were pouring down her face plastering her slightly curly dark hair to her forehead. Her eyes were sunk into the back of her head, and she looked as though she hadn't slept for a week.

"My dear!" Lily moved swiftly to her side and gently guided her to the small chintz settee that dominated the room." Tell me. You're frightening me."

"I don't know how to begin, and I don't understand why he did it this way. He promised to give us more time," sobbed Miss Hardcastle as she gallantly fought for breath.

"Just say it." Lily pleaded. "Whatever it is, it can't be that bad. We can sort it out together. We usually do."

"Not this time, my dear. Nobody can. Maybe not even God." Lily could see Miss Hardcastle taking deep breaths and visually trying to calm herself down.

"That's right. Nice and easy. Now please tell me what's wrong," Lily pleaded.

"It's Philip, my dear."

"Is he ill? Take me to him. Is he in the hospital? Lily could feel her words tumbling away from her. It was almost as though she knew that something terrible was just around the corner and she could put it off, just a little longer.

"He's dead, Lily." Lily felt her heart beginning to race and could hardly comprehend what she was hearing.

"You must have made a mistake. Philip was fine this afternoon. Full of his usual jokes. Insulting the customers and them loving every minute."

Miss Hardcastle took a deep breath and put her hands on Lily's shoulders looking into her eyes.

"He killed himself, Lily. I found him hanging two hours since."

Lily knew that the lump she felt in her throat and the cold icicle melting and trickling down her back weren't real. Logic told her so, but it also told her that Philip had to be alive. It'd only been six hours since she'd left him. She would have noticed if he'd been behaving differently. If anything, he'd been in even better form than average during the afternoon. Lily felt as though she couldn't breathe. Her whole world was running away with her, and she couldn't keep up.

Somewhere in another reality, she could hear Miss Hardcastle calling her name, but Lily couldn't seem to locate her anymore. She'd been here a minute ago so where had she gone? Lily was sure that she had something to tell her, but it couldn't have been that important otherwise she would know what it was, wouldn't she?

Lily woke up to find her head on a cushion and her feet propped up on the floral settee. Miss Hardcastle's concerned face hovered above her.

"I'm so sorry, Lily. I shouldn't have blurted it out like that, but it was such a shock finding him like that, and then there were the police to deal with..."

After a few seconds of blessed oblivion, harsh reality came flooding back to Lily. She didn't know what to say or how to behave and felt utterly bewildered. Miss Hardcastle seemed to have got herself a little more together since before Lily had fainted though she still looked completely drained.

"Let me go and make us both a good cup of tea." She seemed to be trying to regain some of her composure. "While I do that perhaps you had better read this, my dear. He told me to give it to you when...well you know."
Miss Hardcastle handed Lily a small white envelope with Lily's name on the front written in a flamboyant hand. Lily took it with trembling hands and watched Miss Hardcastle retreat to the kitchen area. Summoning all her courage, she ripped open the envelope avoiding damaging the piece of paper inside and slowly unfolded it.
My dear Lily,
If you are reading this, then I have found the courage to shuffle off my mortal coil and leave this earth on my terms. I know that you will be confused and maybe a little upset, but you must understand my dear that living with an inoperable brain tumour that was gradually growing more aggressive was no walk in the park.
Liz and I tried. Our trips abroad were our last-ditch attempt at finding a cure or at least a treatment that would have given me more time, but it was not to be. I know what you thought Miss Armitage. What a filthy mind you have for one so young and yes there was some of that as well which I feel no shame about whatsoever. If you can't have a good time when you know that you are dying when can you?
I have left you the shop and the rooms above. "Bookends" was all about you, Lily. Your energy and passion gave it new life, and I got enormous pleasure from watching it, and you grow side by side. Liz said you were the one and she was right. Don't be too sad, Lily. You and Liz made a stubborn and at times selfish middle-aged man very happy in his final years – much more so than he deserved.
I don't doubt that we'll all meet again somewhere down the track but not too soon, I hope. That's of course if St Peter will open the pearly gates for me.

God bless for now.
Philip Devine.
Lily could barely read the final words of the letter for the tears coursing down her face.
"But why didn't you tell me?" Lily pleaded as she saw her friend coming back into the room with two cups.
"He didn't want you to know, Lily and he was right. What would have been the point? You'd got problems of your own, and he didn't want to see you miserable. He loved watching you in the shop each day and discussing all the new ideas you had with him. I'm sure he went on longer than he would have done otherwise if he hadn't had all that."
Miss Hardcastle had washed her face and pinned her hair back up again. Small details that made Lily feel a little more grounded again and gave her the confidence to speak freely.
"You've known him for a long time haven't you, Miss Hardcastle?"
"I have, my dear. I loved Philip very much and feel no shame in that." Tears glistened in her eyes but didn't fall.
"Why did you never marry?" Lily tentatively asked.
"He was already married to a wonderful woman but today's not the day to go into all that. Besides which I enjoy taking a bit of a risk from time to time."
The two women smiled at each other for the first time that night. Lily felt no shock as she trusted both. She knew that their reasons would have been good ones whatever they were.
"You must feel so sad." Lily took Miss Hardcastle's hand.
"I do, my child. Desperately but I was prepared. It was just the shock of finding him like that, but I understand. Philip wanted to leave this world while he was still himself and not the person that a brain tumour would eventually have turned him into."

Later that night when Miss Hardcastle was tucked up snoring gently in Lily's bed, as Lily hadn't wanted her to spend the night on her own, Lily thought back on the evening's events. She would miss Philip for a long time, probably always in some way but she understood why he'd done what he did and what a brave decision that was. Lily felt desperately sorry for Miss Hardcastle, but she was one of the strongest women that Lily had ever met, and Miss Hardcastle would move forward taking her memories with her. It also looked as though she would move on as a moderately wealthy woman. Who would have thought? Lily Armitage from Peel Street – a successful businesswoman and despite her grief Lily couldn't help but feel a flicker of excitement deep within her soul.

CHAPTER TWELVE

June 1913 to August 1914

Sometimes when Lily had time to stop and think she was astounded at how quickly the last three years had flown. She'd thrown herself into making "Bookends" a legacy of which Philip would have been proud. Besides selling all manner of books it now harboured fancy stationery which seemed to be a hit with most of the Derby ladies and a small section was devoted to needlework and craft essentials. The upstairs room where Lily had lived for a while, she converted into a little cafe providing light refreshments. Its central location in the town gave it an immediate advantage and custom was thriving.
Philip had been a wealthy man and both Lily, and Miss Hardcastle had been able to buy themselves modest but comfortable dwellings. Lily's small house was on the outskirts of the town towards Ashbourne. It had the luxury of a small plot of land at the rear where Lily kept chickens, grew flowers and sometimes even gave herself the luxury of sitting out there after a hard day at work breathing in the fresh air and taking in the view.
She still thought of Philip often, but time had mellowed the acute pain she had felt in the year after his too early death. When she thought of him now, it was with gratitude as she realised how lucky she was. The main blot in her contentment was her feelings about Alex. She'd always known he would be completely supportive of her decision to

take on the shop after Philip's death. He'd guided her through the minefield of jargon and legalities that had followed the suitably elaborate funeral. He'd also been a shoulder to cry on when the harsh circumstances of Philip's passing overwhelmed her.

Lily knew that Alex would make a good husband and he'd been true to his word never pressurising her in any form and allowing her time to find her feet with the business. Without it, they would probably now be married possibly with a child on the way. Lily knew that Alex desperately wanted a family and Lily supposed that she did eventually, just not yet. Also, over the last year especially as things started to settle down Lily was no longer sure that she wanted to marry him at all.

"But why not? He's gorgeous and adores you." Maggie, who remained Lily's best friend, scolded. The two women sat in Lily's garden drinking in the last rays of the sun. Though their lives had gone in very different directions, they shared a bond from childhood and still tried to catch up with each other at least once a month.

"I know, and that's why I feel so bad. It's not even Alex. I just don't think I want to marry anyone."

"Don't let me put you off." Maggie teased. Lily smiled. Her friend had always been able to laugh at herself and keep positive, and she certainly hadn't had it easy. Her husband had been disabled in the mine and Maggie had returned to long hours of work in the mill too soon after giving birth. She'd ended up collapsing and being quite ill. Maggie recovered, but it just made Lily realise how even more selfish she was towards Alex.

She didn't doubt that she would get the respect of the community once she married him. His days in prison had been virtually forgotten and most people, especially the ladies, liked " that lovely Mr Poynton from the high school." Women were now legal equals of their husbands and not just property. Not that Alex had a problem at all with Lily having her own business, so she knew again how unfair she was being. However, Lily knew that society's attitudes were difficult to shift, and most women and men still expected the wife to sit at home by her husband's side, bear children for him and let him have his way whenever he got the urge. Maggie laughed out loud as Lily tried to explain how she felt.

"Well if you don't want him to have his way with you, I don't mind being second best."

"You need to wash your mouth out with soap and water, Maggie Jenkins before your mother hears you."

"That might be a tad difficult as she's been dead well over a year." Maggie smiled.

Lily felt ashamed and felt a blush travelling up her neck to her face.

"I'm so sorry, Maggie. I forgot with her not having been around for such a long time and you know..."

"Aye, I know, Lily so don't trouble yourself. I don't anymore. Leaving my dad in the lurch and going off with her fancy fella to Nottingham. Got run over by a tram she did but neither dad nor I heard from her after she left, so it don't make any difference."

Lily thought of her grandma and the way she was never spoke of in her parent's house. She hadn't thought of her for a while, but now she felt a little sad for her father. Maybe Lily and her dad didn't always see eye to eye, but she couldn't imagine never going to his funeral or speaking of him again.

"A penny for them." Maggie interrupted Lily's train of thought.

"Sorry, Maggie. I was daydreaming. What did you say?"

"If you're at all interested," Maggie pretended to be put out," I wondered what you thought of that suffragette woman who was killed by that horse."
"You mean Emily Davison, don't you? It was the king's horse running in the Derby, and I don't think she died until a few days later. Don't know what she was thinking though. It's not going to do women's rights any good I tell you."
Maggie nodded and stood up dusting down her skirt.
"Well, I'd better be on my way. Don't know how some of these women have even got the time to go running around getting in folk's way."
Lily laughed gently. Maggie was no militant, but she was generous, kind-hearted and utterly right in her opinions about Alex.

Just over a year later Lily was sitting in the garden in almost the exact position she'd sat with Maggie, but this time it was with Alex. It had been a year when little had changed. In some ways, Lily was grateful for that. A year with no earth-shattering emotional problems or tragedies. In some ways a little boring but just what the doctor had ordered.
Alex glanced across at her from the chair opposite, and Lily's mind drifted back to the conversation she'd had with Maggie last summer. Alex still undoubtedly worshipped the ground that Lily trod on, but Lily knew that he couldn't wait forever. It wasn't fair to him as his desire for children had increased if anything and Alex would make a fantastic father. Lily knew that his child would never feel isolated or unloved as he had as a boy.
Lily felt impatient with herself. Sometimes she didn't even know what she wanted. Even "Bookends" was while not exactly a chore was probably no longer the challenge it had been in the early days. She'd employed two extra staff just last month, and most days she didn't even need to be there if

she hadn't wanted to be. It was almost as if when life got too easy, she felt unsettled and needed something else to strive for or a new problem to solve. Armitage women weren't renowned for making life simple for themselves Lily reflected as she thought about her mother and the secrets that they shared.

"Did you hear about the assassination of Archduke Franz Ferdinand in Sarajevo?" Alex said dragging Lily back from her thoughts again.

"I think I heard something about it, but it's not got anything to do with us has it? I don't even know where Sarajevo is. Alex raised his eyebrows and gently teased her.

"Geography's never been your strong point, has it? Maybe I should have been bringing you atlases to read instead of "Alice in Wonderland" all those years ago."

Lily smiled as she remembered how good Alex had been to her family when she'd still only been a child.

"Well I don't have any cause to go anywhere much besides Derby anyway do I Mr Poynton so what's the point?"

"Maybe we'll all see the point soon enough." Alex reflected.

"Are you ok, Alex? You look. I don't know. Sad suddenly."

Alex came across and planted a gentle kiss on Lily's forehead.

"Don't worry about me. Just an old man with his ramblings. I just feel uneasy and don't know why. I just sense that there is something around the corner that none of us sees yet."

"What sort of thing?" Lily felt a little scared at the gravity of his tone.

"Something that could change us all forever, my love."

On 4th August 1914, Britain declared war on Germany in response to their invasion of Belgium. Lily felt a shiver of fear go down her spine as she listened to Asquith's words on the radio. Her eyes drifted over her worried-looking parents and met Alex's. This then was the something around the corner. She wasn't surprised that Alex had had some premonition about this day. He read voraciously and was always interested in what was going on around him. To hear him hold his own with older and supposedly more experienced colleagues made Lily feel proud. But this wasn't now some intellectual discussion or hypothetical situation briefly alluded to in an English country garden on a perfect summer's evening. It was tangible and Lily, herself, was intelligent enough to realise that nobody in Britain would be untouched by what was about to unfold.

A week later Lily and Alex were sitting with Ethel and Bert around their hearth. After finishing work Lily had begun to take the time to drop in on her mum and dad after work. Though she loved her little house, it seemed just that bit too quiet now. It wasn't only Lily as Alex also seemed to gravitate towards Bert and Ethel's home on Peel Street in the evening. It was as though they found some comfort in each other's company.

"I don't know what you're all so worried about?" James came bounding in with his usual boundless enthusiasm. "At school, they're saying that all the fighting will be over by Christmas."

"I hope they're right, lad but that's not what Lord Kitchener is saying." Bert smiled at James.

"What does he know?" James answered as he flung his satchel onto the table.

"Sometimes our James! For somebody who is supposed to be earmarked for Oxford or Cambridge, you take the biscuit." Lily admonished him, but her twinkling eyes and slight quirk of her mouth belied her stern words. James, though he was completely unaware of it was like a breath of fresh air and always lightened the atmosphere. He was still obsessed with all car related matters but was proving to be an excellent scholar and gaining top grades in all his subjects.

"Is there any tea going, Mum?" he grinned.

"Make yourself a jam sandwich to fill the gap," Ethel shouted over Lily's head. James didn't need to be told twice and next minute was clattering around in the small kitchen.

"What do you think, Bert? How long is it going to last?" Alex spoke softly as Lily regarded the exchange between the two men. Alex had always treated her father with respect and seemed to value his opinion. She felt a little guilty as she was honest enough to admit that he behaved far better towards her father than she ever had.

"I think it's going to be a long haul, son, but we've got to believe that we'll come out of it the other side."

"They're asking for volunteers, Bert. There are recruitment posters everywhere in town."

"All I can say is that I thank God James is too young to be considered," Ethel remarked, "though I don't think he'd go even if he could. His heads too wrapped up in his books."

There was a lull in the conversation until Bert split the silence and smiled sadly across at Alex.

"You're going aren't you, Alex?"

"Of course, he's not going, Dad. What are you on about now? He's got to teach. That's where he's needed." Lily could hear her high-pitched voice resounding in her head. Alex could hear the women's voices in the background but wasn't taking in what they were saying. It was almost as though there was only himself and Bert in the room. He met the older man's hazel eyes and could see the pain and respect in them.

"Yes, Bert. I signed up this morning, and I'm leaving for training in a couple of days' time."

CHAPTER THIRTEEN

November 1914

Lily woke with a start. Sweat was trickling down her face. Her heart was beating so fast that if she hadn't known better, she would have sworn that a sparrow had taken up residence and was frantically beating its wings to escape. She felt afraid which made no sense as she'd always felt secure in her little house.

It had just been another bad dream she realised. Struggling out of bed Lily gave a little gasp as her feet met the cold stone of the floor. There was more than a definite nip in the air now, and she wrapped her dressing gown more tightly around her. Pulling back the curtains slightly Lily stared into the impenetrable darkness. The only faint shapes she could make out were the white blobs of the sheep that seemed to continue to graze contentedly regardless of the hour of day or night.

Despite the cold Lily opened the window slightly and breathed in the fresh night air which calmed her. She couldn't even remember what she had been dreaming of apart from Alex's face staring at her with his mouth wide open but with no words coming out. At some point, this had been replaced by Philip smiling at her in the benevolent way of old. At that moment, Lily thought that she must have realised that she was in a dream as his face had been so white and then Miss Hardcastle had appeared with a red rose between her teeth.

"Pull yourself together girl." It was probably that which had woke her as she had always found Miss Hardcastle impossible not to be obeyed. The feeling of terror had slowly subsided, and Lily stood listening to the silence. It seemed almost inconceivable that a few hundred miles away young men and boys were blowing each other to pieces in the name of justice and honour. She still didn't completely understand why Alex had felt such an overriding compunction to take up arms. She knew from little things that he'd let slip about his time in prison that he'd experienced violence at first hand and how much he'd hated it. To put himself in a position where he might very well have to kill another human being face to face to save himself or his men didn't tally with the gentle man he was. On the other hand, though Lily knew how pig-headed and principled he could be at times and if there were a cause he believed in he would be first in the queue. Now, nobody knew where he was or when he was coming home again. Lily pushed the niggling thought that he might never arrive home to the back of her mind.

"Men! Who needs them anyway?" Lily muttered fiercely under her breath. She was quite convinced that if women oversaw the world, there wouldn't be the destruction of peace that was going on now. Of course, she knew that the war was a lot more than boys playing with their toys but sometimes Lily felt that their testosterone-fuelled bodies led to them making rash decisions without little thought of the consequences. She wasn't surprised that Henry immediately leapt into her mind though she rarely thought of him usually. The last she'd heard he'd also signed up. With his connections, Lily thought that he would probably fly through the ranks and would be an officer now at the very least.

Lily half-filled the kettle as she watched the first weak shafts of sunlight heralding a new day and wondered for how many of the servicemen out there today it would be their last dawn. Only last week Chrissie Bennett who lived a couple of doors down from Ethel and Bert had received a telegram informing her of the death of her son in action.
"He died a hero," Chrissie had told Ethel, "dragging one of our wounded lads away from enemy fire. Why did he have to be a hero, Eth? As though that makes it any better. It won't bring him back, will it?" Ethel had told Lily that Chrissie had then collapsed in tears on the pavement and she'd had to go and get Bert and James to help get her inside.
Lily was so deep in thought that she jumped at the insistent banging on her front door.
"Open up, our Lily, you lazybones."
Lily pushed the hair away from her face and reached for one of Alex's old cardigans flinging it around her shoulders. Winter was coming for sure. She smiled as she saw who her early morning visitor was.
"What are you doing here so bright and early? You've even woken the larks. What's so urgent to pull you out from between the sheets at least a couple of hours before normal?"
James gave Lily one of the infectious smiles that lit up his face and rarely failed to make those around him feel better. If he ever achieved his ambition to be a doctor, he'd take the ducks off the water and have all the ladies confiding their deepest worries to him.
"It isn't that early, our Lil."
Lily glanced at the monstrosity of a wall clock that hung in the hallway. It had been one of the rare occasions when Alex had got it wrong having bought it for her last birthday. Not that Lily would ever have told him so as he usually was spot

on with his gifts. James was right. She'd been daydreaming though it didn't matter as she wasn't going to the shop today but meeting up with Miss Hardcastle. They rarely went a week without seeing one another unless Miss Hardcastle was abroad on one of her scouting expeditions for Royal Crown Derby. She had a flair for design and had long left the confines of the office.

"Mum says to come to tea after work, and she won't take no for an answer, so you'd better come, or she'll shoot the messenger."

"I'd better had then, hadn't I as we don't want the golden boy in trouble." Lily ruffled James's hair as she knew he hated it but couldn't resist the rare scowl that crossed his face when she did. "Tell her I might be a bit earlier than five though as I'm not at work today and I'll help her make it. Mind you I won't be staying if you use it as an excuse not to do your homework." James gave her a wink, and Lily laughed. She knew there were no worries on that score. James was beginning to realise the potential that both Bert and Ethel had seen in him from when he was young. He was still crazy about cars, and his dream was to own one as quickly as he could. Lily remembered how he'd so admired Henry's car on that fateful day from when everything seemed to start going wrong.

However, his sights were now firmly set on joining the medical profession. Though James hadn't really known Philip very well his death and the circumstances surrounding it had made a big impression on him. One evening, shortly after Lily had returned to "Bookends" after Philip's death, James came to meet her from work. They walked in comfortable silence for a few minutes until James broke it. "One day they'll be able to cure people who get sick like Mr Devine." Lily couldn't completely hide her surprise though James seemed deep in thought and barely noticed. "And

they'll be able to help people who are depressed like dad."
An image of Philip from one of Lily's nightmares momentarily flashed through her mind to be quickly replaced by one of her father hunched up over the hearth. Lily didn't think that there would ever be a medicine to cure the insidious disease that had claimed Philip and wracked him with such pain that he had resorted to desperate measures. Neither did she see why good money should be wasted on people who sat around and refused to help themselves.
However, she didn't want to slight James who had obviously been thinking this way for a while. She felt privileged that he felt able to open up to her like he did. The feeling of discomfort she had originally felt around him after discovering his parentage had all but disappeared by that time though she still felt uneasy around Ethel from time to time.
"I'd like to think that in the future nobody would have to suffer the indignities and doubts that Philip did." Lily smiled gently at her brother.
"That's what I'm going to do, Lily. Help people like Mr Devine and dad."
"You're going to be a fancy doctor then are you and leave us to go and live on Harley Street?"
"Well I don't know about that, but you just wait, Lily. I'll be the best doctor that Derby's ever seen."
Though the conversation had been a few years ago, Lily remembered it as clear as day. Firstly, because the young man who now stood on her doorstep had never wavered from his commitment to try to make it happen. Also, because Lily had felt ashamed that a child so much younger than herself could feel such empathy with a man whom he only knew in passing and a man who spent most of his working hours staring into space. A man who wasn't even

his father though of course in James's eyes he was and if necessary, Lily would take that secret to her own grave.
At times Lily worried that she couldn't connect deeply enough with people and often felt that she was on the outside looking in and just going through the motions. First, there was her father, then Henry and more recently Alex. She thought that she'd fallen short in her emotional involvement with them all. Events that should have stuck, almost at times felt that they had happened to someone else. Maybe her mother was right, and she was still living with her head in the clouds. However, though perhaps at one time she had been young and at times foolish she felt that as she'd grown into womanhood, she was now able to face her shortcomings honestly. She knew that sometimes she was still quick to judge and at times impulsive, but Lily had always believed that she had a vast capacity for love.
Lily reasoned that maybe love wasn't the all-encompassing emotion that she read about in her novels and could appear in different forms. Her grief after Philip's death had been almost overwhelming. Lily also knew that she loved Miss Hardcastle though she would never say so to her face and Lily loved her mother though she didn't want the same life for herself. Did she love or even like her father? Lily believed that deep down she must as otherwise how could he engender such feelings of anger in her at times and why should she care if he sat wasting the hours that God had given him? What she felt for James was easy. Lily would lay down her life for her brother. Lily laughed out loud as she realised how melodramatic she was again. It must be in the blood, darling. At the very least though she would stand up for James against anyone who set out to hurt him and she would help him in any way she could for him to realise his ambition.

But what about Alex? Maybe that was the biggest question mark in her mind. She missed him and that she couldn't deny. The conversation always flowed smoothly between them, and they never ran out of topics to discuss. He was also the kindest and gentlest of men but his time in prison had given him a steely resolve. She felt that she could spend every day in his company and be content but was that the life she wanted for herself? Was it exciting enough? Did Alex want the kind of life that Lily envisioned or was he content to remain a schoolmaster for the rest of his life? Terrible events were happening in the world as November struggled to a close. Ypres in Belgium had been burned by German bombing and closer to home at Sheerness Harbour, Battleship HMS Bulwark had exploded leaving 788 dead. Maybe Alex was in danger this very moment though Lily had always felt that she would know if he was. But then why would she if she wasn't even sure if she loved him?
That morning, after Lily had seen James on his way, she sat quietly for a while longer looking out over the barren fields that bore just a slight hint still of the frost that had occurred overnight. Lily loved this place but recently had been feeling lonely and lacking in purpose. Most people around her seemed to be either fighting the war in their own way or building a future despite the uncertainties. She was overseeing a shop that now literally ran itself with the extra staff she could now afford to employ. She would be forever grateful to Philip for giving her financial stability and freedom, but on this grey and misty morning, she imagined she could almost hear his voice from the other side of the grave.
"Go and get it, my dear. It might be just around the corner or the other side of the world, but you'll recognise it when you find it." Lily smiled as she remembered his gravelly but cultured voice. Philip had never seemed to have trouble in

taking the first step on many journeys but what did you do, Lily thought, if you didn't know what that first step was anymore.

CHAPTER FOURTEEN

February 1915

"Why don't you move back in with us for a bit, love? It'll be much closer to work, and it would be a bit of female company for me instead of having to listen to these two blabbering away about nothing all night long."
Bert shook his head in mock exasperation at his wife.
"We wouldn't charge," Bert joked, "and your mum could do with a bit of help around the house. You'll certainly liven things up if nothing else."
"Please, Lily!" James pleaded. "Then you'll be able to tell me about everything that's happening down at Rolls Royce. Did you know that Eagle engine you said they'd been testing is based on the Rolls Royce Silver Ghost engine and the Daimler engine that was used in a 1913 Grand Prix Mercedes?"
"I haven't a clue what you're talking about, but I'll think on about the other thing," Lily promised.
A week after Alex had left, the office job at Rolls Royce had turned up and while it was not quite the epiphany that Lily had been searching for, he felt compelled to try for it. Before the war, the firm had made luxury cars, but in January the Admiralty had ordered twenty-five new engines for planes, and Rolls Royce began their significant journey into the world of aviation. While, James somehow, seemed to know a lot more about the inner workings of the company and their products, Lily felt that at least she would be in daily

contact with people who were working positively towards the war effort. It helped her feel closer to Alex and while she didn't really need the money, she felt more satisfied than she'd been for a while.

In the evenings though her house seemed a little bleak and dismal. Not many visitors had appeared over the back end, and Lily understood why. It was just that bit too far to walk in the wet and the frost especially when the nights had started pulling in.

Lily still cherished her property, and in a few weeks, the garden would be full of crocuses and primroses. These would be followed by the bright yellow trumpets of the daffodils that would cut through the gloom and would herald the start of spring. The brilliant red tulips would then unfold their faces to the sun and would dance like young ladies stepping out into society for the first time. These days seemed a long way off when the bitter winds of February made the windows rattle all night long, and Lily lay tossing and turning with unsettling thoughts running through her head.

Her parent's house, while more cramped, seemed brighter and full of life. Neighbours and friends of James were always popping in and out. Ethel was continually bustling about. The malaise that had affected her a few years ago had disappeared, and she seemed to be full of renewed vigour. Even Bert seemed more interested in what was going on around him since the war had begun. Quite often on a weekend night when James hadn't got college the next day, Bert would sit with James into the early hours helping him out with a problem he couldn't get his head around. Alternatively, they would sometimes sit discussing how they thought the war effort was going. Sometimes when Lily was out back helping Ethel, she would hear Bert laugh out loud at something that James must have said. Ethel would smile while Lily would occasionally feel a pang of jealousy. She could never remember making her father laugh about anything, and James wasn't even his flesh and blood. She always immediately felt so sorry for her thoughts that she ended up being extra pleasant to them both for the rest of the day.

As Lily was lacing up her boots ready to begin the trudge home, through an evening where it had already started drizzling, she began to think there were worse ideas than to move back in for a couple of months while she settled into her new job. Lily knew that she didn't always see eye to eye with her father, but at least she hadn't got the problems some young girls had. Kitty, one of the girls at "Bookends", was having a hard time of it at home with her dad coming in drunk at all hours and taking it out on Kitty's mother. Lily only knew this because one evening, after work she had found Kitty sobbing quietly in the back room. It had all come tumbling out, and Kitty told Lily that she was afraid that her father would start on her next.

"He's as nice as pie when he isn't in his cups...honest, Lily but when he's had a few, it's as though the devil incarnate takes him over. I swear to God it's true." At least, Lily thought listening to Kitty, her father had never been a violent man, and for that, they could all be thankful. Lily knew that Kitty would grab the opportunity to be a sitting tenant in Lily's house for a couple of months and that would mean the house would be kept ticking over until the better weather.

Lily felt that the loneliness that had seemed to envelop her even more in the last few weeks might very well have something to do with Alex. He's been one of the very first men in his battalion to be granted leave. At the end of January, he'd arrived home for a precious few days staying at Ethel and Bert's as it wouldn't have been deemed proper to remain at Lily's. Lily had been shocked to see how thin and tired Alex looked as she waved to him from the other end of the platform. As she got closer, she saw that there were purple shadows under his eyes and the mud from the trenches was still visible about his person though he had done his best to tidy himself as best as he could under the circumstances.

"You're looking bonny, Lily. Really bonny." Alex smiled down at her. Lily was going to reply in the same vein but knew Alex would see through it straight away, so she just put her hand in his.

"That's a new one, Mr Poynton. Been hanging out with the Scots have we while we've been away?"

"Must have picked it up from Andy, Andy Stewart. A great young lad from Inverness way. Always cheerful you know, Lily. Never mind what was thrown at him. Kept us all going sometimes with his warped sense of humour."

"And has he got leave as well or wasn't he one of the lucky ones?"

"Got blown up last week along with his jokes. Anyway, best get on. Mustn't keep your mum and dad waiting."

Alex linked Lily's arm as they emerged from the railway station onto the street. Lily had to admit she felt a little shocked at how quickly Alex had dismissed the demise of one of his comrades. She was also surprised to notice the admiring glances of both men and women as they strolled along the pavement.

"They're looking at you as though you're some sort of demi-god," Lily whispered. She was a little embarrassed to be stared at so blatantly though Alex barely seemed to notice.

"Well done mate." A total stranger came up and vigorously pumped Alex's hand. "You're out there doing us proud." Lily wondered why the athletic-looking young man in question wasn't also out there "doing us proud" if it was so crucial to him.

Alex looked at the man as if he hardly existed. Lily wasn't even sure if he realised the man had been shaking his hand up and down a minute ago.

"It's like a ghost town, Lily," Alex muttered, and Lily could feel his fingers pressing more tightly into her lower arm. Lily hadn't really noticed but now looking around she realised that most of the people in the street that morning were women or men over forty. The rest of the men were either in college like James or floundering around in the mud at the front. Lily momentarily wondered how many of them would walk the streets of Derby again.

The four days Alex was home passed in a flash. He talked very little about what he'd seen or done in France and seemed to want to concentrate on simple pleasures like going for a pint in "The Lamb and Flag" or walking along the banks of the River Derwent. On the third day, they'd borrowed bikes from James's friend. Alex oiled them up, and they'd cycled out almost as far as Ashbourne and the gateway to the dales. That was the most peaceful Lily saw Alex since his brief return. When it was time to leave Alex told Lily he didn't want her to go to the station. It would be too hard, so they'd said goodbye on Peel Street. He held on to Lily a little longer than might have been deemed proper before, but rules had changed, and now nobody batted an eyelid.

"When I come back again, Lily, we need to talk, and I will come back." His grey-green eyes met Lily's blue ones for a moment, and then he took her hand pressing his lips lightly to it. With a brief nod, he turned and walked briskly away without a backward glance. Lily watched until he went around the corner and was out of sight. She turned to go

back indoors full of an empty feeling she couldn't quite identify. Ethel took one look at her face and sat her down. "Sit down, love while I make you a strong cup of tea." A few minutes later Ethel came and placed a large mug of steaming tea in her hands. She sat across from Lily and picked up the knitting she had on the table and set to work.
"He didn't sleep in his bed you know?"
"What do you mean?" Lily asked, slightly puzzled.
"When I took him up his tray in the morning, I found him curled up on the floor fast asleep."
"Did he say anything about it?"
"Well it would have been a bit difficult to ignore but if the truth be told he was embarrassed about it. He told me he'd got so used to sleeping on the hard ground that he couldn't get used to the softness of the bed."
Lily couldn't even begin to think about what it must be like for him.
"Did he say anything to you, mum? About what it's like."
Ethel took her daughter's hand.
"All he said, love, was that it was hell. One minute you were joking with the man next to you in the trenches and the next he was dead. He said that those of us left behind couldn't begin to understand what it's like over there."
"He's right, Mum. We can't, but I do know he'll fight tooth and nail to get back to us. I also know the men at his side are the lucky ones. He won't turn his back on anyone if they need help."
"Unless they're on the other side," Ethel said quietly.
The honesty of Ethel's observation was evident in the silence that followed.
Though Lily knew that none of them at home could grasp the reality of the Great War as it was beginning to be called, they knew that it wasn't now all "going to be over by Christmas." This original optimism had been replaced by

uncertainty about the future for them all. Lily's initial confidence that Alex would sail through the war unscathed had been severely challenged. She wondered whether she should have given more of herself to him. Lily remembered thinking this about Henry but in very different circumstances and thanked God now that she had never gone that far. With Alex though she felt that it might have been different.

Maggie had told her that the girls on Pear Street always did well when the lads were on leave.

"A quick shag in the passageway by Benny's and they're set up for the month. Think I'm in the wrong line of work, Lil." Lily was no prude, but sometimes her friend's turn of phrase shocked her though she never let it show. She just couldn't imagine Alex paying for it and then pressing himself up against some writhing girl in a Derby back street. On the other hand, he was bound to have done it with somebody. Being ten years older and with his good looks he had probably had several offers and taken some of them up.

It hadn't been something that they'd talked about and was one of the few things Lily felt uncomfortable talking about with him. She wasn't naive. Even her mum and dad had sex. When she lived at home previously from time to time, she'd been able to hear her father's groaning through the paper-thin walls and her mother's gasps that got louder and faster as the act reached its climax. Lily had mostly lain there rigidly feeling her cheeks getting burning hot and praying for it to be over. Once though she had let her own fingers slip down to that secret place between her legs as she felt the vibrations from her parents bed the other side of the wall. Next morning, she had not been able to look them in the face and had rushed out to work with some mumbled excuse about having to be in early. She'd felt ashamed and a little tarnished by the incident but now thinking about it she couldn't help but feel a little flurry of excitement. She thought about how Alex's naked body would press against her own bare skin. She was slightly surprised when she realised that this was the first time that she'd really thought of him in that way. They'd shared a few kisses and a couple of times Alex had gently touched her breasts but always over clothing. Most of the time Lily felt that they acted more like sister and brother.

The cold air rushing in from the outside as James bounded in brought Lily back to earth with a bump. Alex was back out there fighting in the trenches, and all Lily could do was contribute to the war effort here as much as she could. They'd both made choices and would have to live with them until hopefully, the opportunity arose for them to be acted upon in one way or another.

CHAPTER FIFTEEN

November 1915

"Never say die," seemed to be adopted as the Armitage's family motto for most of 1915. Bert's good-natured black humour that had seemed to have disappeared after his accident returned in force. Though he was too old to join up and wouldn't have been able to because of his bad back and possibly his lack of height he found new purpose in involving himself with the local defence force.
"I'm going out for a bit, love," became a familiar cry as Bert donned his Lovat green uniform and pulled on his red armband bearing the letters "GR" for the present king. His hazel eyes would twinkle, and he usually gave Ethel a wink or surreptitious pat on the bottom on his way out. Lily could scarcely believe that she was living with the same man. He had become undeniably more comfortable to be around and far less prone to uncharacteristic outbursts of anger that he occasionally displayed. There was a quiet satisfaction in Ethel's smile each time she waved him off.
"Maybe now you can see just a few of the reasons why I fell in love with your father." Lily and Ethel had become closer than they maybe would have done if Ethel's secrets hadn't come tumbling out a few years back. At the time Lily had felt that her mum was on the way to a breakdown but unburdening herself to her daughter seemed to have undone a pressure valve. Lily would now go as far to say that her

mum was one of her best friends and she didn't think that there was much that she couldn't share with her.

"It's difficult for me, Mum. I've never really known this person whom you talk about to me, and if I'm honest, I'm jealous. Why couldn't he have been that person for me when I was growing up." Lily knew that she sounded like a spoilt child instead of a mature young woman, but she'd needed so much from him and he'd never been able to give it. Ethel opened her arms and Lily snuggled in like she had used to do when she was small.

"There are things about your dad, love that I can't share even with you. I made a promise to him many years ago, but one thing that you must believe is that he loves you and James so much. He's so proud of both of you."

"Well, so you both should be of James. Who'd believe a lad from Peel Street going to Oxford? He deserves it though, and I don't begrudge him for it."

Ethel raised her eyebrow and gave a little smile.

"You don't mind at all then?"

"Well perhaps just a smidgeon," Lily laughed, "but he's going to the right place. Do you know, Mum, they're even inviting women to give lectures there now?"

"Well, a bolt of lightning bound to strike them before the years out then!"

The two women collapsed in heaps of laughter.

"Seriously, though Lily, he's as proud of you as he is of James. While all your friends have been running about with their head in the clouds or holding down poorly paid jobs what have you been doing?"

"Sitting on the fence!" Lily ventured.

"Fiddlesticks! Without you, poor Mr Devine's business would have gone under a long time ago. You're a successful businesswoman, Lily, who employs staff and is financially secure. How many women of your age can say that, especially from this neck of the woods?"

Lily thought a lot about what her mother had said later that day as she was working through the figures in the office. She knew she should be proud. At the time she'd thrown her heart into "Bookends", and her hard work had paid off both for herself and for the staff she now employed. All of them were working in safe, clean conditions and received a generous wage.

If she tried not to think about Alex too much, she could almost believe that she was content. Lily knew that she wouldn't be working at Rolls Royce forever, but for the moment she felt valued there. The engineers were such intelligent men, and they put maximum effort into what they were trying to achieve. Now this was continuing to benchmark and flight test the Eagle engines. Lily had seen the records of the first orders that had come in at the start of the year for twenty-five engines at £930 each. Mainly because James was always pestering her for more information about the company, she had been trying to find out a little more about the technical side of the work.

She had struck up a friendship with a lad called Richard who often popped into the office for a cup of tea in his break. Richard reminded her lot of Timmy. Rich was very young but passionate and knowledgeable about his work and the company. He appeared to have great respect for Frederick Henry Royce whose genius and passion had already made the young Derby company a world leader in automobiles.

"I've never seen the great man." Lily teased one afternoon as she handed Rich his mid-afternoon snack.

"You're not likely to either, Miss Armitage."

Lily groaned.

"How many times have I told you its Lily to you?"

"It sounds disrespectful though. You're older than me, and a lady."

"Well not that much older young man and I'm not even sure about the last bit."

Richard blushed.

"Anyway, as I was telling you, Lily...I'm not even sure where Mr Royce lives. It's in some seaside town miles away as he isn't in very good health and Derby airs supposed to be bad for him. I don't think he even knows that much about planes."

"That's comforting to know." Lily laughed. "I'm sure our jobs are as safe as houses then, Rich!"

"Don't you worry?" Rich almost fell over his words in his haste to reassure Lily. "Mr Royce and his team won't let us down." Lily shook her head as she shooed him back to work. What it must be like to have that much enthusiasm for what you did and that much faith in someone you hardly knew. She was still thinking about it as she trudged home from work later that afternoon. There was little light left in the sky though this wasn't particularly surprising as the day had been a classic grey November affair.

"A penny for them, love." Lily jumped slightly as Bert caught up with her.

"You made me jump, Dad. I think I must have been away with the fairies."

"Well, it wouldn't be the first time I don't suppose."

Lily nodded, her head down. She still didn't always quite know when her father was serious or not.

"Lily, love. I'm just teasing you. Trying to cheer myself up. Your old man making a fool of himself as always."

"Sorry, Dad. It's been a long day, and I'll be glad to get home. I'm surprised you're still out here if you're going out again later."

"Not sure that I will, love. Not tonight anyway. "There was something in his voice that made Lily stop and look at her father carefully. Though he was smiling it didn't seem to be quite reaching his eyes, and he looked drawn. More tired looking than Lily had seen him in months.
"What's the matter, Dad? You look different somehow."
"Well, I don't think that's probably a bad thing, do you?" Lily could sense the tension behind his banter, and he looked as if he could crumple to the floor at any minute.
"Are you sick, Dad? Shall I go and get help?"
"Let's just get home shall we, Lily? What I am sick of is this war. Thank God James is too sensible to want any cotter with it, and I've got you all safe under one roof." Lily sensed there was more to it than what her dad was letting on, but a steady drizzle had begun, so she said no more. Lily took him by the arm, and they walked silently side by side.
Ethel smiled as the two of them entered the kitchen together but couldn't help but notice the stern looks on both their faces, especially Bert's.
"What's the matter, Bert? You look terrible."
"It's bad news, love." Bert sighed sinking into the chair by the hearth and pulling Ethel into the one opposite.
"It's Mattie, Ethel."
"What? Chrissy's Mattie? He hasn't been gone two minutes. You must have it wrong." Ethel said. Lily crossed the room and put her hands on her mother's shoulders.
"I'm so sorry, love, but I haven't. News has only just filtered through, but he was killed in action, over a month ago now in the British advance at Loos."
Ethel's shoulders began to shake while at the same time she began to rock back and forth. For the first time in a long while, Lily felt afraid for her. Ethel was so strong most of the time, but occasionally it was as if all the stuffing had fallen out of her."

"You've got it wrong, Bert. Please tell me you've got it wrong. How can a mother bear to lose one child let alone two?"

Bert looked as white as a sheet but soldiered on as best he could.

"I'm not sure that she can. Apparently, when Chrissy heard the news, she flew at Roy and if she hadn't been pulled off by the two army guys who came to tell them she could have done serious harm. She then proceeded to go around the house throwing and kicking everything in sight. They had to get a doctor in to sedate her. There's talk they might have to send her to the lunatic asylum at Kingsway if she doesn't come around from wherever she's gone to in her mind."

"That poor man, "Lily whispered as she stroked her mother's hair. "He's lost both his sons and now might lose a wife as well."

"We're so lucky you know," Bert said looking at his wife and daughter. "We might have had our ups and downs, but we're still together. Fewer and fewer families can say that nowadays." Lily could feel her eyes prickling and swallowed to get rid of the lump in her throat. The world was so full of horror now, and her father was right. Lily looked at her mother. Colour was slowly beginning to return to her cheeks. All of them read and heard about the war, but in many ways, it was almost as though it was happening to someone else. It almost seemed necessary at times to put it to the back of the mind so that daily life could continue to function effectively. Derby had escaped relatively lightly up to now, and it wasn't until its ugly face affected someone close that the futility of it couldn't be ignored.

"Don't fuss. It was just the shock. I'll be fine, and I'll go around and see Chrissy and Roy in the morning to see if there is anything we can do. But for now, let's see about getting everybody some tea." Lily felt a wave of relief sweep over her. Her mother wasn't fine, but she wasn't going to go under – at least not this time. Lily caught a glimpse of the young woman that her mother had been back in Kirk Langley. Even after the tragedies of losing her father, mother and sister Ethel had remained strong and wouldn't take any nonsense from anyone. Both Lily and James had benefitted from that strength as had Bert. Ethel was fiercely protective of her family.

Lily glanced across at Bert who was now hovering uncertainly at the foot of the stairs. Some instinct told her that there was something else on his mind. There was perspiration on his brow even though it wasn't unusually warm in the house as Ethel hadn't fired up the oven yet. It was James, who had just come from upstairs after hearing the commotion, who put a hand on his father's shoulder.

"What is it, Dad?" Bert held onto the bannister as if for support. He looked pasty and ill, but his voice was strong as he faced his family.

"It wasn't just Mattie. Billy Knowles from Alfreton way was killed, and Henry Ingram has been reported as missing in action."

CHAPTER SIXTEEN

November 1915

"I'm ashamed that I don't feel anything Lily, but I just don't." Ethel confided to Lily the following day after Bert had gone out on patrol. "I should feel something. He's the father of James for goodness sake, and even though he could be a bit cocky at times, he wasn't a bad man."
"He's only the biological father, Mum, not the father in any real sense of the word. Anyway, I don't blame you. So much has happened in such a short space of time and we haven't seen Henry for a bit. It all seems a bit surreal besides which I sometimes think I was a very different person back then."
Ethel gently laughed. "It isn't that long ago love, but you're right. It does almost seem like another world."
Later as Lily walked along the cobbled street of Sadler Gate, she thought back to the conversation they'd had earlier. Despite his advances, Lily agreed with her mother. Henry wasn't really a bad person. Misguided maybe and lacking in morality certainly but he didn't come close to some of the beer-swilling louts you saw on the street corners after closing time. The day in the alley as Lily had come to think of it had been so out of character for Henry, and while she hadn't forgiven him, she'd since wondered what the impetus was for it. Probably she'd never know now.
The day was unusually pleasant for late November, and Lily felt it lifting her spirits. She had a day off and was heading into town to try and pick up some cheap Christmas presents

as she reckoned that closer to the day she would be snowed down at work and at home. Ten minutes later, after having done a bit of window shopping, Lily approached St Peter's churchyard gates like she'd done many times before. As much to her own surprise as anything she found herself pushing open the black iron wrought gates. Did all churchyard gates creak Lily wondered as she tiptoed across the gravel and then had to stifle a laugh as she realised how ridiculous she must look. Who was she going to disturb anyway? Not surprisingly the churchyard was empty. People would be making the best of the unseasonal weather to visit the park or wander along the banks of the Derwent. The long-term residents of the graveyard weren't likely to care too much either as they would be busy discussing Christmas plans with St Peter.

"You're daft, you are girl," Lily muttered to herself as she tried to remember where her gran and granddad Armitage were buried. She felt a little embarrassed that she hadn't visited in all those years since she'd stood on the fringes and watched her granny committed to the ground for eternity. Lily also felt uneasy as she knew that if this got back to either of her parents, she would be in hot water. Even though she was as close to her mum as she probably had ever been Lily saw the shutters come up fast on the rare occasions that Granny and Grandad Armitage had been mentioned.

"What did you do, Granny that was so awful?" Lily whispered as she regarded the simple inscription on the gravestone. No platitudes about being a good mother or sorely missed. Just a name and date of birth and death. Lily pondered about who had even arranged the funeral. She knew that her dad had two sisters and a brother, but she couldn't ever remember meeting them and had got the impression that they had moved away from the area years ago. Lily didn't need a crystal ball to predict that her parents would have had little to do with it.

The two gravestones stood out from the others as they were the only ones entirely without flowers or decorations of any kind. Some plots had vases full of opulent evergreens full to the brim with red berries and small white flowers that Lily had forgotten the name of cascading down the side. Some hadn't been visited for a while as dry brown sticks protruded from cracked jam jars. The petals of the flowers had long ago been blown away by the wind. Neglected indeed but not completely ignored or forgotten.

Tentatively she took a sprig of evergreen from a vase the other side of the path and a twig bedecked with red berries from another. Searching in her pocket, she found a stray length of light green ribbon and tied the two together.

"If only I hadn't been just a baby when you passed, Granddad. Maybe I would have been the one you were able to talk to." Lily laid the paltry bouquet in front of her Granddad Jack's headstone. For whatever reason Lily thought that it would be too much of a betrayal to do the same for her Granny.

Back on the street, Lily felt an overwhelming sense of sadness. For who or what she wasn't even sure, but the clouds that had now come and blocked the sunlight seemed to match her mood. Lily also felt a sudden almost overwhelming desire to see and talk to Alex. He was the only one she felt might understand and indeed the only one she could have explained her malaise to. But of course, Alex was on the other side of the English Channel fighting for king and country, and there was no guarantee that she would be able to speak to him ever again.

The desultory mood, the seeds of which had been sown the previous evening, blanketed the Armitage household for the rest of the day and well into the evening. Henry hadn't been mentioned again although he was one of the elephants in the room. Lily secretly felt that there might as well have been a herd of them as each member of her family seemed to be immersed in their own private world unwilling or afraid to re-emerge.

Lily knew that her mother had been to visit Chrissy and Roy earlier that morning and it hadn't gone well. Ethel had caught Lily on her way out.

"Roy's a broken man, Lily, and Chrissy just sat in that back kitchen staring at the wall and not saying a dickey bird."

"Well isn't that better for Roy rather than her crying and screaming?" Lily ventured.

"No, I don't think it is, love. Maybe you'll have to go around to completely understand, but it was as though there was nothing substantial left of her. She looked right through me without any recognition. Roy said she sobbed herself mercifully to sleep eventually late last night but ever since she woke early this morning, she hasn't said a word or moved from that spot."

"They can't send her to Kingsway though. Before this, she was always so full of life. She might have turned the air blue on occasion, but they can't commit her for that. That place will kill her." Lily had an inordinate fear of the lunatic asylum along with many others in Derby. To Lily losing your mind seemed far worse than losing an arm or leg though she sincerely hoped that she would never have to prove the theory.

"I'm not sure that it will make any difference to her. Roy said that without their sons he doesn't think that either of them will be enough for each other anymore. I think Chrissy's just decided to retreat from the world and who can blame her really?"

Glancing across at her mother who was now trying to rustle up a stew from the scraps they had left Lily could understand why she was so quiet. Chrissy had been one of her best friends ever since she had moved onto the street even though in many ways they were like chalk and cheese. Her father was sitting in his not so usual place nowadays staring into the dying g embers of the fire. Coal was expensive, and they had to eke it out like they did with everything else. Lily couldn't begin to guess the half of what was running through his head but if she'd been a betting woman, she would have put odds on that Henry was somewhere in there. She wondered what her father really hoped for. Feeling a little guilty Lily felt that in his shoes she might very well not want Henry to survive the war. Then again Lily was beginning to realise that her father was probably a kinder, more forgiving person than herself and she was starting to understand that this wasn't necessarily a weakness. She tentatively touched him on the shoulder. "Tea won't be too long, Dad. It'll do us all good to get a bit of summat hot inside us." She was rewarded with a brief smile as he took her hand and gave it a short squeeze. Despite all the uncertainty and the worry, Lily felt that this war was at least doing her father some good. He was out daily patrolling the streets helping anybody out where he could. The fresh air had brought some colour back to his cheeks, and he seemed to have filled out a little, and his clothes no longer looked like a pile of rags minus a person. While people were dying around him, Bert seemed more alive than he'd been for years.

James was nowhere to be seen. Lily suspected that he would be upstairs where he could be alone with his thoughts. Though he hadn't voiced his concerns to Bert and Ethel Lily knew how worried he was now. Everybody was beginning to realise that this war was going to be a long one and would require vast resources of manpower. Only last week James had confided in Lily that one of his lecturers said that he believed that the existing system of voluntary recruitment would not be enough to keep the army strong.

"Apparently, Lil, a national campaign has been developed demanding that able-bodied men should be compulsorily called up for military service." Lily had been horrified. She knew that James was utterly against the futility of war and had seen no sense involuntarily enlisting like Alex and Henry even if he'd been old enough. All he wanted to do was to become a doctor and treat and heal people not blow them up or see them maimed for life.

"They can't do that, can they? People wouldn't accept it. It's an invasion of personal freedom."

"We might not have a choice but let's just keep it between ourselves for now. Mum and Dad have enough on their plates." So, Lily had kept her promise to her brother though she knew that their mum had noticed his unnatural quietness.

"He's just working hard; Mum and he gets tired." Lily had ventured to send a quick prayer up as the words came out of her mouth. She reasoned that it was only really a white lie and was for the greater good. Asquith might yet be able to turn the tide and just because James's teachers thought something it didn't make it inevitable. Lily was often of the opinion, especially of late, that higher education and a more erudite knowledge didn't necessarily go hand in hand. Usually, more intelligent discussions were held at grassroots level amongst the people who were directly affected.

Not for the first time in recent weeks Lily missed Alex. She got great pleasure from their lengthy discussions about the ways of the world. Not that they always agreed Lily reflected ruefully, but she was proud that Alex viewed her as his equal in such matters. Though he might consider himself a lowly schoolmaster he was one of the most interesting people to talk to that Lily had had the fortune to meet.

That evening Lily felt more tired than she'd done for a while as well as unsettled. The future seemed so uncertain for all of them. She looked around the kitchen and wondered where they would all be in a year or even a month's time. She smiled for the first time that evening as James descended the stairs. It would literally take a bomb to part James's stomach from its tea.

Christmas was just around the corner, so maybe they would be able to put their troubles aside at least for a day or two though Lily dreaded to think where Alex would be spending Christmas Day. A few days after that Lily would turn twenty-six. An old maid, James had teased when she'd mentioned it last week. Maybe he wasn't far wrong, but Lily didn't want to be a casualty of war in that respect. Many girls had married men whom they wouldn't have touched with a barge pole in times of peace. Though Lily wasn't against the great romantic gesture, events in recent years had sobered her, and when she went into marriage, it would be with her eyes wide open.

"Stop your daydreaming, Lily and get those plates on the table." Ethel's stern voice cut through the silence. At least some things never change Lily thought, and she found that reassuringly comforting.

CHAPTER SEVENTEEN

December 1915

Christmas 1915 passed quietly for most of the residents of Peel Street. Lily went to midnight mass at St Peter's. It seemed strange to be walking through the church's gates again within the space of such a short time. She was accompanied reluctantly by James. Ethel said she had too much to prepare for the following day though Lily for the life of her couldn't see what. Both she and her mother had been cleaning on and off all day, and the house gleamed. Lily had gone down to the market late that afternoon and had secured a cut-price goose for their Christmas dinner, and the vegetables had been prepared and were standing in salted water ready to be cooked tomorrow. Admittedly Bert had come in late off patrol and looked more prepared for his bed than a church service, so James had been man enough to step in.
Lily was glad they had tried. The service had calmed her and stepping out into the starry night it seemed almost unbelievable that a few miles across the sea, men were huddled in mud-filled trenches looking up at the same sky and agonising over what tomorrow would bring.
"It's going to be a cold one." James shivered pulling his muffler more securely around his neck.
"At least we're going home somewhere warm with a half decent meal to look forward to tomorrow," Lily answered. Linking arms, they tentatively made their way along the

frost-tinged pavement trying to stifle their laughter as the lady in front of them nearly went a cropper.

"It's like a bloody ice rink out here tonight." The familiar cut glass accent touched with a good smattering of Derbyshire twang drifted back to Lily and James.

"I'd know that voice anywhere," Lily said to a slightly puzzled James. "Miss Hardcastle...Lizzy!" Lily shouted along the street to the figure in front. Miss Hardcastle turned, and her face lit up when she saw who was hailing her.

"Goodness me, dear child. It's wonderful to see you. Where have you been hiding the last few months?" Lily explained about her job, and her parents and how much time it all took up.

"And who's this handsome young man?" Miss Hardcastle scrutinised James with her usual beady stare as he grew redder in the face. At any other time, Lily might have made James stew for a while, but it was Christmas, and goodwill to all men should probably extend to her brother. Lily realised that Miss Hardcastle had not actually met her family many times and maybe not James at all. Though they had become firm friends, it was through circumstances at work and a need for female companionship in a mostly male-dominated workforce that had thrown them together initially.

"And there's me thinking that you've found yourself a new beau." Lizzy winked at James who was just glad that the darkness was hiding his embarrassment.

"No, I'm still with Alex. Well sort of," Lily muttered.

"And he's away fighting to save his country as befits the nobleman he's always been."

"Yes, something like that though I've no idea where he is or when I'm going to see him again."

"Well, when you do give him a big hug from me and tell him to hurry up and make a decent woman of you."
"Well, maybe you can give him that hug yourself. He's always admired you, Lizzy, especially after Philip. Well, you know..." Lily felt slightly uncomfortable as she wasn't sure how much Lizzy wanted to talk about that horrible night, but she knew that Alex would love to catch up if he got the chance. Lizzy and Alex had grown to know each other well with Alex collecting Lily from work on a regular basis, and he'd been fantastically supportive of them both after Philip's death.
"I would love to Lily, but I very much doubt that I'll be around."
"What do you mean?" Lily sounded panic-stricken and clutched James's arm even tighter. "You're not ill, are you?"
"No, my dear. At least not as far as I know," Lizzy linked Lily's free arm. "but I've been offered a job as a buyer at Liberty's in London. Mr Antony put in a good word for me. It's a fantastic opportunity, and it's time to move on."
"But what about your friends and all of your memories of Philip are here."
"Not all of them my dear. We had some exciting times in London, but you're right. A lot of them are here, and maybe that's why I can't stay. I still feel as though I'm swimming against an incoming tide some days and he wouldn't have wanted that. I think maybe down south I'll be able to hold onto the happy times and gradually put the sad ones behind me. Besides which it is a great opportunity anyway, and I can't see me marrying and settling down with babies anytime soon can you?"
Lily felt tears prickling the back of her eyes and knew she was selfish. To get things in perspective, she didn't see Lizzy as much as she used to, but it just seemed as though everybody who mattered was slowly being taken away from

her bit by bit. James seemed to sense her upset as he gave her arm a gentle squeeze.
"It sounds exhilarating, Miss Hardcastle," he said giving Lily a chance to recover, "and I'm sure we both wish you all the best."
"Of course, we do," Lily butted in, "but we will miss you so much." Lily put her arms around her friend, and they hugged each other tightly.
"And you, my dear, when your young man returns from the war you must both come and visit."
Almost exactly a week later Lily thought back to that conversation as she opened the birthday present that Lizzy had dropped off before she'd departed for the big smoke. Lily heard her mother's appreciative gasp as she unwrapped the gift to reveal a beautiful Liberty's dove grey scarf imprinted with delicate bluebirds that looked little like swallows. There was also a card with an inscription. "In winter they must leave, but summer nearly always brings them back home again. Your friend always. Lizzy Hardcastle."
"It must have cost a small fortune, Lily and it's absolutely beautiful." Ethel found her voice.
"Not half as beautiful as you though, Lily."
"Give over will you and stop being so daft." Lily didn't get any further as realisation dawned.
"Well, that's a fine way to greet your future husband, Miss Armitage." Lily spun round to find herself looking into a very familiar pair of grey, greenish eyes that despite the lines of fatigue surrounding them blazed with love. Lily had always secretly thought that girls who talked about their hearts beating so fast they thought they were going to fly out of their chest as slightly melodramatic. Until now, at this moment, she knew exactly what they meant. Alex opened his arms, and Lily folded herself into his body. As she felt

him encircle her, she knew at last that this was precisely where she was meant to be, for, as long as God or Lord Kitchener allowed

The rest of the day raced by. After Alex had been fed and watered most enthusiastically by Ethel and he'd answered a barrage of questions about the war from Bert they'd been not so discreetly left on their own. Ethel went across to Roy's and Chrissy's, and Bert said he'd promised to meet one of his friends from the local defence force for a swift pint. Lily breathed a sigh of contentment as Alex pulled the two wooden kitchen chairs together and they sat holding hands by the fire.

"They're such good people, you know, Lily?"

"I know that and probably appreciate them more since you've been away, and life has suddenly seemed to have become much more fragile."

"James was quiet though. Aren't his studies going well?"

"Oh, there's no problem on that score. He's committed to becoming a doctor. I think it's all this talk about compulsory military service that being bandied about that's unsettling him. He's no coward, but he's always been against the war."

"I know, love but I think the government will vote for the bill. Most of the Liberals don't like it, but I think they'll go with it as seeing it necessary in the circumstances. I certainly think that Lloyd George will push for it."

"But that's so unfair, Alex. It's a complete invasion of individual freedom."

Alex laughed and then tried to quell it as Lily's blue eyes flashed daggers at him.

"I'm so sorry, Lily. Of course, I don't think it fair, and James might be exempt yet if he can prove that he is genuinely against it on moral grounds. It's just you look so beautiful when you get enraged by something." Lily still didn't quite believe people when they talked about her being beautiful. If she'd been pushed, she would say that she was passable. Her mousey brown shoulder-length hair always seemed to have a mind of its own, and Lily thought she was far too pale. She spent quite a bit of time outside and loved walking in the park or beside the Derwent when she had time to herself. Yet she never seemed to achieve that healthy weather-beaten glow that the rest of her family, even her Dad now, seemed to have.

She leant towards Alex and kissed him on the lips. They were both acutely aware that Alex had only three days leave and then he had to travel back to Dover and set sail for France again. Perhaps surprisingly they had talked little of Alex's experiences at the front. Lily had not pushed him as she remembered the first time he'd been on leave and her mother finding him curled up on the floor in the morning.

"Let's go for a walk." Alex pulled her to her feet and grabbed his trench coat off the hook on the back of the heavy wooden kitchen door.

"Maybe the fish shop will still be open, and we can bring some back to bring in the New Year." Lily picked up on his enthusiasm. Who knew what even tomorrow would bring to any of them? Maybe it was pointless worrying, and the best thing to do was take each moment as it came. The evening was surprisingly mild for the time of year considering that Lily and James had been shivering in their boots after leaving Midnight Mass. Without really knowing how they found themselves on the banks of the Derwent where they'd spent many happy hours walking and talking in more peaceful times. Several couples were taking in the night air with quite a few already the worse for wear for drink.

"Happy New Year to you, Miss." A middle-aged slightly inebriated gentleman tipped his tweed cap at Lily. She giggled and whispered to Alex.

"He's a little early, but I'm not going to argue with the sentiment. Who really knows? It could all be over sooner than they think."

Trying to ignore Alex's sceptical look she linked arms with him comfortably. Before the war, they'd sometimes walked for miles, and Lily missed it. She also missed her little house. She knew that living with her parents and James seemed to be the right thing to do now, but at times she craved her own space. Though she'd been popping into the house about once a week to keep it ticking over, she hadn't spent any quality time there in months.

"Would you mind if we wandered over to mine for a few minutes. It won't take long, and Mum and Dad won't be expecting us back just yet, I'm sure.

A clatter greeted them on arrival, but it was only Mr Reynard out on his regular scavenging mission. They watched him lope away across the field at the back of the house. Lily took a deep breath. It was only a couple of miles from Peel Street but even though the house was probably no bigger than her parents there just seemed to be a greater sense of solitude and space that Lily had missed. Unlocking the back door, Lily shivered as the coldness met them. However, last time she had been here she'd laid a fire, and it was soon crackling away, the flames casting a flickering shadow on the stone walls. A bottle of wine was located at the back of the pantry and sitting on the small sofa snuggled under one of Ethel's knitted patchwork blankets they felt as content and secure as anyone could be under the circumstances. Smiling they clinked glasses.

"When this madness is all over, Lily, I'm going to come back and make you my wife and then we can sit here like this every night. It's taken us too long to get here, and I don't want to waste any more time."

"Neither do I," Lily whispered taking the glass out of his hand and tentatively placing it on her breast. She smiled as she saw a look of comprehension slowly dawning on his face.

"You know I'll wait for you, Lily. When I come back, we will be married straightaway. I can be patient."

"I don't want you to be patient Mr Poynton, and I think you've waited long enough. We're here now, alive and we love each other. What more do we need?"

With a groan, Alex pressed her to him, and she could feel his hardness through her clothes. Lily stroked the lines on the face that she knew so well as if by doing so she could smooth away his wrongful imprisonment, his terror and deprivation in the trenches and his years of worrying and wondering whether Lily would ever feel the same way about him as he'd always had of her.

They saw the answer in each other's eyes. Familiarity mixed with passion and understanding meant there was no shame. The war had shifted people's perspectives, and made individuals consider what really mattered to them. As Alex gently peeled away Lily's clothes, he peeled away any self-doubt that she may have had. As he entered her, their bodies began to move in unison as Lily cried out in pain and pleasure and Alex silently wept with happiness the bells of St Peters rang in 1916.

CHAPTER EIGHTEEN

February 1916

After Alex's return to the Western Front, the Armitages stuck their heels in and tried to get on with it. Despite the knowledge of the enormous casualties being suffered in France life for many in Derby continued in much the same vein as it had done before the declaration of war. It was true that most families had someone at the Front, but children still had to be fed, homes cleaned, and jobs done. More prayers were probably said than usual, and people who hadn't been seen at church very much before suddenly found God. After all, the word on the street was that it was a good idea to have an insurance policy.
There were murmurings about some bombing in London, but to most ordinary people London might as well have been on the other side of the world. Of course, there were families like Roy's and Chrissy's who had been devastated by their losses, but most families clung to the belief that their loved ones would come home. At the end of the day, there wasn't a great deal else they could do.
A full month had passed since Alex and Lily had confirmed their love for each other. Sometimes when Lily was snowed down with paperwork at Rolls Royce or immersed in housework, she could almost believe that it hadn't happened. How could she have been so lucky to experience such happiness? Occasionally, Lily began to wonder if Alex had come out with "sweet nothings" to get what he wanted and

then she immediately felt ashamed. In her heart, she knew there was nothing further from the truth, and it was her own self-doubt rearing its ugly head again.

Lily continued to wash the tea dishes as she thought back to that first morning of the New Year. She had been convinced that her mum would berate her for not getting home in time to see 1916 in. That was before she would face all the questions about where they had been until this time. However, Ethel had given Alex one of the brightest smiles Lily had seen in a long time.

"Sit yourself down, Alex and we'll get a good breakfast inside you, love," Ethel said. Bert was busy polishing his patrol boots and looked up as they came in.

"Alright, love?"

"Never better, Dad."

"Well, that's alright then." He went back to whistling and cleaning his boots.

Nothing much had changed since then; Lily smiled as she watched her dad lacing up his boots.

"Off out again, Dad. You'll need another pair of boots soon. Those will have no soles left the amount of traipsing you do."

"Well, it's better than me sitting on my arse in front of that hearth all day." Bert smiled at his daughter.

"Language, Bert!" Ethel chided from the next room.

"Too good for me that one, you know lass. Married beneath her station she did." Ethel appeared in the doorway with her hands on her hips.

"What a load of rubbish you do talk some of the time, Bert Armitage."

"Most of the time, love, if not all the time." Bert winked at Lily as he made his way out and they could both hear him chuckling as he made his way along the street. Ethel shook her head and went back to whatever she'd been doing in the other room. Lily thought again how ironic it was that it had taken a war to slowly bring her dad back to the land of the living.

Lily had half thought of going to see Maggie. Maggie missed Steve as much as Lily did Alex and Lily knew that young Master Robert quite often had her running around in circles. Lily grinned as she thought of the blond tousled haired two-year-old with the face of an angel. Maggie always said it was a good job God had given him that face or she wouldn't have been responsible for her actions. Lily knew that despite all their bluster Maggie and Steve loved Rob dearly. There had been two miscarriages before him, and the doctor had told Maggie she shouldn't have any more children, so he was doubly precious. Lily wondered how many children she and Alex would eventually have. At one time she hadn't been able to imagine herself with any at all, but a great deal had changed in a short amount of time.

"Are you still going out, love?" Ethel called through.

", I don't think so, Mum. Its pitch out there and Maggie will be all locked up now if she's got any sense. I'll pop round tomorrow."

"Probably for the best, love. She might have young Robert tucked up and in his bed by now, though maybe not." Lily laughed. Her mum knew Rob as well as she did. "I'll just finish in here, and then we'll have a cup of tea and take the weight off our feet for a bit."

"Sound good, Mum. Just the two of us for a change. I'll get a brew going."

"Where's James, by the way?" Ethel came through into the kitchen untying her apron as she walked.

"Down on King Street. Royal Crown Derby actually. He's gone to see his friend Dan. Something about going hiking this weekend. Thorpe Cloud was mentioned."

"I really don't know where he gets his energy from." Lily had to smile at her Mum as she could say the same about her. Even when Ethel sat down, she had to have something in her hands to keep busy. Lily saw what her father must have seen when her mother was young. Ethel had the same blue eyes as Lily, and though her brown hair was now streaked with touches of grey at least, it didn't have a mind of its own like Lily's own.

Lily jumped as the door burst open, partly because she hadn't been expecting anybody but also because of the bang it made as it hit the wall.

"For goodness sake, James. Shut that door. You weren't born in a barn. Anyway, why aren't you with Danny?"

"Sorry, Mum but he's feeling a bit off colour. Reckons he's coming down with a touch of flu, so I thought I'd steer clear but never mind about that. Both of you get your shoes on and come outside quick!" Lily rolled her eyes in mock despair at her mother. At times she couldn't believe that her brother was a serious medical student. Sometimes he acted like a ten-year-old. Tonight, she saw the glint in his eye that he usually reserved for if he'd spotted a rare type of car or something similar.

A couple of minutes later as they stood shivering on the front step, they couldn't fail to see the long sinuous shape that was traversing across the dark sky. Lily had never seen a Zeppelin before but knew what they were and what they looked like. Alex had told her that the government thought they were little more than a joke as they hardly ever hit the target they intended. Lily didn't feel like laughing as she stared transfixed as it travelled slowly towards the horizon.

"It's got no lights on. I reckon its lost and just moving on." Lily could hear the excitement in her brother's voice but could also see her mum's frightened face.

"Come on, Mum. Let's get you in. You'll catch your death standing out here. Like James says it's moving on. They won't want anything to do with us. They've bigger fish to fry."

Lily sat Ethel on the sofa while at the same time trying to conceal her own shaking.

"James, get in here and make yourself useful. Get Mum a strong cup of tea and us two as well while you're at it." Lily tried to calm her thoughts and think logically – a tactic that she had used before and sometimes it worked. Firstly, there had been very few civilian casualties in the war so far. Secondly, why would Germany bother with Derby when Birmingham, Coventry and Liverpool weren't far away, and thirdly the Zeppelin had moved on. They were going to be okay.

For the next hour, the three of them sat drinking tea and quietly chatting, with James going outside every so often to see if he could spot any activity. It was the closest any of them had been to actual warfare, and the Germans had suddenly become a genuine manifestation. Suddenly it seemed as though civilians on the Home Front as well as soldiers on the Front Line were at risk. James was buzzing with excitement. While he wasn't in favour of the war, he was fascinated with transport and machinery of every complexion and he'd momentarily forgotten about the danger that they could have been in. Unfortunately, Lily and Ethel hadn't.

However, after an hour or so their minds began to ease a little. There'd been no further sightings.

"It's like we thought," James said sounding a little deflated. !"They've passed over us and gone to bother some other poor sods." Lily began to feel a little calmer, especially when Bert dropped back home just before half-past eight.

"They've gone, so the panic is over. Another one passed over about a quarter to eight when Bill and I were patrolling down the Wardwick but there's been no sign since. Get yourselves to bed early tonight. You all look shattered."

"I suppose you'll be going out there again. Why can't you stay home for once? You've been out hours already. You've got to be tired, love." Ethel said. The truth though was that Lily didn't think that her dad looked very tired at all.

"I'm fine, love. Don't worry. I won't be late, but Bill and I are just going to have a potter around to make sure people are alright. You won't have been the only ones to have been scared witless by the bastards."

"I'll have some supper waiting for you when you get back." Ethel kissed her husband on the cheek.

"Aye. Ok, love. That would be good." Bert gave her a quick hug. Lily and her dad knew that Ethel had no intention of going to bed before he got back. She also sensed how worried her mum was about everything still as she hadn't even told her dad off about his language.

In the end, none of them went to bed. James had calmed down enough to go upstairs and catch up with some of his studies. Lily and Ethel busied themselves making sandwiches for when Bert returned and then they sat sewing and reading. Lily dozed, and she thought her mum did as well. It wasn't unusual for Bert to be out late but when Midnight came and went the tension was almost palpable. James evidently couldn't sleep either, and at ten past twelve, he came running downstairs taking them two at a time. Whether it was a sixth sense or something else, they all knew that something felt very wrong.

"It's the windows rattling. That's what's wrong. There's no wind. The windows shouldn't be rattling." Ethel's voice rose as her panic grew. Lily stared at James who crossed the room and grabbed her hand. They were all now conscious of the booming of the guns getting closer.

"They didn't go away, Lily. They didn't go away." James's face was ashen. It was no longer a game, and she could feel his trembling. Her own heart was racing, and her legs felt like jelly, but she knew that she had to keep it together. Her thoughts flitted to Alex. He must feel like this all the time. Never knowing where the next assault was going to come from or when it was going to happen. Lily silently mouthed a prayer while at the same time running after her mum who had gone dashing out onto the street, probably to look for their dad. She wasn't the only one out there. Several women and some older men were staring at the shrapnel that was bursting in the direction of the river. The long menacing airship could be seen in the distance while the children ran excitedly around the adult's feet as the shells burst far below it.

Ten minutes before Bert had almost finished his patrol and was looking forward to getting home for his supper, he saw a chink of light shining from the Midland Railway site. He was well on the way across the yard to warn them when the Zeppelin struck. Bert was killed instantly along with two others.

The Armitages weren't the only family to suffer that night. Others paid for Derby's mistake of putting their lights back on after it was believed that the airships had retreated. Earlier fifteen people had been killed in brightly illuminated Burton, and the overall cost was eventually to be seventy people killed with thirteen injured and wide-scale destruction and devastation. The raid would subsequently be noted as one of the heaviest of the First World War.

CHAPTER NINETEEN

February 1916

In the aftermath next morning there were murmurings that it could have been worse. Derby having received warnings managed to dim the lights and they missed the first wave of attacks while Burton wasn't so lucky. This was of little consolation to the families who had lost loved ones. The only cold comfort Bert's family had was that he wouldn't have suffered, and he was killed doing a job that had won him back his self-respect.

Lily worried that her mum hadn't taken it all in. Ethel had spent the morning making tea for the many neighbours who came to offer their condolences. James had gone storming out mid-morning.

"We're not a freak show, you know? Haven't you got homes of your own to go to?" He yelled at Mrs Carmichael who had come down from the top end of Peel Street to pay her respects. Lily apologised and made excuses for him though she was of the opinion herself that Alice Carmichael only seemed to darken people's doors when she could sniff bad news out. She'd be busy today then, Lily thought bitterly. However, the main feeling Lily had now was one of extreme tiredness. She'd cried herself to sleep for a couple of hours just as dawn was breaking. It seemed so unfair that when she'd been slowly getting to know her father he'd been so cruelly snatched away. She wasn't a stranger to injustice. Since Philip's death, she had been very sceptical of "God's greater plan" that had been a phrase bandied about quite extensively recently. Lily had begun to think that it was all random as to who was taken and who was spared to live out their natural lifespan.

Lily also had the insight to appreciate that out of the family she was probably the one who was going to try and hold things together. That morning she missed Alex desperately. She thought about his mother who had died giving birth to him and about what life with his father afterwards must have been like. Though Alex always saw the best in people, reading between the lines, Lily correctly guessed that he had been desperately lonely as a child. His father, the local parson, had gone through the motions but had retreated into himself when his wife died. Though he did his best Alex had to grow up quickly. Lily couldn't wait to marry him and give him the love he'd never really had. In the meantime, though she had to look after her mother and brother and hoped she would have the strength to do so.

James had come crashing home shortly before midnight with the stench of alcohol on his breath and clothes. Lily made no comment. Usually, he barely touched a drop and now wasn't the time to berate him for being as drunk as a lord. She gently guided him upstairs. It didn't take much to push him back on the bed and peel his shoes and socks off. Leaving a glass of water on the bedside cabinet, she crept out hoping that their mother hadn't heard the kerfuffle. She left the door slightly off the latch, so she could quickly peek in on him later.

Lily quietly opened the door to her parent's room after lightly tapping on the door. She listened to her mum's steady breathing. Nature had taken over, and her mum's mental anguish and devastation had been suspended. Her small figure scrunched up in the middle of the double bed looked so forlorn that Lily felt a lump come to her throat and turned from the room with tears in her eyes.

It was just over twenty-four hours since all hell had broken loose in Derby, but this night couldn't be more different. Not a soul was roaming the streets. Many were still lying awake either counting their blessings or wondering how they were going to get through the next day and the one after that. Lily quelled the gas light and sat in the back room looking out of the window at the racing clouds highlighted by the moon. The kitchen was chilly as the range hadn't been lit for that long that day. Her mother had received her visitors in the front room and had brought out the china reserved for special occasions. Lily smiled softly for the first time that day. Even amid tragedy her mother kept to the proprieties. She pulled her shawl more tightly around her and eventually drifted to sleep thinking about her father.

In the days before the funeral, both Ethel and James surprised Lily. Apart from having a sore head the day after James was full of apologies for his behaviour.

"How could I have been so selfish, Lily? I was just so angry I wasn't thinking straight. After all, I'm the man of the house now!" Lily smiled at her brother. He wouldn't even be eighteen until October later that year, but in many houses across the country, the same scenario was being played out. "I'll leave college and get a real job. Don't worry, Lily. I'll look after you and mum." Lily was touched by his naïve concern though it was the last thing that either Lily or Ethel wanted for him.

"You will do no such thing. What you will do is work even harder at your studies and become a fine doctor. I'm still not short of a bob or two you know!" James looked slightly relieved as Ethel came in from the front room with a duster in her hand.

"What do you think you're doing, Mum? I thought you were still in bed and I was going to bring you a cuppa up."
"I'm not ill, Lily. Just sad and lying in bed isn't going to make me feel any better. We'll just have to keep putting one step in front of the other and see where it takes us. After all, we're only one family in many hundreds to experience loss." Ethel held out her arms to her two children, and even though they both towered above Ethel's slight frame, Lily felt comforted and about five years old again. For the next hour, household chores were forgotten, and Ethel sat on the small sofa with Lily and James squashed either side of her. She told them tales of Bert from when they'd just met, through his time at the colliery and beyond. She spoke of the joy he got from his family and how grateful he'd been to find a purpose in life again.

Though James appeared not to notice Lily realised that her mum had not spoken at all about her dad's childhood or about when she and James were born. She hoped that James would never find out the truth. Lily didn't see how he could, as apart from Ethel, Lily and Alex were the only two people left who knew. Lily wondered if Alex had been right when he'd voiced his opinion that Bert had always known that James was Henry's but had chosen to ignore it. At one time she would have thought it impossible but in the last year or, so she had come to realise how strong her parent's love was. She had also begun to appreciate how hard life had been for her father and wondered even more about his childhood. What had happened all those years ago that even now after his death her mother wouldn't talk about it?

A few days later the funeral took place at St Martin's Church in Alfreton. The weather had turned again, and there was a smattering of snow on the ground. As Lily, James and Ethel got out of the car a weak shaft of sunlight struggled through the clouds.

Lily had expected there to have been a handful of people and was surprised when they got inside the church that it was over three-quarters full. The service was simple and as Lily attempted to keep her emotions in check and sing along to "All things bright and beautiful" she thought about how much she didn't know about her father. Her mum had told her that as a young man he had loved the countryside, hence the choice of hymn. On his days off and when he could escape from the clutches of his mother he'd beg or borrow a bike and head out to the Derbyshire Dales. Lily had laughed as her mum had told her how once they'd acquired a tandem and Ethel had sat with her feet up on the crossbar peeling an orange while Bert pedalled furiously away at the front, entirely oblivious. There had been many such stories told over the last few days, and there had emerged a picture of a virile, athletically built, gentle, young man with hopes and dreams much as Lily had.

"It was just when the black dog got to him that it was hard." Ethel had tried to explain to both Lily and James. "He'd start to doubt his self-worth and sometimes lose his temper at the smallest of things. It got a lot worse after the accident when he couldn't work anymore at the only job he knew really."

After the service and burial, the congregation was invited back to the village hall for light refreshments. Lily had to smile as she saw Agnes Massey in the steady throng of people making their way there. The last time Lily had seen her was at Grandma Armitage's funeral though she was almost sure that Agnes hadn't spotted her. Most people in town though knew of Agnes with many agreeing that she was quite the professional funeral-goer.

Ethel seemed to know most people and Lily noted how they all showed her great respect. Lily felt proud of her mother as she weaved in and out of the tables acknowledging the guests though Lily thought that she looked utterly drained.

The hardest part for them all had been seeing Bert's body committed to the ground. Lily still had the indents of fingernail marks on her palms which had happened as she watched her father making his last journey, at least on this earth. She now just wanted the day to end so that the three of them could get back home, close the curtains and leave the "I'm so sorry" brigade on the outside. Even as she thought it Lily felt bad. After all what else was a person supposed to say at a funeral? "Good riddance?" Lily felt hysterical laughter bubbling up and turned to James who was just purloining another sausage roll. She doubted that anything would curb his appetite.

"Go and get Mum. She looks exhausted. I'll sit here and save her a seat." Lily wearily sank down on the nearest available chair. She felt utterly shattered and a little nauseous. It was so hot in the hall considering the freezing temperatures outside.

"Excuse me for interrupting, but I had to come and say hello." Lily looked up and fixed an automatic smile on her face. Her head was throbbing by now, and she desperately wanted some fresh air but if nothing else she knew how to conduct herself in public. After all these people had tried to turn out and pay their last respects on a genuinely dismal day. A tall young man with blond hair stood in front of her. Holding his hand was a young boy of about five years old. He was studiously staring at Lily in the unconscious way that only children possess. Now Lily genuinely smiled. He was a gorgeous looking little boy with thick unruly dark brown hair and a cheeky grin.

"I'm sorry, but you've got me at a disadvantage. There are so many people here today that I don't really recognise. I didn't realise that my dad knew so many people."

"Everybody in the colliery liked your dad, Miss Armitage. He'd help anybody out but quiet like. No song and dance with Bert. Even when he got Alan and me out, he was the same. I'll tell you one thing for sure though. If it hadn't been for Bert, we wouldn't have made it. Pulled us out with his bare hands he did. I just had to come and pay my respects when I heard. Really sorry I was, Miss."

Realisation suddenly washed over Lily.

"You're one of the boys he pulled out all those years ago."

The young man shyly held out his hand.

"John Cartwright, Miss and this here's my son, Ritchie."

"Pleased to meet you, Miss." The small boy stuck out his hand as he'd seen his father do.

"Well, Ritchie. You're not short on manners, and I am very pleased to meet you as well." Lily solemnly took the young lad's hand in her own. The knowledge that this young boy would not exist but for her father overwhelmed her. A little while later when John and Ritchie had taken their leave, Lily realised that however long she lived, she was unlikely to anything as significant as saving a life. Two young men were out there with families of their own all down to her dad. In the last few months, Lily had found more out about her father than she'd previously done in her twenty plus years. She felt ashamed as she thought about how she hadn't even tried to understand why he acted the way he did. James had shown far more understanding and not for the first time Lily found that entirely ironic.

Lying in her bed later that night unable to sleep she was filled with an overwhelming sense of loss for the man that in some ways she had never known until it was almost too late. As Lily closed her eyes and willed herself to sleep, she vowed that she would find out all that she could about her dad and maybe in that way she could put both their ghosts to rest.

CHAPTER TWENTY

March 1916

The period immediately after the funeral was unsettling for them all. Lily returned to her job at Rolls Royce. Only one bomb had hit there, and the damage had been limited. Lily's first workplace had been spared. Timmy told her that when the air raid siren sounded at Crown Derby, they were in the middle of firing a kiln that had to be doused.
"We were worried it was going to be spoilt but it fired well, and the bosses decided to mark the whole kiln load with an airship and moon mark. To remember the event, you know, Lily!"
Lily was glad for Timmy. His enthusiasm for his job hadn't diminished, and at the funeral, he'd told her that he was going to be married next year. However, Lily wasn't sure that Derby wanted to remember the event. The whole concept of Germany attacking from the air had brought the war much closer to civilians, and the Zeppelins had been nicknamed "baby killers."
James had completely changed his tune about joining up.
"I'm going to make sure those bastards pay for what they did to our dad." James had reverted to being the angry young man who had surfaced just after Bert's death. Lily appreciated though that now his anger was different. It was not the hot-headed anger of a young man who hadn't really seen much of life. It was the colder calculating anger of a young man who in a single night had seen and suffered more

than he should have done. It looked as though he might get his wish as on the 27th January the Military Service Act had been finally passed. All single men aged eighteen to forty-one who were outside of a protected occupation were now part of the army reserve and liable for immediate call-up. Some women were almost ecstatic.

"Bridget Sowter says she can't wait for her bloke to be called up. "Ethel confided to Lily one sunny morning in early March. Ethel was busy starching James's shirts for college. Lily was momentarily taken back to that day years ago when Alex had appeared at their back door with books for her to borrow. Little did they all know then what lay in the future for them all. Nothing had been heard of Alex since he'd left them last time, but Lily knew she had to put that into the back of her mind as it wasn't unusual. Her mum and James both needed her to hold it together now. She dragged her attention back to the present.

"That's a horrible thing to say, Lily said, "especially when there are women like you that have lost their husbands to the war."

"I can't say that I blame her, love. I don't think that she gets those black eyes of hers from falling downstairs, do you? It'll give her a bit of a respite from Hugh's mean ways." Lily's shock at her mum's blunt comments must have shown on her face as Ethel continued. "She's not going to be the only one either. You must remember and understand, Lily, that I was one of the lucky ones. Whatever you thought of your dad he never lifted a finger to me all the time we were married, and God knows he had cause to at times. It might not have always looked like it to you, and maybe we both did some daft things in our time, but we did love each other."

Lily knew that this was the truth and had come to appreciate that there were aspects of her father's past that's he knew nothing about at all. However, she felt disappointed that her mum almost felt as though it was the right of a man to hit their wife if they didn't toe the line. She merely nodded at Ethel and turned back to the range where she was busty chopping vegetables for their supper later.

"Leave it, Lily. There'll be time later. Put the kettle on. There are things it's time for you to know and it's my responsibility to tell them to you. I've been putting it off frightened to upset you more, but I owe it to your dad." The next hour was one of the most surreal of Lily's life and one of the most illuminating.

"I know that you went to your Granny Armitage's funeral." Lily immediately felt disloyal though why she couldn't really say.

"I'm sorry, Mum. I thought you'd never know, and I didn't see the harm."

"It's alright, love. To be fair, I didn't know for sure until recently."

"Agnes?"

"Agnes," Ethel confirmed.

"I don't know, Mum, why I went. I'd got no intention of it, and when I got home, I felt guilty about it. There was no way I was going to tell you and especially Dad."

"It was unfair of us, Lily, especially of me. Your dad could never have told you, but I could have. I chose to keep my promise to your dad which I don't regret, but now he's gone. " Ethel closed her eyes and looked so pale Lily felt that her mum might pass out but when she opened them again, they were full of resolve. "There's no easy way to say it, Lily. Betty Armitage wasn't a good woman. She wasn't a good wife and not a good mother. To call her a domineering cow would be an insult to the livestock my dad used to keep on his farm. She was bitter, twisted and lacking in any compassion."

Lily felt afraid of the venom she could hear in her mother's voice as well as a little taken aback. If Ethel had been born into a different class, Lily had always felt that she would have been able to hold her own with the best of the aristocracy. There was a certain refinement and breeding about Ethel that Alex had commented on and that Bert had obviously seen.

"Your mother's a princess to me," he'd confided to Lily on one of the rare occasions he'd had a drop too much to drink. Lily smiled as she thought back to the earnest tone of his voice as he'd tried to get his point across while trying to conceal that he was one or two too many over the eight.

"Jack, your grandad was weak. He chose to close his eyes to it all. An ostrich with its head in the sand comes to mind, but I hope he rests in peace. As for Betty, I hope the worms got her, and she's rotting in hell wherever that might be."

"Mum! Please stop." Lily grabbed Ethel by the hands. Maybe the strain of the last few weeks had finally come to a head. She'd never seen her mum like this ever. Ethel's eyes were blazing with anger, but she took a shuddering breath and looked steadily at her daughter.

"Don't worry, love. I haven't gone mad, at least not in the way you think. It's just been bottled up inside of me for so long. Your dad was so proud of you, Lily and he didn't want you to know. He didn't want you to think him weaker than he thought you already did. I wanted to tell you. I wanted to shout and scream the truth to the world so that you knew what he had gone through, but I kept my promise." Lily wasn't sure that she wanted her mother to continue because whatever it was must be serious for her to talk the way she had been doing. Even when she had told Lily about Henry, she hadn't got herself into this much of a stew. It was clear that whatever it was it had been kept to herself for a long time. Even if Lily had asked her mum to stop, she didn't think that she would be able to. A few minutes later Lily wished she'd tried harder.

"Your dad was abused, Lily, by Betty, his own mother. Can you begin to imagine that? The one person whom, even if everybody else lets you down, should still be there for you." Lily felt cold even though the range was blasting out heat into the small kitchen. Not for the first time since her dad had been killed, she desperately wanted Alex at her side. The ball that she'd kept her emotions tightly wrapped up in since the funeral was rapidly unravelling.

"Why are you telling me this now, Mum?" Lily sobbed. "Don't you think we've all got more than enough to cope with anyway? Dad's gone. We don't know if Alex is still alive and if he is it looks as though our James will be going out to join him later this year."

"Don't you think I realise all that, love but there's never going to be a good time."

Lily wiped her face with her sleeve and took a deep breath. In some ways, she felt separated from what she had just heard, and a small part of her hoped desperately that somehow her mother had got it all wrong. How could a woman abuse her own son? If nothing else as her dad grew older, surely, he'd had the strength to resist her. She'd heard horrible tales about men abusing their wives and, in some instances, even their daughters. She wasn't so naïve to think that physical violence and abuse didn't occur. Some women also acted as though their husband had the right to do what they wanted. The thought that this could have been her mother if her father had been a violent man, made Lily sick to the stomach. It was a path that she knew that she would never tread.

"Your dad was abused mentally and physically through most of his childhood, and it didn't stop until he got a job in the pits. The cruel bitch was afraid of him walking out and her not getting his money, so she eased off." Gradually, the mist that had seemed to cloud Lily's mind slowly began to evaporate. She thought of the loneliness that Alex had experienced as a child and realised that there were far worse things on earth for a young boy to suffer and her dad had been subjected to them.

"What did she do?" Lily almost whispered as though by not saying it to loudly would make it go away.

"Your dad couldn't even tell me everything. Quite wrongly he felt too ashamed, but I know, apart from the shouting and the hitting that most of the family experienced, Betty picked on Bert to go to in the middle of the night when she thought everyone else was asleep." Lily was horrified. Despite everything that she had experienced over the past few years she found this the most shocking.

"Why didn't he shout out or scream? The others would have heard him and come to him surely."

"Perhaps they would. Who knows? That's why he didn't though, because of them. All he would say was that if Betty hadn't done it to him, she would have turned to one of the others." Ethel was almost in tears herself now. "Don't you see, love? He was protecting his brothers and sisters like he thought he was protecting you and James by not speaking of it."

Later Lily walked along the banks of the Derwent towards Darley Abbey. It wasn't a particularly pleasant afternoon, but she welcomed the keen wind and the few drops of rain she felt as she walked. Her head was beginning to clear slightly, and she blinked back tears as she thought of a little boy lying awake in the middle of a cold dark night waiting to take his medicine as her mum had explained Betty used to call it. She then thought of the virile young man she'd seen in photos imaging him pulling those two young boys to safety ignoring his own injuries and the pain he was inflicting on himself. She visualised his despair as he couldn't reach the third. Lily began to understand his depression. Sometimes the world got too much to bear so that the only way you could escape it was to retreat from it. She wondered where her father had gone to in those long hours sitting in his chair by the hearth not speaking a word. Again, she felt a little ashamed of James understanding their dad more than she had. She hadn't at times even attempted to and her face burnt as she remembered how she had poured derision on her father's behaviour. Lily sat on a bench by the river and watched a moorhen's red legs frantically paddling away to keep abreast of the current. Tears rolled down her cheeks caused by the pain of realising that she could never get her dad back to make amends and to tell him that she loved him. Walking back in the twilight she remembered the last time she'd seen him. He'd looked tired, but his eyes shone with enthusiasm for what he was doing and the people he was finally able to help. In the midst of death, he'd been genuinely alive, and that was the image Lily determined she would hold on to in the weeks and months of regret that she knew lay ahead.

CHAPTER TWENTY-ONE

April 1916

Lily spent the next few days feeling that she had been knocked for six. Her mother's revelations lay heavily on her and as the weeks passed after the funeral Bert's loss seemed to be felt even more keenly. As time relentlessly marched on it really sunk in that Bert was no more. They couldn't pretend anymore that he had gone off to the Home Guard and would be home later for tea.

His death and funeral, at first, seemed to have a surreal quality as though some random joker was going to pop up and tell them it had all been a mistake and that service would resume as normal. They all realised now that wasn't going to happen, and Bert's death had made them understand their own mortality far more than anything the war had yet served up.

The general atmosphere in the whole of Derby seemed to be downcast. Even though many families had lost people to the war, they'd still had an inherent belief that they would be safe at home. They didn't see themselves as important enough for the enemy to take much note of them. The Zeppelins had brought the war to the Homefront, and now everybody was feeling vulnerable.

Some started to blame people for leaving their lights on though there had never been any official regulations enforcing the turning off lights. Others felt angry because it was believed that Liverpool had been the intended target for the bombs and not their own town.

"The bloody Germans couldn't even get that right." James ranted as he came blustering in one evening late in early April.

"Get your coat off and have a warm. Tea will be on the table in twenty minutes." Lily tried to calm her brother who had become a virtual stranger since the attacks.

"So, you're ok about that are you, Lily? It should have been the bloody scouses and not us that got blasted."

"Of course, I'm not saying that it's alright. How do you think that I could believe that, but people in Liverpool have families just the same as us or hadn't you thought about that?"

"We don't know them, though do we? Oh, what's the point? I'm just going to get washed up." Lily took a deep breath as she heard James cursing as he turned the outside tap on too full. He'd probably have soaking wet boots now as well which wouldn't improve his humour. Lily did understand his anger, but he was so hard to live with now. She knew that it was hypocritical, especially with Alex at the Front, but she found women and children being attacked in their own home even more horrifying than the tales they heard coming back from France almost daily. Lily just hoped that life would settle down eventually though she wasn't naïve enough to ever think that it could return to normal.

At least James was channelling his anger into his studies instead of into a bottle like many others were doing. After his tea James would go up to the bedroom and study almost fanatically for hours. Several nights before turning in Lily had gone in to find him slumped over his books with the light still flickering.

"I've just seen him in the yard." Ethel said as she came through the back door and sank wearily down on what they still called and probably always would "Bert's Chair" by the hearth. "He's not the only one suffering though is he, love?" Ethel smiled weakly at her daughter. "I've just been to see Flossie Bembridge. The doctors say her Jimmy will be lucky to last the month. Lung cancer they reckon it is. It's not all about the war. Bad things happen all the time. At least our James isn't out on the street making more trouble."

"Who's causing trouble, Mum?"

"Oh, it's nothing that serious I suppose, but you know that new order that came in the other week."

"The one that was received by the Chief Constable so that he could decide which public lighting we're allowed to show?"

"That's the one. Well, it seems that some people are having none of it. Them up Littleover way are the worst bunch. No surprises there I don't suppose."

"I suppose not, Mum, but they're not the only culprits. Emily Jackson who lives just down the lane from me in Markeaton reckons that it isn't important if her lights are showing at night. Apparently, she says it doesn't matter if you live in the country."

"Daft beggar!" Ethel chided. "It's not even the country. She'll be getting herself killed and you in the bargain if she doesn't straighten her head out."

"It's not very likely now is it seeing as I'm never hardly there," Lily said.

"I know we're putting on you, love. Me and James but it's just…"

"You're really not Mum. I don't want to be down there away from you all at the minute. Maybe when the lighter nights appear but for the minute I'm just fine here. In the thick of the action as Dad would have said. He would have been in his element now, wouldn't he?"

"We'd never see him, " Ethel sighed. "He'd be out there in that uniform putting the world to rights. They're going to set up motor control stations as well now. Ever since that report in the "Mercury" that the occupants of a vehicle had signalled to a Zeppelin at Stanton they're going to be investigating the intentions of the occupants of all vehicles, even bikes, in future raids."

"And the Home Guard is helping?"

"Playing quite a part in it I've heard."

"Dad was a different man in those last two years wasn't he, Mum?"

"Not a different man, Lily. Just the man he was before he lost his way a little." Ethel sighed and slowly rose to her feet.

"Well this chit-chat isn't going to get tea cooked, and we don't want to give the young master of the house out there anymore cause for complaint. I'll just go and change my skirt, and then I'll come back down and help you finish off." As Ethel made her way to the bottom of the stairs, she touched Lily briefly on the hand. "You're a good lass, Lily. I don't know what I'd do if you weren't here." Lily turned her back to Ethel and began fiddling with the tea plates not trusting herself to answer.

Later that evening when Ethel had gone to bed and James was in the back bedroom studying Lily sat in the old winged armchair by the window. In her hands, she held a copy of "A Portrait of an Artist as a Young Man," written by James Joyce who apparently was an up and coming young Irish author. It had been published at the back end of last year, and Timmy had somehow managed to track a copy down and give it to her as a late Christmas present. Lily had been really touched by the gesture as Timmy had admitted that he hadn't a clue what it was about but thought it might be her sort of thing and that she'd be able to fathom it. His cheeky grin always uplifted her spirits, and she promised him she'd get back to him with her verdict

She now handled the book reverently. To Lily, books were works of art and held infinite flights of imagination that seemed to make the impossible possible. She realised that she hadn't read a "proper" book since leaving "Bookends." The distinctive smell that only new books had brought memories of Philip rushing in. A small part of her still felt that his suicide had been selfish. Now there were hundreds of virile young men being killed in the name of war every day and thousands more being maimed. If they had been given the chance of one more day to see and hold their loved ones again to say goodbye, of course, they would have taken it. Deep down though she knew that Philip had committed the act he did not just out of the fear of the pain he knew was to come but to save his loved ones from seeing him go through that pain.

Lily longed desperately for Alex to be sitting beside her. A new book or author had always been exciting for both of them and reading one they would sit well into the early hours discussing and pulling it to pieces and enjoying every minute of doing so. Her mind drifted back to when she was still at school and Alex would pop round her parents' house with his latest offering. Ethel and Bert had always enjoyed his visits, at least before the Maisie Dawkins incident. Lily smiled as she thought back to how flustered Ethel used to get when that "nice Mr Poynton" came calling. Bert used to sit in his chair taking it all in, and Lily wondered why it wasn't until now she had realised that the look on his face had been pride. Not derision or scorn as she'd mistakenly once thought but pride in his daughter because she did understand and love for his wife because she didn't.

Lily felt tears building up and angrily brushed them away. Not for the first time she wished she'd tried to understand her father better. He and James had nattered on for hours some evenings. Sometimes though when she heard the two of them talking, they might as well have been speaking in another language. "Psychoanalysis" and "lobotomy" meant very little to a young Lily with admittedly her "head in the clouds" at times.

Lily felt a little like that now. There were too many thoughts racing around for her to make sense of any of them. Trying to grasp and retain the logical part of her brain she reasoned that she hadn't been party to all the facts. She began to laugh hysterically – party to all the facts! What a joke that was. How could anyone tell an impressionable young girl that her brother was the result of an affair that her mother had had and that her father had been abused by his mother, that impressionable girl's own grandmother? It wouldn't exactly make a relaxing story. Once upon a time…

Lily held her knees close to her body and rocked backwards and forwards.

"When the wind stops the cradle will fall and down will come baby, cradle and all…" She could feel tears coursing down her cheeks which seemed strange as she hadn't laughed this much in ages. Alex, her father, Philip, even Henry. Where were they all now? Perhaps she might have a tiny winy idea about her father and Philip. Something to do with being cold in the ground. Maybe that was where Alex was as well now. Keeping good company. He'd always enjoyed intelligent conversation. Bless the lamb.

"Lily! Lily! Stop. Oh, God Lily. Please stop." What was James doing there, Lily thought. She didn't believe he'd been invited to the party. Perhaps he'd slipped in without the others noticing. The more, the merrier she supposed. Though she couldn't really see what was going on anymore. Everything seemed a little blurry. Still, they would have to let her know about it all when they got back.

She vaguely felt a stinging sensation on her right cheek.

"God, Lily! I'm so sorry. I've been so selfish. Take deep breaths, darling. It's ok. Nice and slow. I'm here now." James always did have a soothing voice. He'd make a good doctor. Oh, that was good she could see him a bit more clearly now. Something must have got in her eye. Lily felt a little better though she wasn't sure how she had been feeling before, so she wasn't going to worry about it. She was more concerned about James. She wondered why on earth he was crying.

CHAPTER TWENTY-TWO

April 1916

Lily woke up to sunshine streaming through the thin cotton bedroom curtains which seemed strange as the sun never reached this side of the house until at least midday depending on what season you were in. She turned her face towards the warmth.
She'd get up in a minute, but it felt good. Still half asleep she heard a gentle tapping on the door, and her mother came in balancing a cup of tea on a tray with a slab of bread and dripping.
"You're awake, love. That's good, and you look better." Lily was finding the start to this day all a little confusing. She couldn't remember even being ill. The last thing she recalled with any clarity was sitting by the downstairs window intending to read a chapter of the book that Timmy had given her for Christmas. She vaguely remembered someone shouting but that had probably been the Breeze brothers arriving home late from the pub. It wouldn't have been the first time they'd come in roaring drunk.
Lily squinted as Ethel opened the brightly coloured gingham curtains and the sunlight hit Lily's eyes. At first, she couldn't make sense of anything but then noticed the grandfather clock, which Ethel's father had bequeathed to her, ticking steadily away in the right-hand side of the room.
"My God. Mum! It's one o'clock in the afternoon. What were you thinking letting me lie here till this time? Why am

I lying here anyway? Why didn't I wake up?" Ethel came around to the side of the bed and put her hand on Lily's shoulder gently but firmly pushing her back onto the pillows.

"Shush love. Calm down. James went out early this morning and told Rolls Royce you wouldn't be in today. Told them you're feeling a bit under the weather."

"But we had an important order coming in today. Then there's all the paperwork."

"They were fine about it so don't worry about that. The bosses said they were surprised you came back to work so soon after your dad's death anyway and that you should have taken more time off. They said for you to take the rest of the week off."

Lily looked a little more relieved and pulled the blanket up to her chin. With her tousled hair and traces of sleep still in her eyes, Ethel thought that she looked like a little girl again. Ethel many times wished that she could turn the clock back. How differently she would have handled things, but she comforted herself with the reasoning that there weren't many people who had no regret about their life. No use crying over spilt milk she would admonish herself. Her duty now was with the family she had left, and like James, she also felt a little guilty. She'd recognised the pain that Lily was in but because her pain was so immense, and Lily seemed to be coping she'd pushed it to the back burner. Something to be dealt with when she felt readier to offer the support that deep down, she knew that Lily desperately needed.

In many ways since the Zeppelin attacks, they had all been trying to function in their own little worlds keeping their individual feelings close to their chest in case sharing them caused more pain. Well, no longer Ethel promised herself. We are in this together, and we will deal with it together. Maybe in a roundabout way, things coming to a head with

Lily were a blessing in disguise. At least James had been civil when he'd left this morning and had even suffered a hug from Ethel without pushing her away.

Lily did take the week off work and during that time the three of them really talked probably more than they had ever done. Ethel and Lily had become close because of Ethel's revelations about first Henry and then Betty. Both Ethel and Lily agreed that telling James about Henry couldn't do any good at this stage. Nobody even knew if Henry was coming home again. Lily wasn't a cruel woman, and despite Henry's behaviour she didn't like to think of him as another casualty of war. However, she had to admit that now it was more comfortable not to have him around.

Ethel did tell James about Betty though there was only so much she could say to either of her children Bert hadn't revealed all the details even to her. It seemed likely that a lot of Betty's evil secrets had gone to the grave with Bert. Both Lily and Ethel expected James to fly off the handle, so they were amazed at how calmly he seemed to take in the information.

"I always knew that there was something more on his mind apart from the boy he wasn't able to save in the pit. It always seemed so strange as well how he didn't talk about his parents to Lily and me."

"So, he told you about the abuse?" Ethel challenged James.
"No, but I knew there was something and that it must be pretty dark for him to be as depressed as he was."

Both Lily and Ethel thought back to the many hours they had spent in the back kitchen preparing meals and washing dishes while Bert and James had sat by the fire talking together in muted tones. They had assumed it was about James becoming a doctor or the war or politics. James was well versed on matters to do with the government and had a social conscience that tied in with his ambitions. On reflection, Lily thought that maybe James had known Bert better than any of them in the last few years. She saw that knowledge reflected in her mum's eyes as well. It made them both even more confident that it would crush James if he ever found out the truth about his parentage.

The time away from work gave Lily a bit of space to reconsider what she wanted to do for the war effort. She still felt a little weak and prone to dizzy spells now and again but mentally felt strong enough to assess her options. Though she hadn't seen Maggie for a while, she had heard from one of the girls at work that she'd gone nursing. Her husband's disabilities had proved to be worse than first thought, and he'd passed away only a couple of months after Lily had last seen Maggie at the Markeaton house. Lily greatly admired her friend as apparently; she'd turned her life completely around. She'd moved to London and was training hard to become a member of the Queen Alexandra's Imperial Military Nursing Service, and she was a respected member working for the British Army. Many other young women didn't hold the badge of respect that the QAIMNS seemed to offer and were sent to serve with the Belgian or French forces instead. Lily worried for her friend though as it appeared that she was often put into dangerous positions. Another part of Lily was slightly jealous in that Maggie was at least experiencing the horror of war first-hand and was making a real difference to the wounded troops out there. However, Lily didn't know if she would have the patience to follow in her friend's footsteps. If nothing else Lily had always been very perceptive in the knowledge of her strengths and weaknesses. She thought back again to the terrible arguments she'd had with their dad at times, and she felt ashamed at the lack of respect she'd shown at times. Lily decided that she would think about it just a little longer. She felt so tired these days and didn't want to rush headlong into another project and then realise she had got herself in too deep.

A few weeks later a typically blustery day in late April Lily got a bit of a boost when an old friend dropped by to see her. "It's a wild one out there tonight, Mum." Lily took off her overcoat shaking it free of water before she hung it on the back-door peg. "I'll just go and freshen up, and then I'll help you with tea. Our James seems to have got his appetite back at last."

Ethel was busy stirring a large pot of rabbit stew on the range.

"Don't worry about that tonight, love. I've set a fire in the front room so go in and get yourself warm. You've got someone waiting to see you." Lily was intrigued. She couldn't imagine who would be significant enough to warrant her mum making use of their precious coal. Besides which she couldn't think of anybody at all who would want to visit her. She heard James's laugh filtering through from the front. It was apparently somebody he felt comfortable around. At the same time, she hoped whoever it was wasn't going to take up too much of their time as all she really wanted to do was have an early tea and an early night. However, as soon as she opened the door and heard that unique accent her tiredness evaporated. James beamed at her.

"Had a good day, Lil? I've spent a fabulous hour sitting here talking to Miss Hardcastle. You wouldn't believe the tales she has got to tell about London. We didn't miss you at all." Lily caught the surreptitious wink that James threw in the way of Lizzy Hardcastle.

"Now James I wouldn't exactly say that, but I agree it's been a delightful afternoon so far and it's been a pleasure to get to know you better in the light than peering at each other in a rather dreary and cold churchyard. Lily smiled and held her arms out to her old friend.

"Lizzy! What are you doing here apart from flirting with men far too young for you?"

Miss Hardcastle gave Lizzy her trademark slightly coquettish "butter wouldn't melt in the mouth "look.

"Well, I don't know about that, dear. Your brother brushes up pretty well." Lily laughed out loud. Something that she couldn't remember doing for a long time.

"Well, you haven't changed. Shameless as ever." James got up from the settee where he had been entertaining their afternoon visitor.

"I think I will get out of your hair and let you two young ladies discuss me behind my back."

"You flatter yourself, dear brother." Lily gave James a playful shove. "Go and get on with whatever it is real men are supposed to be doing." As soon as James had left the room the two women fell into each other's arms again.

"Let me look at you, Lily." Miss Hardcastle said stepping back and holding Lily at arm's length. "You look well child but tired."

"It's been a difficult time Lizzy, but you look absolutely wonderful. Libertys and London must be suiting you."

Lily's keen eyes had noticed the navy-blue Wanamaker coat with a large cape collar of coney fur draped over the back of the settee. Lizzy was also sporting a new hairstyle. Lily thought that it was called a bob and had heard that it was a new trend that had come in from Paris though she had yet to see any of the female population in Derby taking up the mantle.

"London's fine. I think whatever happens to the old girl she will always come through. A wonderful city Lily. Full of vibrancy and ambition even in these hard times."

"But?" Lily queried sensing that there was more.

"Well…Liberty's my dear. Maybe not quite so fine."

"I thought that it was doing fantastically well despite the restrictions of the war." Lily sounded surprised.

"Oh, the store is in good shape, child. Richard Shaw, the architect you know, was so right when he wrote to Mr Arthur Liberty. "You find things, most of them beastly and you leave them glorious in colour and full of interest." Lily let Lizzy ramble for a few minutes. Sometimes her intellect carried her away to places Lily couldn't follow and often didn't want to. She knew that her friend would disclose what was on her mind in her own time.

"Lasenby you know? Mr Liberty's middle name. Peculiar name but a visionary of his time."

"But?" Lily insisted sticking to her guns.

"Well if you really must know it's that woman. She hates me, Lily. Right from the start, she hated me, and I'm sure she's sleeping with the boss. Everything I do she criticises, and I don't get any back up from the other women, and I don't get invited to any of their get-togethers. All scared of the boss lady, so they don't open their mouths and they steer clear of me as if I had the plague."

"So, you're giving up?" Lily sounded slightly stern. "I thought you were made of stronger stuff than that."

"I'm not giving up, Lily but I'm changing direction. I'm not afraid of her or any of them but I feel like a fish out of water. Daft as it sounds, I miss Derby and its people. I feel that I belong here. After Philip…well you know I didn't think I could settle here again, but I've put some ghosts to rest in London."

"So, you're moving back here?" Lily didn't want to sound too hopeful and push Lizzy into doing something on impulse though she would love her friend to come home.

"Probably, Lily but not just yet. There are affairs I must sort out, and I'm going to make sure I walk out of Liberty's with my head held high and with what's owing to me. I also don't want to leave the department in a mess. I'd like to do something a bit more useful though than advise ladies, with too much time and money on their hands, what to wear to keep their husbands from straying."

"To be honest Lizzy, I have been feeling much the same recently. I have no idea where Alex is, our James will almost definitely be signing up later this year, and nothing is going to bring dad back."

Lily felt the first stirring of excitement as Lizzy continued. "One thing we have got, thanks to Philip, is money or at least property. If we give up our jobs, we will also have precious time. Let's try and do something that would have made Philip proud." Miss Hardcastle hugged Lily tightly to her.

"I knew there was a reason for me coming to see you today apart from to see a dear friend and her handsome brother. Let's think about it, my dear. Let's really think about it."

CHAPTER TWENTY-THREE

Early May 1916

As spring continued to cast a net over the parks and countryside around Derby Lily felt more positive. The changing of the seasons stopped for no man and spring had always been Lily's favourite time of the year. Her favourite flowers, the daffodils, provided a welcome splash of colour as they waved in the breeze, with their faces towards the sunshine.
Lily still grieved for her dad and knew that she always would have regrets about her relationship with him while growing up. Talking to her mum had helped her in some ways as at least she now appreciated how much her father had loved her.
"In many ways, you and your dad were like two peas in a pod. "Ethel said when they were both sitting by the hearth one evening. Ethel was knitting. She was rarely seen with idle hands. Lily was perusing the "Mercury" for any information about developments in the war. At one time Lily wouldn't have necessarily been overly pleased with the comparison, but she'd learnt a lot about Bert since and recognised his proud, stubborn spirit in herself and was glad of it. Ethel continued, "Maybe that's why you clashed sometimes. Neither of you was prepared to back down when you'd got a bee in your bonnet." Lily smiled.

"Maybe you're right, Mum, but that's not always such a bad thing is it?" Lily didn't quite know how to interpret Ethel's sceptical look and didn't try too hard.

"Have you thought any more about what Miss Hardcastle said?" Ethel inquired.

"You're allowed to call her Lizzy, Mum, but yes I have one or two ideas ticking away, but nothing's set in stone yet. To be honest, I think we'll be looking more towards the autumn before she's tied everything up down there."

"So, you're staying with Rolls Royce for now?"

"For now, I think, but I'm cutting my hours back a bit. It'll give me time to mull over a few plans and besides which I feel so tired most of the time. You know I won't see you short."

"You don't owe us anything, Lily, but you know that James and I are grateful for what you bring in."

The following week Lily moved back to her own home. Much as she enjoyed the company of her mum and James, she was beginning to feel that she wanted her space again and she knew that James would be glad of the extra room to spread his books around. Her mum had convinced her that she would be fine or at least okay and besides which Lily would still see them every day.

The worry about Alex was still on all their minds, but it wasn't uncommon for letters to go astray and even officers only got so much leave. Lily determined to put all her energy into making her own home as comfortable and cosy as possible. Both Alex and Lily had agreed that it would be their first married home. What had swung the decision for them was the large garden and attached field that came with the property that would allow them to grow their own produce and maybe eventually even keep a few hens and the like. Alex had joked that they would also keep a pig and a goose and fatten them up for Christmas. Well, at least Lily had thought that he was joking. Hypocritical it might be, but she'd rather take her chance down at the market than raise the fatted calf themselves.

So, it was that the first warm day of the year saw Lily throwing herself into the digging and preparing of a vegetable patch around the back of the house. She'd felt unsettled ever since she'd woken up and this physical work was just what she needed to provide a distraction. She just hoped that no visitors would appear to see her attire of an old pair of hobnailed boots she'd found in the bedroom cubby hole and God forbid, a pair of beige cotton breeches. Quite a few girls were now daring to try the new fashion, and it certainly beat the hobble skirt for comfort and practicality.

By late morning Lily was hot and sweaty, and her muscles were aching being unaccustomed to such prolonged physical work, but she felt satisfied with her morning's labours. As she sat with a well-deserved cup of tea Lily could already envision the rows of beans and peas that she was going to plant at the back of the border. The sun was almost as high in the sky as it would get at this time of year and just at the angle to dazzle her eyes from where she was sitting. Lily rested her head against the back of her chair and was just about to drift off in the warmth when she caught a glint of something flashing through the trees. Not really understanding why Lily rose and went towards the five-barred gate that separated her house from the lane outside. She managed to identify Michael emerging from the trees. It must have been the silver buttons on his uniform reflecting the sun that caught her eye. Lily felt as cold as if she'd been standing there in the chill of December. Michael skidded to a halt, on his bike, just in time before he hit the gate.

"Whoops. That was a close one. Morning Miss Armitage. A lovely one it is as well. Just right for gardening."

How young he was thought Lily as she took in his mop of ginger hair and heavily freckled face. Too young to be immersed in the war or understand what it was all about though wasn't that true of most people? Michael handed over what he'd come for, and Lily stood watching his figure recede into the distance as he made his way to the next customer. Maybe customer wasn't quite the right word, Lily thought. Customers usually acquired what they needed or wanted.

Lily strolled back into the house and placed the telegram on the hall table. It was much darker in there than in the rest of the house as the window was north facing. It seemed such a shame Lily thought to waste such a beautiful day. She turned away from the table and quietly shut the door behind her as she emerged once more into the sunlight. Lily took deep breaths of the sweet fresh air, picked up her fork and began to attack the earth. By early evening as the light was fading, she had a perfect vegetable patch dug out and manured ready for when Alex came home.

Come home Lily was sure that he would. Even as she sat in her favourite patchwork effect armchair holding the opened telegram, she felt the same. Lily stared at the letters MIA repeatedly. The telegram wasn't such bad news. Now, if it had read KIA-Killed in Action – there would be no hope. Missing in action meant that Alex could be out there anywhere. The written telegram described how a grenade had exploded close to Alex and four of his comrades as they were coming over the top of one of the trenches. Two of them had survived though limbs had to be amputated. The other two were picked up in pieces from off the battlefield. Lily knew that the rest of the platoon would have done everything they could to retrieve their bodies and bury them in temporary graves close to the front line. Of Alex, there had been no sign.

Lily couldn't begin to explain it to herself, but she didn't feel as shocked as she thought the situation might warrant. Ever since she'd moved back to her own home, she'd felt even closer to Alex. This was where they would begin what hopefully would be a long life together. She'd come back to start to prepare for that next step in her life. Ever since she'd moved back, she'd felt as though she had been waiting for something and this morning it had arrived. The Army hadn't found Alex, so that meant that he was still somewhere out there alive.

At eight o'clock that evening Ethel quietly pushed open the kitchen door to see Lily sitting there in the same armchair with the few letters that Alex had managed to send before his last leave. Ethel and James went to sit on the settee opposite to Lily.

"I was worried, love. You said you were going to pop round tonight. You're not, poorly are you?" Lily quietly handed the telegram to James. She knew that her mum still struggled with her reading at times, though she was much improved since Lily had begun helping her. James read the telegram out in a quiet but steady voice. He didn't speak, but his stricken look spelt volumes.

"Oh, love. I'm so sorry." Ethel pulled Lily to her feet and embraced her daughter wishing that she could take all Lily's pain onto herself.

"Mum, don't worry. I'm not going to crack up as I did at yours. We need to stay strong. Alex's comrades adored him because he is a decent officer and man and Alex looked after them as though they were the brothers he'd never had. They all would have searched hard for him which means there's still hope, Mum. While there's hope I won't give up."

Ethel looked her daughter in the eyes.

"I know that you won't, Lily. Your dad wouldn't have done either and neither will we. Put that kettle on James, and then I'm going over the way to fetch Dr Ogley."

"Mum! What for? I'm not ill."

"I know that you're not Lily, but you are tired. I know you weren't sleeping well at ours. Don't think I didn't hear you rattling around in the middle of the night. Dr Ogley can give you a mild sedative – just to make sure you get a good night's sleep."

"Agree to it, Lily." James attempted a half smile. "You know she's going to do it anyway and if you're going to stay strong, you need to stay healthy."

"Ok. Ok, Dr Armitage but only because you might just possibly know what you're talking about." Half an hour later Lily was tucked up in bed with Ethel fussing over her and Dr Ogley prodding her. James was hovering on the landing not sure what to do with himself. They all liked Alex, and he'd been a great help to James before he'd gone off and enlisted. James didn't feel as optimistic as Lily appeared to be. He also didn't think that he was as good at concealing his feelings as their mum, so he kept out of the way and carried on pacing.

Lily was so grateful to them both and happy that they'd said they would stay overnight. It was comforting to think of somebody else being in the house now. However, she wished they would leave her in peace just for a little while. Lily was vaguely aware of Dr Ogley's voice saying something to her mum. He'd always been their family doctor, and they all trusted him implicitly. Lily smiled as she thought back to a time when she thought she hated him. James had been quite ill as a toddler with bronchitis and Lily had been convinced the doctor had come to take her brother away and never bring him back. Dr Ogley had gradually brought her round with his patience, kindness and not least his party trick of juggling oranges when they'd been lucky enough to have some.

"Lily." He now said in a gentle voice. "Just a couple of questions and then I'll leave you and your good family in peace."

"What is it that you want to know Doctor?" Ethel butted in.

"Have you been feeling extra tired recently, Lily?"

"Oh yes, Dr Ogley. She has. Only the other day…"

"Mum! Please. I can speak for myself you know. I told you I'm not going to lose my mind this time." Dr Ogley chuckled and then quickly tried to convert it into a cough."

"Yes, I have, Dr Ogley. For just this last two or three weeks especially. We've all been under quite a bit of stress recently like most people."

"I do know that my dear and I'm truly sorry for it. Just one more thing. Have you experienced any dizziness or sickness recently?"

"To tell you the truth. Now that you mention it, I have been feeling a bit sickly but only this last couple of weeks really."

"Mostly in the mornings?" Dr Ogley smiled gently.

" I suppose the answer is yes, but I don't think that it's anything serious."

"Well, it depends on how you look at it, my dear. It's certainly a common condition, especially in young women."

"She is?" Ethel almost squeaked and James from his position still on the landing looked bewildered.

"She is Ethel." Dr Ogley then turned to Lily and calmly took her hand. "You are experiencing, young lady, the most natural thing in the world. I would estimate you to be about three months pregnant. Give or take a week or so."

It had never even crossed Lily's mind. With all the stress her body clock had been all over the place. She hadn't remotely considered the possibility. It had only been the once, and they had taken precautions. Lily looked more shocked than when she had received the telegram.

"I'm going to be a mother?" Dr Ogley closed his bag as he made his way towards the bedroom door smiling at James's equally shocked expression as he passed him by.

"I think, my dear, you can safely say that is a real possibility."

CHAPTER TWENTY-FOUR

May 1916

Lily spent the following few days trying to decide what she felt about her present predicament. It wasn't ideal, and she really didn't know how people were going to judge her and her family. She couldn't help thinking back to a few years previously when Amy Mellor had been spirited away in the night because of her "sin" of falling pregnant outside of wedlock. Maybe the war had changed people's perspectives in some ways. There was a lot of talk being bandied about encouraging people to live for today because you never knew what tomorrow was going to bring or if you were even going to see a tomorrow. However, Lily wasn't at all confident that this philosophy extended to unmarried mothers.

What made her even more apprehensive was the memory of how Amy's mother and father had talked about their daughter, as though there was no question of her staying at home while she was pregnant never mind bringing up her own child once it was born. Lily knew that there were ways and means that desperate women took when confronted with the same dilemma. Most of them took place in seedy backstreets somewhere under the "guidance" of an illegal practitioner and in unsanitary conditions. Some women had paid the ultimate cost of their lives during or after these backstreet abortions. Luckily, Lily didn't see this as an option. She reasoned that at least she had money, but even if she hadn't Lily didn't think that she would be able to get rid of the life that was growing inside her. At the same time, she fully understood why some girls couldn't face going through with it, and Lily would also argue that women should always be able to have a say in what happened to their own bodies. She felt that if Alex knew he would be overjoyed even though it had all come a little earlier than planned. She smiled as she figured that he would probably have her at the altar within a week. Lily had felt lonely many times in her life, but in those first few days after finding out about her pregnancy, the feeling almost overwhelmed her. She missed Alex so much and felt that he was the only one she could have admitted to entirely the various emotions that were encompassing her. Thankfully the weather had taken a turn for the better and Lily spent many hours outside tending to the garden or going for long walks in the park or along the Derwent.

Ethel had been unusually quiet after Dr Ogley's revelation. Both she and James had stayed the night as they'd promised. Lily woke up to find Ethel hovering over her bed with a breakfast tray, but she didn't stop to chat which was unusual. Later in the morning, James had knocked tentatively on the bedroom door only to poke his head round to say that he and Ethel were going home.

"Mum says she's got things to do," He said to Lily almost apologetically.

"I'll come down and say bye at least." Lily began to push back the bedcovers and search for her slippers with her toes.

"She says to take your time getting up. We'll see ourselves out apparently."

"What do you think's going through her head, James?" James spread his hands out as if he were offering supplication to the Lord above.

"Who knows, Lily? When she gets in one of these quiet moods its best just to let her be and mull things over. She'll come around." Lily beckoned to her brother, and he gently took her hand.

"I believe that you are getting wiser by the day than any of us, James Armitage. Putting mum aside for the moment what do you really think about your wanton sister?"

"Don't put yourself down, Lil. I can't think of anybody more loyal to this family than you, and I know that you'll keep the bairn and you'll do it proud. Whether Alex returns home or not."

"You don't think he's coming back do you, James?" James smiled sadly as he moved away from the bed.

"I really hope that he is, Lily, for all our sakes.

Lily determined that whatever anybody else thought she was going to do the best that she could for herself and the baby. Though she felt a little sick still in the morning and the waistband of her navy work skirt was maybe a little bit tighter than usual there were no more visible signs of her condition.

In the past, Lily had occasionally contemplated what it would be like to have a child. It was such a commonplace occurrence while at the same time being utterly overwhelming in the way it would shape and change a person's life. At times Lily almost felt outside of the situation and could scarcely believe that she was going to be responsible for bringing a new life into the world.

It was four days before Lily saw Ethel again. In the interim Lily had kept busy and the house was clean, and the garden was coming along nicely. It was while hoeing a few of the spring weeds out, to make it easier to cultivate the ground later, that Lily spotted Ethel hovering by the gate. Lily brushed her tousled hair back from her sweaty forehead and slowly made her way along the path trying not to think of the result of the same journey that she had made a few days before.

"You can come in, mum. That's if you want to."

Ethel pushed open the gate and looked her daughter in the face. Lily could see the unshed tears shining in her eyes and the slight quivering of her bottom lip. She also had dark shadows under her eyes as though she hadn't been sleeping.

"Mum. Don't take on so. We'll sort it out. We always have before."

"I wouldn't blame you if you didn't want to speak to me anymore, Lily, never mind let me in your house. I abandoned you when I of all people should have known how much you needed someone."

Lily shook her head. She hated to see the pain in her mother's eyes knowing that she was partly responsible for it. "I knew that you'd come when you were ready," Lily said quietly.

"I won't let you down again my love. I swear on my family's life. Whatever anyone says from here in I'll be right at your side. I've no excuse but it's just this whole thing has brought back all the feelings of desperation and loneliness I had when James was on the way. Not knowing who to turn to and not really being honest with anyone. It nearly drove me mad, Lily and I doubted whether I would ever be able to live with the guilt."

"But you hadn't a choice, had you? You would never have got rid of James. There's no other choice that you could have made, and it's like that for me."

"You're going to definitely keep it then, love? "Ethel asked with a slightly worried look on her face.

"I'm not sure how I feel about any of it, Mum, but I couldn't give it away especially when I see what you went through with James."

"It was a little easier for me though in some ways at least. To all intents and purposes, I was a married woman and James belonged to my husband as far as anyone else was concerned but I'm with you all the way Lily."

In the couple of months that followed Lily made some changes. On Ethel's advice, she left work. There had been some murmurings in the back room that Lily had found hard to ignore though it may have been paranoia as to her face her work colleagues didn't seem to treat her that much differently. A couple of the office girls had even enquired when the baby was due, and they all still looked very concerned for her over Alex. Lily was far from naïve and realised that in general, unmarried mothers were heavily stigmatised against. Maybe it was because she was engaged, and Alex was missing that she elicited some sympathy.

In any case, Lily saw very few people after finishing at Rolls Royce. She kept herself to herself and continued to concentrate on transforming her home with the slight difference that there would now be three of them to consider and not just two. Lily knew that in many ways she was lucky. Many of the unmarried mothers in Derby would end up putting their children into residential care under the provisions of the Poor Law. At least she was financially secure for the moment. The work at Rolls Royce had been as much to fulfil a need to contribute to the war effort a little bit, but the extra money had been useful to give to her family.

Though Lily now spent a great deal of time in her own little bubble trying to keep positive and healthy, she couldn't help but be aware of what was happening in the world in general. James visited regularly. After the initial shock of his sister potentially having a baby outside of wedlock his enthusiasm returned.

"I can't wait to be an uncle, Lily. It seems to me all the fun and none of the hassle."

"I'll be expecting you to step up to the plate young man." Lily ruffled his hair one evening as they sat on the patio outside drinking in the last rays of evening sun. She had to pinch herself when she thought about James turning eighteen later in the year. She knew that he still had going to the war in mind and she often wished they could go back to when they were children. At times James still could be that annoying brother who cut worms in half and offered them to Lily for her tea. Yet in many other ways, Lily realised that James had grown into a perceptive young man beyond his years.

One afternoon sometime in early July James appeared, to help Lily weed out the new vegetable patch that was thriving. Lily by now was about six months pregnant and beginning to find some tasks increasingly tricky to negotiate. It was made worse by the searing heat that had been with them for a few days. James had brought news of another battle which he sensed was going to be significant.

"We're going to smash them in the air, Lily. We've got 386 fighters pitted against their 129 German aircraft." Lily worried about how enthusiastic he seemed to be now about the war. When their dad had been alive, James wanted no cotter with it. In some ways, though his knowledge was spot on. The Battle of the Somme along with the one at Verdun were to be two of the most decisive battles of the war with massive loss of life. Future historians would see 1916 as the year when the armies of Britain, France and Germany bled to death.

That sunny afternoon, though, in Derby the war seemed very far away. Since the Zeppelin attack at the beginning of the year, there hadn't been any more trouble from the skies. Lily was feeling more preoccupied with the preparation for the birth. She was still apprehensive but now felt an overwhelming need to protect her child from whatever was to come. Often, she would find herself talking to her baby as if it was in the same room which in a way it was.

In the depths of the night Lily would toss and turn trying g to get into a comfortable position while thinking about Alex. Despite at times tears not being far away, Lily refused to cry. Once she did it would almost be like admitting to herself that she had a reason to grieve. So, Lily bit her lip, closed her eyes and entered a dream world where Bert and Alex were calling to her but from so far away. If only she could struggle through the mud a little further, she felt sure she would be able to reach them. However, hands were rising from the ground and grabbing her ankles. She felt herself gradually slipping away from them and being sucked into the earth. Strangely she felt as though a heavy weight was being lifted off her chest and it didn't seem too bad at all anymore.

CHAPTER TWENTY-FIVE

July 1916

It turned into a long tiresome summer for Lily. She was used to being active, and as her body became even more cumbersome, she became even more frustrated. James and her mum couldn't have been more helpful, but Lily hated how much she had to depend on them. Ethel wanted Lily to move back in with her and James, but that was one point on which Lily wouldn't budge. She'd come back to her own house to make it a home for her family. Lily didn't say it to her mum for fear of hurting her feelings, but she felt that if she moved back, Ethel would ultimately take her over. Ethel had taken on the role of the grandmother in waiting with gusto and as time marched on seemed to be more excited than Lily over the whole affair.

Lily couldn't quite pinpoint when her feelings for the child she was carrying had changed. This period of enforced inactivity had given Lily more time to think than was healthy. Her dad had been on her mind. She wondered what he had really been through as a child. It seemed that even her mum hadn't been privy to all the sordid details. Lily hoped that growing up, her father had found someone to share his pain with. He'd never really talked about his siblings, and in most ways, his childhood family was an enigma to both Lily and James.

Now that the nights stayed lighter longer Ethel had got into the routine of popping round to see Lily in the evening. Lily had told her it wasn't necessary to come every day, but she might as well have been talking to a brick wall. When Ethel didn't want to hear something, she selectively ignored it, so Lily resigned herself to receiving a casserole or the leftovers from James's tea most nights.

"There we are, love," Ethel said on one such evening towards the end of July. "Get that down you, and it will do you and the little one good." She placed that day's offering on the table. Lily couldn't quite see what was underneath the blue and white checked cloth but had to admit that it smelt delicious. Ethel's eyes were bright, and the pallor that she had exhibited after Bert's death had lifted. Lily thought that her mum looked five years younger. Ethel was still obviously worried about James joining up later in the year, but for now, she had a definite purpose in life again which was to see her first grandchild brought safely into the world. Following the usual routine, Lily ate though she rarely could finish it all. Her mum really did think that she should be eating for two. They would both then do the washing up and later would close the curtains against the fading light. James would be along later to escort his mum home, but he always gave the two of them a little time together each night to talk about "women's stuff." Mostly they talked about their respective days and news about the war or people they knew. Tonight, though Lily was unusually quiet which of course didn't escape Ethel's notice?

"What's the matter, love? Are you feeling poorly? I'll go and make us another cup of tea if you like." Lily shook her head and motioned for her mum to sit down again in the armchair opposite to her own.

"I'm not poorly, mum but I do feel worried," Lily admitted.
"Well of course you do. It's only natural and with Alex not being around."

"Well, yes, of course, I'm worried about that. I always am, but it's something else. I know it might be silly, but I just can't shake it."

"Lily. Just spit it out. We've now shared far more than most mothers and daughters so whatever you say it's not likely going to shock me."

"Really!" Lily looked doubtfully at her mother. "What if I tell you that I'm worried about this child turning out to be like Granny Armitage?"

"Oh, Lily. Of course, he or she isn't. Why would you think it?"

"Alex used to talk a lot about something called genetics. You know what he's like. Knowledge for knowledge's sake and all that." Lily smiled when she thought back to how eloquent and passionate, he could be about so many subjects. "Anyway, he said that we inherit certain features as well as possibly behaviour traits from our ancestors. Our mums and dads I suppose in the first instance. Suppose I bring a child into the world and when it's older it turns into another Betty Armitage. Suppose I become that person? I'm only young. There's still time for it to rear its ugly head."

Lily could feel hysteria mounting. These thoughts had been pent up in her so long she thought that she would burst if she didn't get them out into the open. Lily felt shaky inside and clenched her hands to try and conceal it. She'd vowed not to cry but was closer to it than she had been for months.

"Lily. Look at me. I know you better than maybe you know yourself. Your child is going to have a loving, caring mother who will fiercely protect it, as best as she can, from all that's bad in the world. She or he won't be insecure as your grandmother was and they will go on to treat their children in the same way as their lovely mother did them."

Lily took a few deep breaths and calmed down slightly though she was a little puzzled over one of her mother's comments.

"You almost sound as though you are making excuses for her, Mum."

"Never think that. I meant everything I said to you before. I'm glad Betty's gone. She was a mistress of manipulation so at least your dad had a few years grace without her hanging onto his shirt tails. But she did have a tough upbringing. That's something that your dad touched on after she'd died. To be fair, you deserve to know as much as I do now especially now that you're going to have a family of your own soon."

During the next hour as the fading light turned to darkness, Ethel talked to Lily and eventually James who came in a little later. They both listened intently. It turned out that Betty Armitage hadn't been a Derby woman as Lily had assumed. She'd been brought up in the notoriously hard area of the East end in London. Her father was a hard-drinking foul-mouthed individual who worked in the docks, and her mother worked in factories sometimes up to fourteen hours a day. Betty being the eldest was left to look after her siblings and rake in as much extra money as she could. She'd clean windows, run errands or make matchboxes to scrape together a meagre amount so maybe the family could have some extra stale bread that day. Her brother, Bill, who was the next eldest, would do the same as well as chopping kindle and selling it when he could. The family struggled to survive losing Baby Benjamin to measles when he was only a few months old. Later, Lottie, Betty's only sister died of diphtheria.

Lily especially was fascinated.

"But how did dad know all this? I can't see him sitting having cosy fireside chats with Betty." Lily asked.

"No of course not," Ethel said with a tinge of bitterness in her voice. "It was Jack who used to talk with him. Usually, after he'd had too many down at the pub. Who knows what was going on in Jack's mind at the time either?"

Ethel continued to paint a picture with words for Lily and James. When she talked about a family of nine living in a single room with no clean water for washing and drinking Lily felt a little guilty as she glanced at her own well-furnished home. She imagined that it would have been a mansion to an EastEnders family back then.

James got up to light the lamp before it got completely pitch, and Ethel's face was revealed in the soft glow. Lily thought that she looked almost as though she wasn't here at all but back in the past along with that family.

"That's not very good. I agree, and maybe we don't always appreciate what we've got, and we should, but it still doesn't explain how a woman can go and abuse her own flesh and blood." James's angry voice cut through to Ethel and seemed to jolt her back into the present.

"James is right, Mum. People have got it tough today as well, but it doesn't turn them into abusers."

"Of course not. You're both right. But let me get through to the end, and then you'll both know as much as I have ever done."

The two siblings nodded and listened as Ethel let vent to feelings that she'd been hanging onto for a long time. Lily already knew, but Ethel told James how much she hated Betty for what she had done to Bert. It also came out that a couple of years after Betty's funeral Bert revealed to Ethel that he was pretty sure that Betty had been abused by her own father.

"So, it is in the blood?" Lily was almost tumbling over her words in her anxiety. "What goes around comes around. We're all tarred with the same brush."

"Lily. Calm down. Think of the baby. "Ethel put her hand over Lily's.

"I am doing, mum. Thinking of the baby. What happens if it turns into another Betty Armitage?"

"Lily please snap out of it and let Mum finish. But please don't say that dad forgave her. That would be too much to stomach." James said.

"Your dad never forgave her for what she did." From the coldness of her tone, Lily and James knew it to be true. "But he did believe that she was scarred from the past, and it deeply troubled her. His theory was that she felt so unworthy herself that she wanted to make others fear her to escape her feelings of self-hatred."

"Blimey!" James said in admiration. "My dad was quite a thinker back in the day."

"Your dad was a very clever, brave and modest man. That's why that you, Lily, can never be anything like Betty. You are your father's daughter. Just as your father would never have dreamed of doing the same to you. He turned the numbness and sadness that he felt as a boy into anger and eventually channelled that into strength and compassion. Never let me hear any of you ever call your father a weak man again."

Lily felt the warmth of her grateful tears coursing down her cheeks. Through them, she smiled at her dear mother and brother. These tears were allowed because for once they weren't about Alex but for their son or daughter. She knew the truth of what her mother said. Lily was her father's daughter. Even during their disagreements, it had always been so. Lily silently thanked her father and promised to bring up her child to be confident and secure so that they would never feel unworthy. They would always feel loved just as Lily now knew that she always had been.

CHAPTER TWENTY-SIX

August 1916

As August 1916 ended the sultry heat of the past few weeks seemed to be abating much to Lily's relief. She felt as though she could breathe again, and her energy seemed to have returned. The house was spotless, and there was plenty of late summer colour in the garden. The vegetable plot was doing well and having fresh produce readily available made all the hard work worth it.
Lily though was becoming increasingly restless. She hadn't really heard very much from Lizzy who was still down there in the big smoke trying to sort her life out enough to return home. Lily didn't expect to see her in Derby until the backend. All the preparations for the baby were done, and now all Lily could do was wait, which wasn't a state of being that came naturally to her.
It was a beautiful morning. Sometimes such mornings would make Lily ache with sadness. It didn't seem fair that folks were going about their daily business and soaking up the sun while boys and men were laying down their lives in the trenches. Today though Lily welcomed the sunshine. It was a perfect day for walking, warm but with a gentle breeze. She decided to make her way into Derby, spend some time by the river and then maybe go and see how "Bookends" was getting on.
Though Lily still technically owned the business she had little to do with it now. She had found a very competent

manageress in the shape of a middle-aged lady called Jane Thomas. Jane had definite plans about the way the business should be developing in these challenging times. Lily liked most of them and even the ones she wasn't too sure about she was prepared to give a go. If Philip hadn't given her a bit of a free rein when she had started, many of the initiatives Lily had successfully engineered would never have got off the ground.

With an overcoat over her arm in case it got chilly, she set off with a definite purpose in her step. Once she got onto the banks of the river, she was feeling a bit puffed so decided that she would sit for a few minutes to get her breath. One of her favourite pastimes was to watch the people wandering along its banks. Often, she would make up stories in her head about them. Maybe the girl on the opposite bank, who was running as though her life depended on it, was meeting her lover for an afternoon tryst. Perhaps, the old gentleman sitting on the bench, two down from her, with worn out patches on his jacket, was one of the town's homeless. Lily chuckled to herself. Of course, the girl could merely be late for work, and the man could be a millionaire who gave most of his money to charitable causes.

Sometimes Lily would see somebody she knew on her travels and would walk a little way with them catching up on the local gossip. Today though the people passing were mostly strangers though she thought that the figure of the gentleman sitting on the banks of the river about a hundred feet upstream seemed vaguely familiar. She screwed her eyes up against the sun to try and get a better look as he slowly got up and began to walk in the opposite direction. There was just something about the set of his shoulders and the leisurely walk, but it just couldn't be. Lily's heart was hammering. She needed to get up and walk the other way and put it down to a vivid imagination. But curiosity at times might as well have been Lily's second name, and she just had to know for sure.

The gentleman wasn't walking fast. He stopped several times for a few seconds as if to get his breath and look out over the water. So, Lily didn't have to hurry to catch up. She was now so close that if she'd stretched out her arm, she could have tapped him on the shoulder. Lily knew that she should leave it. The pulled-up collar of the trench coat, and trilby made it virtually impossible to get a look at his face. Why he wanted to be so trussed up on such a warm day, Lily couldn't understand. Yet she had to know even at the risk of making a fool of herself.

A nanny with a baby in a pram was approaching from the other direction. She looked flushed, and a little harried as the baby in her charge certainly didn't have a problem with its lungs. A moment later a rattle catapulted out of the pram and landed at the man's feet.

"You've got your hands full with that one my dear." The gentleman's soft, cultured tones drifted back to Lily, and she watched transfixed as he gave the rattle back to the young lady pushing the pram. Lily froze. She couldn't be here. She shouldn't be here. The pram advanced towards Lily, and the man turned around to wave goodbye to its occupant. Lily felt an overwhelming panic that temporarily rendered her speechless and motionless. The man joined her in the moment until he quickly regained his composure.

"Lily my dear. You don't know how happy I am to see you." At first, Lily thought that she was going to faint, but the next minute the blood came rushing back to her head. He had been the last person that she thought she would see on the banks of the Derwent today and in many ways the last person she wanted to see.

"Henry. You're back." Lily croaked.

"Yes, my dear, I am, and I must say that you are a sight for sore eyes."

"We all thought that you were dead." The words were out before Lily realised how that must sound. To her surprise, a smile crept across Henry's face, and for a moment Lily glimpsed what she had seen in him in the first place. He'd lost a lot of weight though, and there was pallor to his complexion, but his eyes were bright with interest as he looked Lily up and down.

"You don't change, Lily. As forthright as ever. Maybe you don't realise how refreshing that can be. Who's the lucky fellow?" Alex continued. By now Lily was only a few weeks away from giving birth.

"Alex. Alex Poynton but he's away in the war now." Henry nodded.

"I heard that he was missing. I'm sorry Lily. I really am. It doesn't surprise me though that you got together. Even during our brief affair, I always thought that there was a flicker of something going on between you both. "Lily wasn't usually lost for words, but she was really struggling with the whole situation. She had to admit that part of her was resentful that it was Henry standing there and not Alex. It seemed so unfair that Henry looked relatively unscathed while Alex was out there God knew where. Lily turned to walk away because she really didn't know what else to do.

"Lily. Please wait. I know this must have been a shock for you. I didn't think that I would see you either, at least not out here, but I was going to come and see you once I'd got myself on my feet." Lily slowly turned and looked him in the eyes. She wasn't afraid of him. In fact, he seemed different, more subdued and she supposed that he'd gone through a lot like they all had.

"Why would you want to see me, Henry? What would be the point? We've all moved on as best as we can, and there are more important things to be mindful of now."

"Please, Lily. Just give me ten minutes. We can go somewhere where there are lots of people, and I won't lay a finger on you. I really am not that man anymore." Much as she almost didn't want to, Lily believed him. She was also curious as much about what he could tell her about life in the trenches as she was about what had happened to him. Seeing him had also brought her a little hope as Henry had been missing almost as long as Alex and here, he was.

Half an hour later saw them both sitting in a quaint café just across from the library. Both were on their second cup of coffee. Despite herself, Lily was both equally fascinated and horrified at some of the stories Henry had to tell. He'd always been an impressive raconteur and hadn't lost his touch. The upshot of the conversation was that Henry hadn't been injured but had been diagnosed with tuberculosis of the brain.

"This was after I'd collapsed in the trenches without a bullet in sight. At first, they thought that it was just exhaustion but eventually the military doctor on duty probed a bit deeper and a lot of things made more sense when he'd made his diagnosis. He didn't write me off, Lily but gave me a straw to grasp onto." Lily thought of James who would probably be out there himself shortly administering to the sick and injured. She worried about him but knew that he would make a real difference to the morale of the troops out there. It turned out that Henry, having the financial means to fund it, had ended up in a sanatorium in Switzerland. There the rest, in the pure open air and away from the stress of war had led to an improvement in Henry's condition.

"But why did nobody hear anything about all this? We thought that like Alex you were missing in action."

"Lily. Let's be truthful. Did anyone even care where I was, and records go missing or get misdirected all the time. I had nobody to run home to, and the quiet and isolation from normal life was a blessing." Lily didn't know quite how to answer him. He did have one of the most precious things that you possibly could have at home in the shape of a son. Lily doubted that he would ever know that though she was surprised at the guilt, she felt from keeping it from him.

"So, are you cured?" Lily asked trying to distract herself from thoughts of James.

"Switzerland has given me a chance, Lily. I'm a realist. 80% of people that get tuberculosis or the white plague as it is sometimes called die. Maybe the care I received might just tip the odds in my favour though. You never know."

"I really hope so, Henry. I really do. In a world where death is all around us, it's good to hear that someone might defy the odds even if…"

"I know what you're going to say, Lily. It doesn't make it better, perhaps but you can't believe the agony I have put myself through over the way I treated you. All I can say is that I was somebody else that day. A man that even I didn't recognise, and I hate myself for it." Though it didn't make it right, Lily had gone through so much more since that day that the whole incident had faded into insignificance. She had always remained puzzled by it though as the Henry she had witnessed that day had seemed like a stranger and acted entirely out of character. Henry had flaws, many of them but he had always behaved like a gentleman around her previously. After hearing him talk about his illness, Lily began to wonder if the beginnings of his disease had been stirring then and his irrational behaviour had been outside of his control.

Lily never did make it to "Bookends" that afternoon. After leaving Henry, she'd decided to carry on walking to try and clear her head. She thought about what a strange afternoon it had been, but at least she had made some kind of peace with Henry and was less confused than she had been. She wondered whether she should tell her mum and reasoned that she would have to. Henry hadn't really made his plans clear, but he was probably going to be around for a while. Lily didn't like to think about how the news would be received too much. Maybe when her mum heard the whole story, she would soften a little. Lily had to admit that for her mum it had been a lot easier when Henry hadn't been around. However, for whatever reason, Lily slept more soundly that night than she had for weeks. Next morning, she woke up feeling refreshed and prepared for whatever the world was going to throw at her next.

CHAPTER TWENTY-SEVEN

September 1916

Lily knew that she had to tell her mum about Henry, and she would. However, she felt she just needed a couple of days to get her head around it herself. The baby was also making life increasingly uncomfortable, and though Lily was naturally apprehensive about giving birth, she felt it had now got to the point where the baby was better out than in. Besides which she was feeling excited about meeting their son or daughter for the first time.

If Lily was honest with herself, which she invariably was, she hadn't been overjoyed when she'd first found out that she was pregnant. Though she wanted children someday, she hadn't seen it happening until another couple of years down the line. She'd also dreaded the reaction she would get from those outside the immediate family. Derby women had never really entertained the image of the delicate wallflower. Most of them didn't suffer fools gladly, and the war had made them even more resilient. With that had come a brusque kindness that Lily had encountered time and again over the past few months.

She didn't flatter herself that it was much to do with her, despite the Armitage family being well thought of in the street. Alex had been a pivotal member of the community, and many families had children that he'd taught and taught well. Far from the mud sticking from his time in prison it had been the Dawkins family who had suffered scorn.

They'd eventually decided to move over to Ashbourne where Maisy's uncle ran a farm, and the last Lily had heard they were making a living from the land. Lily hadn't got it in her to wish them harm despite what Alex had gone through. Maisy had been young and foolish and got herself into a hole that she just kept digging deeper and deeper until she couldn't get out. Lily had teetered on the edge of that hole many times herself.

Alex had become something of a local hero without asking for the mantle. The dignified way that he had behaved after coming home had led to many invites to "come around for tea anytime, Mr Poynton" and casseroles and stews placed outside his door ready for when he got home. Lily still smiled at how embarrassed he'd been over "all the fuss." However, in most of the women's eyes, Alex could do no wrong and so, by association, neither could Lily.

"We'll look after Mr Poynton's young lady until he comes home," seemed to be the general philosophy. Lily felt eternally grateful for their optimism as more frequently her own seemed to be constantly tested. Some days she just didn't see how Alex could still be alive. Surely somebody would have heard something somewhere. Other days she would wake feeling more positive and ashamed at her selfishness. She was far from being the only woman left without her man at her side. Only last month Laura Mathers from just up the street had given birth to a healthy son and was now walking him up and down the road every day managing to find a smile or a "hello" for everybody she met on the way. Lily knew that her husband, Eric was operating one of the first tanks that had been used in the war to try and break the deadlock in the Battle of the Somme. Back in July 100,000 British soldiers had passed into no man's land expecting to find the way clear for them but the German machine guns had survived the previous artillery onslaught, and the infantry was massacred. That day had seen the most substantial casualties of the war with 20,000 British dead and 40,000 wounded.

Lily wasn't sleeping well either. She would often wake in the middle of the night panicking that she couldn't even visualise Alex's face anymore or that she couldn't remember what his voice sounded like. This would then get mixed up with the feelings of grief she still had about her dad and most mornings she was glad to see daybreak.

This morning was one of those mornings. Despite the lack of sleep, Lily felt more restless than tired. The only thing that she was tired of was waiting – waiting for news of Alex, waiting for her baby to arrive, even waiting for Lizzy to come home from London. Lily needed something concrete to do, but the garden was going back a little now. Anyway, James had done most of the work in it, especially over the last couple of months. The house was spotless as very few people apart from Ethel and James visited.

Lily decided that this would be the day she would make it to "Bookends" and offer her services for a few hours. She knew that Jane was struggling a little with the paperwork as Ethel had popped in the other morning to see if she could pick anything up for James's birthday which was only a couple of weeks away. It also meant that Lily could look for a small gift herself. Feeling better now that she had a definite plan in mind, she had a light breakfast of toast and a boiled egg, fresh from the coop she had installed in the back garden and set off for the river.

Lily still chose to walk that way if possible, and it didn't take her too much off track. Even as a child she'd always had an affinity for the waters of the Derwent. She and James would spend hours on its banks playing poo sticks or feeding the ducks. Now the continuous flow of the river calmed her. It rolled on making no apology to anyone and would always be there when she needed it. All Lily could do now was put one foot in front of the other and see what the future threw up. She realised that in many ways she was fortunate. She was relatively financially secure, and she had the emotional support of a loving family. Though it didn't ease the pain the awareness that most families had lost a loved one somewhere along the line made Lily feel a little less lonely. She had already witnessed the indomitable human spirit, and she determined to concentrate on bringing her baby into the world and making the best life she could for it in such an uncertain world.

Just as Lily was about to leave the river path and head into town, she heard a familiar voice beckon her from behind. She knew without turning who it was.

"Lily! Wait up." Henry appeared at her side, a little red in the face and slightly out of breath.

"You certainly give a fellow a merry chase nowadays, Lily."

"Henry! I didn't expect to see you again so soon." Lily wasn't sure that was the complete truth. On their meeting a few days previously, Henry had mentioned to Lily that he often walked the banks of the Derwent on the advice of his doctor to get plenty of fresh air and exercise. Had she subconsciously come down to the river today in the hope of seeing him? She pushed the idea away fiercely and put down any lingering doubts to baby hormones. James in all his wisdom told her that sometimes women could behave quite unpredictably when carrying a child.

Henry fell into step with her and Lily found him surprisingly easy to talk to. His war experiences and illness seemed to have robbed him of some of his self-confidence which Lily didn't see as a bad thing. This Henry was a far quieter and more reflective man than Lily remembered. That slightly superior air that he had supported almost unconsciously seemed to have dissipated. Before Lily knew it, they had arrived at "Bookends" where Henry left her to carry on into town to conclude some business and to see his specialist. For the rest of the afternoon, Lily immersed herself in the shop. She began to realise how isolated she had become since finding out about the baby and how much she'd missed the hustle and bustle of the routing of working life. By the end of the afternoon, she had won Jane's undying gratitude as the paperwork was now looking a lot healthier. She'd talked knowledgeably and enthusiastically to two new customers and was confident that they had liked what they saw and that they would return. Perhaps most importantly she'd regained that sense of pride she'd had at creating the business in the first place, and she sent a silent prayer of thanks to Philip.

Lily decided that she would call in at her mums on the way home to break the journey. It had been a long day, and at the least, she'd be offered a good cup of tea. She might also catch James before he headed out again to study with friends which he often did in the evening. By the time Lily got To Peel Street, there was quite an autumnal nip in the air, and she couldn't wait to open the door and be enveloped in the warmth of the kitchen that usually reached a peak around teatime. The air that met her was cold and uninviting. It was evident that tea hadn't even been thought of and the room was rapidly darkening as the little sun there had been disappeared for another day. Lily felt a little uneasy but reasoned that maybe her mum was around some neighbours. She was a well-liked member of the close-knit community that lived on the street and was often asked advice on all manner of things. Oh well, Lily thought, it looks as though I'll be making the tea then. She sorted out some light and lifted the kettle off the range to go and half fill it with water. "I thought that you might drop by when I went to your house, and you weren't there."

Lily nearly dropped the kettle onto the red brick coloured tiles as her mother's voice came to her from the other side of the room.

"Mum!" You made me jump. What are you doing sitting here in the dark? Are you feeling poorly?"

"I'm of perfectly sound mind, Lily but I don't know if the same can be said of you." Lily began to feel a little scared. Ethel had been coping so well- perhaps a little bit too well.

"Mum! What is it? Go and sit in the front room. I'll go and stoke the fire up and then I'll bring you in a nice cuppa."

Lily made a move towards her mother but was stopped in her tracks by Ethel's cold accusatory tone.

"I went to town today after I'd called at your house. You weren't there were you, Lily?"

"No Mum. If you remember I said I was going to pop into the shop sometime this week. It's good to keep busy."

"Well, you don't seem to have a problem with that do you, Lily?"

Lily felt even more uncomfortable and prayed that James would be home soon. He'd know better than her how to deal with this uncharacteristic irrational behaviour. Lily made as if to kneel on the floor in front of her mother.

"Don't you touch me. You filthy bitch." The venom in her mother's voice startled Lily to the core.

"Mum…" but Lily didn't have time to say more.

"Is it even Alex's baby, Lily? Be honest. It was all very convenient wasn't it" You'd been dragging your heels over him for years and then suddenly you're pregnant and engaged. You've played him for a fool haven't you, my girl? Well, you won't play me that way."

Lily felt utterly bewildered but also angry.

"You've got no right to speak to me that way, and I've got no idea what you have got into your head but whatever it is it's wrong." Lily brushed back tears as she grabbed her coat off the peg behind the door.

"I'm going to go and meet James. Perhaps he'll be able to calm you down as I don't know what's got into you."

"Into me! Into you more like. Henry never could keep his paws off a good-looking woman." The vitriol and bitterness that Ethel had been harbouring for years came spilling out as a barrage of insults. This was fuelled by the pain she'd tried to hide for almost the past twenty years. Lily felt dizzy and sick to the stomach as she listened to Ethel spewing out language that even the hardcore miners would blush at. Yet at the same time, some understanding began to filter through to Lily about what was happening in this bizarre situation. Her mum must have seen her with Henry. Lily knew that she should have said something earlier but had been waiting for the proper moment. Looking at her mother's almost unrecognisable features contorted with grief and anger Lily doubted whether there would ever have been a right moment.

"I thought he was dead, Lily and God strike me down, but I wished him dead. Now he's back and sniffing around the Armitage women again like a dog on heat."

"You might not believe it, Mum but Henry's different now and even if he wasn't you've got no right to question my love for Alex or Alex's baby. I was going to tell you that Henry was back, and I would have done in my own time. It's not me that's in the wrong here, Mum. How can you speak to your daughter like that? Dad will be turning in his grave and how can you wish a fellow human being dead when you've witnessed all the pain and tragedy that we have been through." Ethel took in a couple of shuddering breaths and looked Lily in the eyes.

"You're right. I shouldn't have spoken to you like that, but I'm not going to lie to you. If Henry was dead, it would all be just that bit easier and don't I deserve that, Lily?" All the fight seemed to have evaporated from Ethel as quickly as it came. For a moment Lily saw before her not her mother but an ageing bewildered lonely woman who had taken too significant a share of life's cruel blows. Lily was desperately hurt by her mother's comments, but her voice softened as she took her mother's hand in her own.

"Why would it make our life any easier, Mum? It wouldn't bring Dad back or take away any of our pain."

"No, it wouldn't Lily," Ethel's voice now just sounded plaintive rather than angry "but Henry had his suspicions you know. I told him that James was Bert's, but he's an intelligent man. If Henry was dead, he'd never be able to tell James ever that he was his biological father. We'd all be safe."

The cold air from outside swirled around their feet but reached them too late. The silence in the room was deafening, punctuated only by the steady ticking of the grandfather clock. James's stricken look bore into them as they both dropped into a chasm from which they were sure they would never return.

CHAPTER TWENTY-EIGHT

Autumn 1916

It was as though James had dropped off the face of the earth. He hadn't been seen in college or town. Lily had heard the expression "weak at the knees" but had always thought that it was an overly dramatised expression until she saw James's face on the night that changed everything for them.
She tried to imagine how she would feel if she had been delivered the same news. It wasn't just that Bert wasn't James's biological father but also what had led up to that. He'd had to face the idea of his mother having an affair which previously he would have thought impossible. He'd had to face the knowledge that Lily was his half-sister. Lily had struggled with the relationship though the heart to heart she had had with her mum had helped her come to terms with it. As for James being her brother nothing had changed for her there. They'd been brought up as full brother and sister, and Lily knew that he would always be her little brother and she needed to reassure him that was the same at least.
Ethel was beside herself with worry and renewed shame. The way James had merely stared at them both and then turned his back to them and walked away without a word had been more upsetting to them both than if he had ranted and raved.

"You don't think that he will do something stupid, do you, Lily?" Ethel asked on the third day of James's absence.
"What exactly are you getting at, Mum?"
Ethel looked a little embarrassed.
"Well, you know…like…"
"Like Philip you mean, don't you? Sometimes, Mum, I don't think that you know your son at all." As soon as the words came out of Lily's mouth, she regretted them but couldn't take them back. Lily knew how much James revered human life. At least he had done before Bert's death, but Lily still believed that it was his ambition to make life more tolerable for those who were in great pain or depressed as their father had been.
"I'm sorry, Lily. Of course, I know that he wouldn't. He's too focused on going to war, but I don't know how he'll cope with his morality then."
Lily continued to vigorously scrub the kitchen floor because she hadn't got an answer. She tried to envisage her brother sticking a bayonet into someone's guts to save his own life, but she couldn't seem to make the image work. She knew that Alex had killed men face to face. When he'd been back on leave the last time, they'd talked about it. Alex had said that it was an almost automatic survival instinct and men were learning how to survive like never before on the front line. He'd admitted though that later after the heat of the battle had diminished, he would think about that man's family and the life that he would never have because of Alex's actions.
"We're all pawns in a game that none of us seem to understand anymore," he'd said wearily as he set out again to re-join his regiment. Lily scrubbed even harder as she reflected on the pain that this war had already caused and the ideology of "it will be over by Christmas" was a distant memory lost in the blood of those at the Front.

The following morning Lily got up early and was glad to do so as sleep seemed to have permanently evaded her and the baby was indeed making itself felt. At least he or she is going to be a strong one she reasoned as she poured her tea and puzzled over what she could do to find James. She wasn't even sure if that was the right thing to do either. Maybe he needed to be on his own for a while, but his birthday was coming up, and after that, she suspected it wouldn't be long before they lost him to the war effort. She tried to get into his head and work out where he would have gone if he didn't want to be found. He could afford to take some time off college as he was well ahead with his work. Also, if he'd stayed in Derby, he wouldn't have been able to lie low for long before a well-meaning friend told of his whereabouts. Derby people were some of the most kind-hearted people going but not so good at not letting the cat out of the bag. Lily couldn't stop thinking about it all morning, but by the end of it, she felt that she had a pretty idea of where he was. She decided to keep it to herself a little longer as she thought that he might be in the right place. If he didn't show up by the time of his birthday, she would tell her mum for sure.

By the end of the week, Lily felt exhausted. Her time wasn't that far off, and the baby was giving her little opportunity to rest. Her mum was beside herself with worry, and Lily felt she would have to say something soon. She had to admit that she was also a little hurt and slightly insulted that James hadn't stayed around long enough to talk things through with her. They'd been there for each other through so much, and his rejection of her saddened her more than she let anyone see.

She also felt a little angry at her mother as since Ethel's revelations Lily had had to carry the burden of her mother's secret with her. Many times, as she tossed and turned the night away, she agonised over whether it had been the right decision to keep it from James. She supposed that her mother hadn't given her much choice but knew that there was now a breach of trust in her relationship with James and many fractures never healed completely.

James turned up with Lizzy on the 4th October two days before he turned eighteen. If looks could have killed Lizzy would have been dead the minute, she stepped through the front door. Lily had never seen her mother look so coldly at another person before. It all made sense to Lily though. James had needed to put space between himself and his family and where better to do it than in the Big Smoke. Despite the age gap, Lily had appreciated how well James and Lizzy had clicked on Lizzy's last visit. Though there would never be any romantic involvement, they held each other in a lot of respect. James admired Lizzy's forthright nature and the strength she had shown in the hand that life had dealt. Lizzy was fascinated by James's ideas about the treatment of depression and admired the drive in one so young.

"Don't worry, Ethel. I won't darken your doorstep for long." Lizzy gave James a brief hug and kissed Lily on the cheek. "I'll see you soon, Lily. I'm nearly sorted now so we'll have a lot to talk about."

"We'll see about that." Ethel had got the mettle between her teeth.

"Mum! Stop it. You've got no right to speak to Lizzy like that. It's our faults that James walked out for not keeping our traps shut. You should be glad he had somewhere to go." Lily realised that she was nearly shouting.

"Calm down, Lily," Lizzy said. "I don't blame your mum but at the end of the day James is nearly of age, and he needed a place to stay to come to terms with what he heard.

But don't worry I'm going now. I'll see you soon, but now I think that your brother needs you more than I do."

Lizzy shut the door gently behind her leaving the three of them facing each other in silence. The cold air eddied around their feet reminding Lily of that fatal night when the sins of the mother had again come to rest upon the children. James stood there rigid. He hadn't spoken since entering the house, not even to say goodbye to Lizzy. Ethel moved towards him, but he put up a hand to fend her off.

"Mum, I'm sorry, but I can't do this yet. I'm not sure that I would have even come without Lizzy bullying me into it, so you had no right to speak to her in that tone."

Lily heard the quiver in her mother's voice as she spoke. "I'm so sorry, James. I never intended for you to find out like that."

"Did you mean me to find out at all, Mum? I don't think so, and you know what that would have been the right decision." Lily recoiled at the bitterness in his voice. "My dad will always be Dad and that swine; Henry Ingram can rot in hell." Lily bit her lip. She had an insane urge to laugh. There was such a lot of rotting in hell going on in this family from time to time. She fought desperately to control herself as she recognised it for the hysteria that it was as she'd experienced it when she had heard of Philip's death and again when she got the news that Alex was missing.

James continued, "Henry Ingram will never mean anything to me apart from being the bastard who laid my mother and almost my sister. Thank God you got out when you did, Lily."

Lily thought that maybe Henry was getting the rough end of the stick. Apart from the one incident, which she was increasingly feeling had been a result of his illness; he had never forced himself on her. The same was true of her mother. Much as it would have helped to believe it and then

Ethel could have been exonerated from blame Lily knew that at the time her mother had been as willing a participant as Henry. From what she had learned from Ethel Lily knew that Henry had strong feelings towards her mother and Ethel might have led him to think there was a future with her. Ethel believed that Henry would have married her if she had been free. Wisely Lily kept her mouth shut.

"Are you at least going to take your coat off and I 'll make you a nice cup of tea?" Ethel reverted to the old standby. The beverage that would make everything better regardless of the situation though Lily didn't think that it was going to work this time. Despite her misgivings, she began to fill the heavy kettle up.

"No need Lily. I'm not staying."

"But what about your birthday?" Ethel almost pleaded.

"I don't feel like celebrating, Mum. I'm just going to have a quiet night round a friend's house.

"What will you do then?" Lily tentatively touched his hand and breathed a sigh of relief when he didn't pull away.

"I think you already know the answer to that. I'm going to sign up as soon as I can and go out and get those bastards that took Dad from us."

"Please, James. We can't leave it like this. Who knows when we will see you again? I know you think I'm a whore and perhaps I am, but it didn't feel like that at the time." Ethel was almost beside herself. James' voice cracked as he tried to reply to his mother. Lily could see how close to breaking down he was, and she was swallowing hard to keep herself together as well.

"Never use that word again. Do you hear me, Mum? I would never think of you like that no matter what's happened. I'll write when I can but now, I need to clear my head, and the army will hopefully give me that."

James turned to go out of the door. He glanced briefly at Ethel who looked as though all her blood had left her body. She was so pale. His gaze then fell on Lily.

"Good luck with the little one and Alex. See you soon, Lily."

James shut the door quietly behind him, but its resonance seemed to shake the house. Ethel sat down by the hearth, and it was as if all the fight had gone out of her. To Lily, it was a painful reminder of how her Dad would sit for hours staring into space. Lily raced upstairs, at least as fast as she could. She threw open the doors of the small oak cupboard that stood by her bed. Grabbing the two Charles Dickens books she and her mum had bought from "Bookends" she lumbered back downstairs and ran into the street not even pausing to put on a coat. Ethel didn't even seem to notice. Thankfully James had stopped on the corner to light a cigarette. Lily hadn't even been aware that he smoked though maybe it was a bad habit picked up from his time in London. It would be another black mark against Lizzy if her mum ever found out. Lily was quite breathless when she managed to pull level with him.

"Get back inside, Lily. You'll catch your death. "James took off his overcoat and draped it round Lily's shoulders. Lily thrust the books into James's hands.

"Happy Birthday, James." Lily could see the glistening of his eyes and throwing caution to the winds she flung her arms around him. James buried his head in her shoulder. It reminded Lily of how she would comfort him when he was little and had woken from a nightmare. The difference now was that this nightmare was real and wouldn't dissipate in the light of the day.

From a distance, the two of them could have been mistaken for lovers so tightly did they hold each other. Neither James nor Lily were aware of how long they stood there before they broke apart. The light was fading as Lily watched James walk to the street corner, raise his hand and then he was gone. With a heavy heart, Lily turned in the opposite direction. She wondered whether she would ever see her brother again.

CHAPTER TWENTY-NINE

October 1916

Lily felt desperately lonely in the days following James's departure. They'd become especially close in the last few years, and she could hardly bear to think about what he might face at the Front. On the rare occasions that Alex had opened up about what he had seen in France Lily had been shocked to the core. He'd talked about young boys holding their entrails in as they lay sobbing in agony and crying out for their mothers. What perhaps shocked her, even more, was that Alex seemed to regard these men as the lucky ones. His logic was that at least they died relatively quickly. He talked about soldiers who could no longer function, who had impaired sight and hearing for no discernible reason. He believed that even if the soldiers survived the war, they would never be able to return to normal life. A couple of them under Alex's command had become so confused and overcome with terror that they'd broken cover and ran straight into the line of enemy gunfire.
Even though Lily knew that all this was happening not that many miles away she still sometimes felt as if she was in the middle of some nightmarish story. Apart from the Zeppelin attack and its tragic consequences, Derby didn't appear that much different to what it had done before the war. People had got used to not seeing as many youngish men on the streets and even those families with loved ones at war

seemed to manage to push it to the back of their minds as they went about their essential daily business.

Lily sat in the front room in Peel Street with her hands on her belly staring out into the road. Ethel had insisted that Lily stayed home while she went shopping. Both knew that the baby was close to coming, but Lily had only begrudgingly taken Ethel's advice. She felt more estranged from her mother than she had been for a long while. The upsets and recent quarrels had left their mark, and Lily felt tired of it all. She hadn't believed most of the well-meaning advice she had been given throughout her pregnancy. Avoiding salty or spicy food in case, they gave the child a sour disposition didn't quite tally with Lily. Neither did the advice about avoiding reading exciting books or looking at stunning pictures. However, she did think that maybe the information about avoiding quarrels might have some credibility to it if they made her feel this bad.

Lily hadn't been able to get comfortable at all for a couple of nights, and she kept getting small contractions. The midwife had told her they were nothing to worry about, and they weren't particularly painful, but she felt anxious. She was also concerned about how she thought about the baby she was carrying and wondered whether it was even fair to bring a child into a world that was so fractured.

Also, though Lily was so weary, she felt restless and needed to get out into the fresh air even if it was only to the top of the street and back. Since James had left, she had seen virtually nobody apart from her mother. Raising herself awkwardly from the low armchair in which, perhaps unwisely, she had earlier eased herself into she reached for her coat. Pain more enormous than anything Lily could have imagined ripped through her body causing her to stagger forwards. Luckily the table stopped her fall as she instinctively flung her hands in front of herself. Lily could feel herself shaking as her abdomen relaxed and the pain lessened. She felt a warm trickle running down her leg, and she took deep breaths to still her panic as she was in no doubt that she was in labour.

When Ethel came back any animosity, Lily had felt previously for her mother evaporated. She concentrated on getting through the contractions as Ethel calmly got everything ready. Lily felt a little concerned when Ethel told her it was too early to call for the midwife, but she knew that she had to trust her mother in this.

With Ethel's help, Lily managed to pull herself upstairs to the bedroom where the afternoon dragged past in a haze of pain and occasional lucid moments between the contractions. This was when Ethel persuaded Lily to eat and drink a little so that she would have plenty of energy left for the final stages of labour.

"Oh God, Mum! I can't do this. I don't want a baby." Lily cried out after a particularly intense contraction.

"Well, like it or not, love, you haven't got much choice just at this moment." Ethel smiled as she wiped Lily's brow with a damp cloth for the umpteenth time. "You're doing really well, love. I was swearing like a trooper when I was having you and had got to about this point. Your dad said that the air in the house was blue that day."

Lily felt the pain receding again slightly though she knew that another wave was just around the corner. Lily squeezed Ethel's hand tightly.

"I'm so glad that you're here, Mum. I couldn't do it without you, and all the others have left us."

Ethel's eyes glistened as she looked down at her daughter. "I wouldn't be surprised if your dad isn't looking down on you today and willing you on."

"Well if he is, I hope he isn't looking too closely."

Despite the grief, they both still felt keenly, and the pain Lily was in they both started laughing. A little hysterically maybe but it had been a while since laughter in any form had been heard in the house. Unfortunately, Mrs O'Donnell chose that moment to enter the Peel Street residence. They'd been lucky to find her as many births were attended by an unregistered midwife, and doctors, overall, didn't feel that obstetrics was part of their routine duties. Lily had Lizzy to thank for Mrs O'Donnell's presence, and even Ethel had to begrudgingly admit she had been a good find. Apparently, without knowing too many of the details, Lizzy had met her over in Dublin when she had been on one of her "business" trips. When Mrs O'Donnell moved to this side of the water to be closer to her sister, they had struck up an alliance. Secretly, Mrs O'Donnell terrified Lily, but she trusted Lizzy's judgement and knew that she was in safe hands. Laughter was soon forgotten as Lily gritted her teeth and got on with the job in hand. At times the pain was so severe, she felt she would lose consciousness, and from time to time mixed up images of her father, James, Alex and Philip would float before her eyes and then get garbled in the cream and green curtains that adorned the bedroom window. She puzzled as to how they could all be in the same place at the same time. This confusion, however, was forgotten in the wake of another massive contraction. Hands seemed to be invading Lily's body at every turn and from every direction. She felt enormous pressure on her abdomen and was convinced she was going to split open before her baby arrived in the world.

"That's it, Lily. You are doing so well. Stop pushing now and blow little breaths. Mrs O'Donnell's firm Irish brogue cut through Lily's fog of agony.

"I can see the head." Ethel's excited voice joined in the cacophony. "Come on love. We're nearly there."

All very well for them to say, Lily thought. It was her who was doing all the hard work. Yet she did now feel a sense of urgency and determinedly rode each wave of pain with a purpose. Lily felt a slithering and wetness, and before she really knew what was happening, the baby was expelled from her body.

"Well done Mrs Armitage. You have a beautiful baby girl." Mrs O'Donnell placed the baby on Lily's chest where its startled blue eyes reflected Lily's feelings exactly. She tentatively touched her daughter's hand and was slightly surprised when she felt a finger wrapping around her own.

"She's so strong," Lily whispered almost reverently.

"Just like her mum then." Ethel smiled. "What are you going to call her, love? You've kept us in the dark over that one."

"Only because I wasn't sure but now, I've seen her I am. She's going to be Alexandra Ethel Dorothy Poynton."

"A bit of a mouthful but we'll get used to it I suppose." Lily put her hand gently over her mothers. Ethel's brusque manner didn't fool Lily for a moment. Dorothy, Ethel's younger sister, had died many years back when Ethel was only sixteen herself. From the stories, she had heard Lily knew how close the two girls had been growing up.

"I'll be off then," Mrs O'Donnell poked her head around the bedroom door, "but I'll be back early tomorrow, so no late-night parties please."

"We wouldn't dare." Lily smiled and wondered why she had been so afraid of Mrs O'Donnell, to begin with. Lizzy Hardcastle and Mrs O'Donnell were like peas in a pod. Formidable women but with a heart of gold to match.

The three women present would always have a special bond after the experience they had shared. Alexandra, indeed, was far from being Mrs O' Donnell's first birth but new life seemed even more precious in an age when hundreds of men were losing their lives every day.

A couple of hours later after she'd been washed and tidied up, Lily sat in bed holding her daughter. Every part of her body ached, but it was a satisfying ache. She had laboured to bring this new human being into the world, and her tiredness was a celebration of that. The agony of the birth itself was already receding in Lily's mind as was nature's way. Without this mechanism, no woman in her right mind would go on to have another child.

Lily still felt desperately sad that her father would never get to see his first grandchild and desperately afraid that Alex might not get to see his daughter or James his niece. On the other hand, she felt more peaceful than she had done for a long time. She'd barely admitted, even to herself, how scared she had been about the whole process of giving birth as well as worrying about whether she would bond with the baby.

Lily stroked Alexandra's soft cheek. She was aware that babies couldn't smile when they were first born, but Lily was convinced that Alexandra had one lurking not too far away. Lily drew her daughter even closer to her breast as if by doing so she could protect her just a little longer from the wider, at times cruel, world that lay in wait for her.

"Whatever happens, my darling I will be there for you if it is humanly possible," Lily whispered as she planted a kiss on top of Alexandra's soft downy head. All Lily's fears about not being able to love her own child had dissipated as soon as she looked into her baby's eyes.

As the last of the light faded in the October sky, Alexandra closed her eyes as if to indicate that she felt loved and safe exactly where she was. She'd barely cried, apart from when Mrs O'Donnell had given her the customary slap on the bottom to introduce her to her new world. Lily knew that with or without a husband she would do all in her power to make sure her daughter grew up into a healthy fulfilled individual. The war might have taken many things away from them as a family, but today the scales had tipped the opposite way. That night Lily slept like a baby herself, at least for a few hours, until her daughter's cries for food pierced the calm. So, this is motherhood Lily thought as she wiped the sleep out of her eyes and reached for her daughter. Lily couldn't remember ever feeling as content as she did at that moment.

CHAPTER THIRTY

December 1916

The weeks following Allie's birth, as she came to be known in the Peel Street household, flew past. Lily had tried to mentally prepare herself for motherhood, but the reality was far harder than she had envisaged. She felt overwhelmed at times by the responsibility of having this small human being almost wholly reliant on her for all her physical and emotional needs.

Luckily, Allie was a placid, well-behaved baby. Far more congenial than either Lily or James had been at a similar age if Ethel were to be believed.

"You were a proper little madam at times," Ethel told Lily one cold evening in early December as she sat rocking Allie in front of a dwindling fire. "Even then you knew what you wanted and went into a tantrum if you didn't get it."

"I'm not sure I believe that. I 'm sure James was far worse behaved than me, "Lily smiled across at her mother from her place at the other side of the hearth.

"It was close. I'll give you that. At least when I finally got you to sleep, you would stay down for a few hours."

"And James?" Lily enquired.

"He was a nightmare to get off. Your dad would often think that I'd gone to sleep myself when I didn't appear downstairs for a couple of hours, but sometimes that's how long it took before I could creep away."

"He didn't get better as he got older?"
"Let's just say I had bags under my eyes the size of saucers in the first couple of years after his birth."
Lily smiled. James had always been able to burn the candle at both ends, and it appears he had started young. He would have been very handy to have around to mind his niece from time to time while Lily and Ethel got a bit of shut-eye. The last year had taken its toll on all of them and had noticeably aged Ethel. Lily glanced across at her mother as she got up to finish ironing Allie's nightgown. Ethel looked tired, but there was a light in her eyes that Lily hadn't seen for a long time. Being a grandma suited her down to the ground though Lily wasn't sure that was the only thing that was responsible for her mother's renewed vigour. Only last Monday as Lily had returned home from her daily walk with Allie, she'd seen her mum and Roy Bennett in animated conversation outside his front door.
After the death of their second son, Roy's wife, Chrissy, had been admitted to Kingsway as they had all feared. Within two months she was dead. Died of a broken heart, Roy had decided, and nobody would have seen fit to argue with him. Lily wasn't sure that Roy and her mum yet saw what other people did. They saw themselves as two friends who had both suffered tragic loss and got comfort from spending a little time with each other. However, time seemed to have taken on a new dimension since the beginning of the war and accelerated events accordingly. Experiences became much more intense as daily tragedies were almost expected. Humanity had sunk to a new all-time low where depravity and unmentionable acts were routinely carried out, but there were also significant acts of kindness and courage that helped redress the balance a little.
If something did develop between her mum and Roy Lily honestly didn't know how she would feel about it. By all

accounts, he was a good hard-working man and kept his fists to himself, unlike many others on their street when they had had one too many down at the local. Ethel did seem more at peace, and Lily figured she would let events run their course and deal with the outcome when the time came. If nothing else the war had taught people to live in the moment and not waste precious time worrying about events that were out of their control.

"Are you still going out in the morning, love?" Ethel's voice brought Lily sharply back from her mental wanderings.

"Only if you're not busy, Mum. I don't want to put you out.""

"This little one could never put me out, could you my darling?" Ethel planted a kiss on Allie's forehead. "If you feed her before you go, she'll sleep for a couple of hours anyway. You go, love. They say it's going to be a sunny morning but cold with it. Wrap up, and it will do you good to catch up with your friends."

Lily knew that her mum wouldn't be quite as amenable if she'd realised where Lily was going. Lily had to admit she felt a little guilty but balanced that with the knowledge that her mum would be in seventh heaven having Allie to herself all morning.

Ethel was right. The morning was glorious for early December and just being away from the confines of four walls for a while put a spring in Lily's step. Lily noticed him before he saw her. She stood for a moment or two watching as he settled on his regular bench overlooking the Derwent. The war had changed him physically as well as mentally. If anything, he was now slightly underweight though Lily guessed that his illness had probably been a contributory factor towards that. The look suited him though and enhanced his features. Ironically, he looked younger than he had before enlisting, and Lily was glad to see that his complexion was no longer as pale as when she had first spotted him on the riverbank after he'd come back home. For a moment Lily hesitated realising that she could still turn back. There could be any number of reasons why she hadn't been able to make it that day. Since Allie had been about six weeks old, she'd seen Henry most days. They both seemed to walk along the banks of the river about the same time each morning. Henry for his daily constitutional, as he liked to call it, and Lily to give herself and Allie a breath of fresh air. Every morning they had exchanged a few words with their conversations seeming to get longer every time they met. This was the first time though the meeting had been arranged and they couldn't pretend that they had accidentally bumped into each other.

Henry's right hand raised in greeting. Lily took a deep breath and chided herself for being so faint-hearted. After all, she was merely meeting a friend, and she realised that was exactly what they had become. Maybe a friend she would never be able to take home or be a hundred percent honest with, but she reasoned many friendships survived under that criteria.

"You're looking better every time I see you, "Lily smiled down at Henry as she drew level with him. Henry rose to his feet and kissed Lily gently on the cheek in greeting.

"I feel better every time I see you Lily, and I have started to be cautiously optimistic that I might beat this disease completely."

"I'm so glad, Henry. I really am. It makes a refreshing change to hear some good news." Henry offered Lily the crook of his arm which she tentatively took.

"Let's walk, Miss Armitage and forget about this bloody war for five minutes. Let's talk of cabbages and kings and things nonsensical and fun." Lily couldn't help laughing at Henry's flamboyance.

"Well, Mr Ingram, we are in a positive frame of mind this morning."

"Why wouldn't I be, Lily? It's a beautiful morning, and I'm in the company of a beautiful young woman. We can't always be talking about the war, Lily and what you and I have lost because of it. We owe it to the lads out there to make the best of each day that they're giving us."

"Of course, you're right, Henry, but don't you sometimes feel guilty?" Lily looked worried.

"I feel guilty for many things, my dear and you know that better than anyone but contracting TB and having to be drafted out of the army isn't one of them."

"I don't really mean that, Henry. You've stood up and fought for your country. Nobody can take that away from you."

"Then what, Lily?"

"Sometimes I still get moments of pure happiness, especially since having Allie and meeting up with you again. I forget about Dad and Alex and James. On a beautiful day like today, I can even forget there is a war going on across The Channel." Lily shook her head in apparent disgust. "I must be such a horrible and frivolous person and completely self-obsessed."

Henry stopped walking and spun Lily around to face him placing his hands on her forearms so that it was almost impossible to avoid looking at him.

"Can you not see how far from the truth that is? Think about everything you've done for the people in your life, including me. What you're describing is called survival, Lily. We all need to have those moments to counteract those feelings of loss and loneliness that haunt us in the middle of the night. Those feelings help us to chase our demons away so that we can stay strong for the people around us."

Lily knew that Henry was right. Both had yet untapped reserves of strength to face what might be in front of them, and they recognised that in each other.

"There is one thing though that I'm not sure either of us would be brave enough for."

"And what's that, my love?" Henry said with a puzzled look. Lily coloured slightly at his turn of phrase and then brushed it away as a figure of speech.

"My mother! She would kill me if she knew I was here with you today." Henry looked a little startled.

"That came a bit out of the blue but yes she very probably might and me along with you. You can't blame her, Lily. She's a wonderful woman, your mother and she has had many crosses to bear."

"You really cared about her, didn't you Henry?"

"I did, very much so, but it's all water under the bridge now and looking back I don't think that I recognise the person I was back then. I couldn't imagine ever trying to take a woman away from her husband now. If I'm sincere, which I always try to be with you now, I don't think that your mother and I would have worked out long term. Ashamed as I am to admit it, it was more the thrill of the chase and the secrecy that made it exciting. In the end, we didn't have that much in common, and it ended up feeling a bit empty, for both of us, I think."

Lily was surprised that she didn't feel more uncomfortable about Henry's revelations but since they'd both reunited, she thought they'd got to know each other so much better. She realised that Henry was probably the person she revealed the most about herself to.

"And what about me, Henry? What made you decide to wine and dine me?" Lily teased trying to lighten the mood causing Henry to laugh with genuine amusement.

"I wouldn't exactly call it that, my dear but you intrigued me and as I got to know you more, I realised I had far more in common with you than I would ever have had with Ethel." Lily felt more strongly than ever that Henry had a right to know that he had a son, but she also knew that she couldn't be the one to tell him. There were far more critical emotions involved than her own. As things stood, Lily wasn't sure if life could ever be the same again for any of them. James might never speak to their mother again, but Lily didn't think so. Out of the two of them, James was far more level-headed, and Lily refused to believe that he might never return to them. Anyway, until she knew what had happened to Alex, she hadn't the energy to worry herself to death over James. He was a grown man, and Lily had to trust that he would do the right thing in his own time.

Alex was always in her thoughts. Some mornings she woke up convinced that she would never see him again while at others she harboured a flicker of hope that he had been taken prisoner or was holed up in some foreign hospital somewhere. Lily sometimes had to take deep breaths as she felt panic overwhelming her as she thought of all the different scenarios, none of them pleasant. What frightened her more was that at times she was convinced she had forgotten what his voice sounded like. In many ways, Henry seemed far more real than Alex now.

"You're miles away, Miss Armitage. Am I really that boring to be with?" Lily looked at Henry's slightly sardonic expression. At that moment she saw in Henry, the gentleman she had once been attracted to what seemed like years ago now. What was that quote she vaguely recollected from one of the many books she had perused when working at "Bookends?" Something about the past is a foreign country and doing things differently there. There was much truth in that she reflected as she thought about herself and Henry, then and now. She smiled and gently squeezed the arm that was linked with hers.

"Far from it, Henry. Now let's walk and enjoy this beautiful morning while we can."

CHAPTER THIRTY-ONE

Spring 1917

Miss Hardcastle eventually returned to Derby in full flow. Lily wasn't sure that Lizzy knew how to live her life any other way. Ethel was at least civil to her much to Lily's relief. Her mother was usually generous in spirit, and it had only been because of hurt feelings that Ethel had treated Lizzy so harshly previously.

"Don't worry about it Mrs Armitage," Lizzy reassured them both when she arrived on their doorstep one unseasonably warm March morning. The kettle was on almost before Lizzy walked through the door. Ethel was of the school of opinion that a good cup of tea could go well towards making amends whatever the situation.

Lily made some excuse about having to see to Allie who was now far more demanding than she had been as a newborn. At last, she managed to settle Allie down. Lily smiled as she gazed down at her daughter. For the moment the fears about Granny Armitage's inheritance breaking through seemed irrelevant. Lily wouldn't allow herself to believe that this innocent could ever develop into something resembling a monster. Lily had thought a lot about what her dad had gone through as a boy and whatever excuses she had tried to make up for Granny Armitage had behaved didn't wash. However, Lily couldn't seem to shake the depression she'd been feeling for a few weeks. She'd almost given up any hope of hearing news about Alex. She'd also been so busy with Allie that she hadn't had the opportunity to meet up with Henry again on her own. That probably wasn't a bad thing as Lily didn't want Henry getting the wrong impression. Maybe Lizzy returning would give Lily the boost she needed.

When Lily returned to the kitchen, the two ladies were on first name terms and deep in discussion.

"I don't need that rambling house all to myself, and we would be actively doing our bit for the troops. What do you think Ethel? It would do us both good to get out there again."

"What are you two witches conniving about?" Lily teased them.

"Turning Lizzy's country house into a temporary hospital. There's injured still coming over from France and Belgium all the time," Ethel said.

Lily for a change was lost for words. Lizzy was never one to let the grass grow under her feet, but this seemed huge.

"But where would you live and who's going to run it?"

"Well admittedly, I'm not too sure about the living part, but I've done my homework Lily. I've approached some women who would be prepared to volunteer, and I know Dr Sykes at the hospital would direct me to where I could recruit paid staff."

"Who's Dr Sykes?" Lily felt entirely at sea.

"I got to know him a little while after Philip died. Like your James, he's interested in treating people who are depressed and …well let's just say I needed him at the time." Lily knew that Lizzy had suffered after losing Philip so tragically, but perhaps she had neglected to realise just how much, as she had been caught up in her grief at the time. Lily knew why Lizzy had uprooted and gone to London. It might not have been a resounding success, but she understood the feeling of a place being too painful to remain in for any length of time with everything reminding you of the one you had lost.

"It would be good for us all, Lily." Ethel implored." There'll be cooking and housekeeping to do as well as the nursing."

"What about Allie?" Lily asked, but deep down she knew that she was warming to the idea.

"She comes as well of course. There's plenty of room, and I could easily live in one part of the house, and you and Allie could have another for when you needed a bit of privacy." Lily could see that Lizzy had the bit between her teeth and Lily had to admit the idea of doing something concrete for the war effort was what she had been looking for, for a while. Naturally, Allie was her priority, but it would probably do them all good. Lizzy's house was out of Derby more towards the Derbyshire Dales and Ashbourne. Lily had only been out there a couple of times, but she remembered it as having oceans of space both inside and out. She could see it as a place where a soldier's mental scars, as well as physical wounds, could begin to heal.

"Well we'd have to plan it, and we'd have to have rota. I couldn't be out there seven days a week and neither could Mum." A few years ago, Lily would have just plunged in without thinking and ran with it, but time and experience had taught her to be a little more cautious. However, she thought that between them it could become more than a pie in the sky idea. Lizzy had always been at the helm of the organisation when she worked for Crown Derby. Lily had worked wonders into turning around "Bookends", and Ethel had a wealth of experience gained from running a home and bringing up a family on a shoestring for years.

"I knew that you'd think it a good idea, so I've already got the ball rolling. I've got the Red Cross involved, and we're going to be a Class B auxiliary hospital."

Lily again was amazed at the energy of her friend. She'd never really asked, but Lizzy was probably older than Ethel but had the drive of someone half her age.

"What does that mean? Class B?" Ethel asked looking more animated than Lily had seen her for a while. Maybe it would take her mind off Roy for although Lily had nothing against the man, she wasn't sure if she was quite ready for anybody to fill her father's boots.

"It means that we will be looking after convalescent and ambulant patients," Lizzy replied.

"I really don't know how you've got this off the ground so quickly," Lily said in admiration. "I didn't think that the War Office were accepting any further offers of private houses for auxiliary hospitals."

"Officially, they're not but I initially expressed an interest quite a while ago, and it helps that I can contribute quite a lot of funding towards it. We desperately need something like this up here. Why should London have it all?"

Lily was curious about how much money Philip had left Lizzy, but she would never ask. She did know that they had had an exceptional relationship and knew that Philip would have approved of what they intended to do. Lily smiled at the two women who were looking at her expectantly. Lily appreciated more than ever how much she relied on them and needed them in her life.

"Well ladies, it looks like we are opening a hospital, so we'd better get on with it."

"I told you that she would say yes." Lizzy positively beamed at Ethel. Lily could feel genuine laughter bubbling up from a place within her that she thought she had lost forever. It all seemed a little crazy to her but in a right way and she couldn't wait to get started.

Three months later found Lily sitting in a meadow watching the gregarious swifts showing off their mastery in the air. Allie sat a few yards away studiously plucking the petals off a daisy. Lily smiled as she remembered doing that herself to determine whether Billy Trinder loved her or not. She must have been only about four and wondered why that memory had suddenly hit her. Maybe it was because she suspected she was like a lot of people in war-torn Britain. Eager to get back to an age of innocence when human beings weren't intent on blowing each other up. It was an idyllic day, and Lily could almost believe that death and destruction weren't playing out just over the water.

Shielding her eyes against the sun Lily could detect a figure in the distance coming out of the back gate of Lizzy's house that entered the field. She was almost sure that it was Helen Irvine. Lizzy had been fortunate to enlist her services as Helen had been a military nurse and a member of the Queen Alexandra's Imperial Military Nursing Service. Not that Lily had yet much to do with Helen, but she'd gleaned from Lizzy that Helen had literally lost all the men she had ever loved in the first two years of the war- the young man she had loved as well as her brother and two close male friends. She had apparently thrown herself into her nursing to ease the pain of her bereavements or at least give her less time to think about them.

"Hello," Helen said as she approached Lily. "I'm not interrupting, am I? I just needed five minutes away from it all, and it's such a beautiful day."

Lily patted the picnic blanket beside her inviting Helen to sit down. Originally Lily had bought it for Allie, but Allie had scuppered that well-made plan and was accelerating across the field on her hands and knees in desperate pursuit of what was anyone's guess.

"Sit down and take the weight off for a few minutes. You deserve it. I never see you stop when you are up at the house.

"None of us do," Helen smiled, "but I won't say no. Your daughter certainly seems to be enjoying the day anyway. Your husbands at the front I guess!" Helen settled in hugging her knees up to her chest.

"I'm not sure where he is," Lily admitted. "Missing I think is the official term."

"Oh goodness. I'm sorry. I'm pretty good at putting my big foot in my mouth. Alan always said I should think before speaking, but he was usually laughing when he said it."

"Alan?" Lily queried.

"My fiancé. He was one of the many killed at the Somme."

"Oh, now it's my turn to be sorry." Lily blushed. "I did know. Lizzy told me so who's putting their foot in their mouth now."

Helen laughed as she pushed a stray lock of blonde hair behind her ear.

"It's fine. I talk about Alan all the time. If I didn't, it's as though he never existed. I was there you know- not in the trenches of course – but in the military hospital out there. When they brought him in, he looked as peaceful as a baby."

"How awful for you." Lily felt terrible for her new friend.

"It was, but later it helped. Gave me some sort of closure. As much as I think I'm likely to get anyway."

"How bad is it out there?" Lily ventured. Many of the soldiers who ended up at their hospital wanted to talk about anything else, but the war and Lily felt a bond with this girl even though they had seldom spoken before.

"I suppose you could argue that Alan was lucky. A bayonet went through him. Quick they said. He didn't have time to think about it. Thousands of them out there are dying lingering deaths from infected wounds. These here…" Helen nodded in the direction of the house "are the fortunate ones. They might be missing an arm or a leg, but help got to them before gangrene took them completely."

"I'm hoping that's where Alex is. In some military hospital somewhere being cared for by a wonderful nurse such as yourself."

"Oh, get away with you." Helen pushed Lily playfully on the shoulder. "My Alan though knew an officer called Alex Said he was a great guy. Always came back with a bagful of Woodbines for them when he'd been on leave, but he wasn't an Armitage. Poynton, I think Alex said his surname was." Lily felt her world drop away, and Helen's voice seemed to be coming from far away which didn't make much sense as Helen was sitting there right next to her."

"Lily! Are you alright? You left me there for a moment, and you've gone white as a sheet." The black dots slowly disappeared before Lily's eyes, and Helen and Allie came back into view. She tried to take deep breaths and keep any panic out of her voice as far as possible to avoid upsetting Allie.

"I'm ok, Helen. Really I am." Lily could see though that Helen didn't completely believe her. "But that's my Alex you're talking about. Your Alan knew my Alex, and that's the closest I've been to him in a long time."

Helen was far from stupid and rapidly put the facts together. "So, you're not married but no matter. You would have been if this war hadn't got in the way."

"Did Alan say anything else about him?" Lily's heart began to beat faster. "Did he know what happened to him?" Lily could see Helen thinking something through and waited with bated breath.

"Actually, I think there was something. When I eventually got back to England, there was a letter waiting for me. Alan didn't know you see that I'd conned my way into the hospital over there. He would have been furious at the thought of me putting myself in danger, and our paths never crossed until…well, you know. Anyway, Alan wrote it a couple of days before he was killed. I think he had some premonition about what was going to happen as there was lots of sentimental talk in it which wasn't really like Alan. I can't be sure as my mind was all over the place, but I think he mentioned an Alex in it."

"Have you still got the letter?" Even though Lily wasn't profoundly religious, she sent a silent prayer heavenward.

"All of them yes. Tied up with a red ribbon. Nothing original there but Alan's letters move on everywhere with me. If he hadn't been killed, he might have gone on to be a reporter or journalist. A proper eye for detail he had and a way with words. I struggle to write enough to put on the face of George V. Tell you what. Can you meet me later? Perhaps we'll go for a drink somewhere if you can find someone to look after Allie and I'll bring the letters with me."

"Please, Helen I'd be so grateful."

"No problem. It's been lovely to chat like this, but the stinking bedpans aren't going to wait much longer. See you around eight in "The Elephant and Castle.

For the rest of the afternoon, as Allie slept blissfully unaware of what an uncertain world she was living in, Lily set about cleaning floors, changing bed linen and swilling out bedpans. However, if anyone had asked her at the end of the day what jobs she had been doing that afternoon, she wouldn't have been able to remember one to tell them for sure.

CHAPTER THIRTY-TWO

June 1916

"By gum, it's good to get the weight off our feet. It's been a hard one today." Lily knew that the nursing staff had been involved in admitting two amputees that afternoon. She vaguely remembered one tow-haired young lad cracking jokes left, right and centre. Matron had to curb him at one point as the ward was at risk of running riot and the air was getting bluer by the minute. The other slightly older man who had come in at the same time had hardly spoken a word all afternoon apart from to thank the nurses for their administrations.
"A lovely gentleman that one who came in with the noisy bugger. " Helen continued. "You mark my words. He's got breeding that one has." Usually, Lily would have been curious about any new patients they had admitted and would be one of the first of the volunteers to try to help them find their feet, but her mind had been elsewhere all afternoon. Lily pulled up a chair opposite Helen and tried to show some interest. She didn't want Helen thinking that the only reason she wanted to be friendly with her was for the slim chance she could tell her something about Alex. Lily sensed that Helen could be a good friend, and much admired her for her positive attitude in the face of such adversity. Lily wondered how Helen had coped with all her dreams being dashed to the ground and how she had managed to turn her life around.

Lily still carried the memory of the tragedies of her father's and Philip's deaths but knew that, especially in her dad's case, she hadn't fully come to terms with it. Maybe Helen had found that sturdy box in a hidden place of herself where she pushed all negative thoughts and the awful things that life had thrown at her. Lily knew that her own father's death was still locked away somewhere deep inside of her and she had yet only been brave enough to lift the lid a fraction.
"What are you having, Lily?" Helen was foraging in her purse. Lily quickly put her hand over Helen's.
"No don't be silly. Put your money away. I'm buying after I've dragged you all the way out here when you could be curled up at home in front of the fire."
"Well if you're offering, I won't say no." Lily faintly smiled. That was another thing she liked about Helen in the short time they had known each other. No going round all the houses to get to the point.
Five minutes later nursing their drinks, Helen rested her back on the bench she was sitting on and gave a deep sigh.
"Alan and I used to come here before he went away but it was different then. Loads of handsome young pups were propping up the bar, and usually it was so noisy we had sore throats when we came out because of trying to talk above the clatter."
Lily could see her point as a man who couldn't be under seventy lifted his beer glass in their direction. A couple of younger lads were talking intensely in a corner by the window that looked out onto the square. One of them had a crutch propped up on his side of the table. The other young lad appeared to have no visible disability, but both Lily and Helen understood not all limitations were physically manifested.
Lily felt a wave of sadness sweep over her. She wondered if this public house would ever again be full of young men

enjoying themselves after work with nothing more to worry about than where they were going to take the family on the weekend.

"Penny for them." Helen's voice cut through Lily's reverie. "Sorry, Helen. I was thinking."

"A dangerous pursuit today. Not to be recommended." Lily thought how true that was and felt her heart begin to beat faster as Helen took a bunch of letters out of the deep pocket of her utility coat.

"I had a rummage when I got home, and Alan's officer was called Alex Poynton, so there's little doubt that's your man. Alan mentions him quite a few times." Helen handed a couple of letters over to Lily who tentatively took them.

"I can't read these Helen much as I want to find out what I can about Alex. They're personal."

"Don't worry. Lily. I like you, but I'm not daft enough to let you know everything about "how's my father." I've just picked out a few pages where Alan talks about your Alex. There's nothing on them that will make you blush." Helen grinned at her new-found friend.

"Have a butchers at them while I go and powder my nose." Lily picked up the first page with slightly trembling hands and rapidly scanned it for a mention of Alex. Her eyes devoured the lines anxious to glean anything from the scribbles.

"The lad's mood was down more than usual today, but Alex returned bringing with him Woodbines and chocolate which helped lighten the mood a little. Great bloke. Won't let us call him Sir or anything pretentious. Says when we're in the trenches we are all lads together. We don't even get to see most of the other cocky bastards. I'll be home with you soon…"

Lily gently folded the page and wondered whether Alan had made it home one last time. She picked up another page.

"Alex nearly got himself killed today. The bloody fool went over the top to drag two of our wounded back in. Tommy didn't make it, but Ken got sent home with a bloody hole the size of a crater in his leg. Happy as Larry he was. A bloody hero – that's what Alex Poynton is. Not sure I would have had the guts."

Lily felt a horrible lump constricting her throat. From what Helen had told her already about Alan she suspected that he would have been by Alex's side given a chance. What these poor boys and young men were going through out there couldn't begin to be imagined by those left behind. She felt a sense of pride in Alex and a strange kind of relief. It was clear the war hadn't changed him. He was still the selfless and caring man she had fallen in love with. Lily took her time picking up the final sheet of paper not being sure what she would find.

"Bloody massacre yesterday. The rain lashed down, and in the end, it felt as though we were breathing mud. The Germans took full advantage. So many of our lads didn't get to see the sun come up this morning. After the storm, it was a glorious day, and it made everything seem even worse as we pulled our dead back in. No sign of Len or Alex though. They've bloody disappeared into thin air. Don't worry about me, darling. Keep thinking of me, and I'll see you soon…"

"Here get this down you. You look as though you need it." Helen thrust a large gin into Lily's hands, and Lily had no hesitation in taking a large gulp.

"It's all there is," Helen said quietly. "A couple of days later Alan was brought in off the battlefield but don't give up hoping Lily. Never do that."

Lily felt ashamed of herself because although she hadn't said it to anyone, she had virtually given up hope of ever seeing Alex again. If Helen who had lost so much could be so optimistic, then it was Lily's duty to try and do the same.

"Thank you, Helen. I mean that." Lily smiled though tears weren't far away. "I was losing him. Terrible as it might sound there have been some days when I haven't been able to remember his voice. Your Alan has made him seem real again to me."

"I'm glad I could help but don't feel too guilty Lily. Alan was supposed to be the love of my life, and some days I can't even remember the colour of his eyes. I think it's a kind of protection mechanism. A bit like after you've had a baby you swear, you'll never go through that again but then time passes and blurs the edges of how you felt at the time. Not that I've had personal experience you understand." Lily had to smile at the slightly indignant tone of Helen.

"I never thought you had so don't worry I'm not going to give you a reputation as a scarlet woman.

"You'd better not Miss Armitage, or I'll have your guts for garters." Helen tried to remain indignant, but it wasn't working, and both young women collapsed in tears of laughter. Well, that's what they both convinced themselves of after.

The two of them chatted for another half an hour putting the world to rights. When Lily came away, she felt she'd known Helen for years, and she was convinced that she had made a true friend. Lizzy would always be her closest friend, partly because of what they had both been through together, but Helen was more of an age with Lily. Lily also suspected that Helen had a wicked sense of humour and could be thoroughly good for her.

She woke up the next morning feeling refreshed. She knew that after settling Allie off she had cried, but they had been healthy tears that she had kept battened down inside her for far too long. The tears hadn't just been about Alex but also about her father and the rift that now seemed to exist with James. However, Lily knew there was little she could do about any of it, at least at this moment in time, so she determined to concentrate her efforts on doing the best she could for Allie, her friends and the soldiers in their care. She knew she could do all that well, especially now harbouring a flicker of hope that Alex might be out there somewhere.

As she walked into Lizzy's former massive sitting room that had now become a temporary ward, she smiled at Helen who was busy tending to one of the latest arrivals

"Come over and let me introduce you to Officer Wade. A right handful he is, I'll tell you." Helen laughed giving the handsome young man an all too obvious wink. The young man in question looked amused but also slightly embarrassed, and Lily couldn't really imagine him giving anyone the run-around.

"Forgive my friend," Lily said pulling up a chair opposite to the man's, "but I think she had one too many last night, and it's quite gone to her head."

"I beg your pardon," Helen protested, "but I could drink you under the table anytime."

A smile lit up the man's grey-blue eyes which a moment before had seemed full of sadness. Helen gently squeezed Lily's shoulder and whispered.

"I'll leave you two together for a while if that's alright while I get on with a few jobs. I'll be back soon."

Lily smiled at the man who had watched the interaction between the two of them with interest and stuck out her hand.

"I'm Lily. Lily Armitage."

"Charles. Charles Wade, "her companion returned the gesture, "though actually, I prefer Charlie. That's what all my friends call me, but Charles seems to sit better with my superiors and my rapidly accelerated rise to authority."

"Charlie it is then, but if you don't mind my saying, so you don't seem too enamoured of your rank."

"Oh, don't get me wrong. My parents always had me earmarked for the army, so I guess they're proud and I saw myself taking this route. It's just I haven't exactly earned this meteoric rise up the ranks. I've just acquired it on the strength of those it was meant for going and getting themselves killed." Lily heard the depression in Charlie's voice and couldn't blame him but also felt sure he was an excellent officer.

"I get your point. I do. Being given something is never as satisfying as working towards it and achieving it that way, but my fiancé is an officer and got to it the same way as you did. It doesn't mean that you both don't deserve it. You have to be recognised as the right person for the privilege even in these troubled times."

"Not that it's going to matter much with this." Charlie pulled a face as he flapped his empty left trouser leg back and forth. "Can't see me hopping into battle, can you? Unless of course, they're going to use me tactically. As a surprise element, you know. Stun the Germans into astonishment for a few moments while we gain the advantage."

Lily had to laugh. Black humour had become a way of life for people dealing with what before might have seemed unimaginable.

"What did you do before all this craziness came crashing down on our heads?" Lily was genuinely interested. It was clear to her that Charlie was a gentleman of some breeding from his accent and the way he carried and conducted himself. He didn't come across as thinking himself superior at all though. Entirely the opposite was true if anything. Lily couldn't ignore the sudden passion that had come into his eyes.

"I was a teacher for my sins. My charges were mainly young men in their teens whom I tried to imbibe with a sense of responsibility and a love of learning. Why I bothered I don't know. I should imagine some of the poor little sods have become casualties of the Great War of ours. An inappropriate name for it if you ask me, Lily. There's nothing great about it whatsoever.

The two of them sat in comfortable silence for a few minutes admiring the view from the large picture window that let so much light into the room.

"My Alex was a teacher." Lily was the first of them to break the quiet. "He cared deeply about his pupils just as you do."

"Literature was and still is my great love." Charlie pushed a stray lock of ash blond hair back from out of his eyes.

"I loved to see the light go on in a young person's face when they really got to understand a character and began to empathise with them."

"It's what drew Alex and me together in the first place. He would lend me books, and then we'd discuss them afterwards." Lily was intrigued to find such a like-minded soul in such an unusual set of circumstances.

Helen appeared in the doorway ready to give Charlie his medications and settle him in for the evening but quietly withdrew when she saw the animation on both her friend's faces. Lily and Charlie talked until the sky started to take on inky indigo. Neither of them seemed to notice the bustle of the ward going on around them. They were in an in-depth discussion about J.M. Barrie's "Peter and Wendy" and Barrie's seemingly ambivalent attitude towards women and childhood and adulthood when they realised what time it was.

"Well, my young friend I can't remember an evening that I have enjoyed quite so much- at least not recently.

"Oh dear, Mr Wade," Lily laughed as she pointedly looked around her, "we really must get you out more. Seriously though Charlie I have to go." Lily was a little worried about what Allie had been doing all this time, but she knew that her daughter had an army of clucky women on hand to attend to her every need. Lily really would have to put her foot down with them but reasoned that a little spoiling couldn't possibly harm Allie at such a young age.

"I think it's time for me to hit the hay as well."

"You'll be out like a light I guarantee you but let's do this again soon. It makes a change from all the baby talk I sometimes feel myself drowning in."

Charlie gently inclined his head.

"It would be my pleasure as it doesn't look as though I'm going anywhere just yet. As long as your Alex doesn't get the idea that I'm snaffling his woman while he's otherwise engaged."

"To tell you the truth, Charlie. I wish I had got the opportunity to test his reaction on me spending the whole evening with another man, but I have no idea where he is anymore. From what I've gleaned from Helen I don't think the rest of his regiment know either."

"What regiment would that be?" Charlie looked interested again, and tiredness had seemed to take a back seat for the moment.

"The Sherwood Foresters," Lily replied.

"Well, it's true that we have gone through the wringer and we've had a little more than King John or Robin to contend with."

"We?" Lily gave Charlie a puzzled look.

"The Foresters were my regiment as well Lily. If your fellow's name is Poynton, which seems likely from what you've told me, the last time I saw him he was certainly alive and kicking."

Lily felt a hand gently touch her shoulder and time seemed to stand still as Lily and Helen sat in the fading light as Charlie talked about the Battle of Passchendaele and all that had gone wrong before he was wounded.

Lily heard the emotion in Charles's voice for this was Charles the officer speaking, back in the thick of it. He talked about the unexpected weather coming upon them and the heavens opening with the low cloud stopping the British planes from pinpointing German strong points. Horses and tanks got stuck in the unforgiving mud and men drowned as water rapidly filled the shell holes.

Lily had believed Alex to be in France never mind Belgium, but at the end of the night, she knew that he had survived that day at least. Charles had been left for dead on the battlefield, but he was confident that Alex, along with several others, had been taken as prisoners of war and had been destined for one of the detention camps.

As she lay in her narrow bed later that night, Lily felt that she should have been horrified by what was going on across the water. And of course, she was but, in a world, where the fragility of life had become even more apparent the knowledge that Alex had been seen alive gave her renewed hope. She drifted off to sleep with a small smile on her face with Alex's voice resounding firmly in her head.

CHAPTER THIRTY-THREE

June 1916

Next morning Lily felt a little more sombre. It had been late before she'd fallen asleep even though she had drunk a little more than was good for her. She'd heard stories from other men in the hospital about the harsh regime in the detention camps, and she knew that many men died from malnutrition and worse. She and her mum were also worried about James. Even though so much was still unresolved between them all Lily truly believed that he wouldn't be cruel enough not to let them know he was alright if he could.
"You look tired, love. Rough night with Allie?" Ethel remarked as her daughter came downstairs a little later than usual.
"I don't think I did sleep that well, Mum, but don't worry. It was nothing to do with Allie. She was good as gold." Lily marvelled every day at what a placid, happy baby Allie had developed into. The worry and trauma Lily had experienced when pregnant with her obviously hadn't translated itself to Allie. Lily reflected on what Alex would think of his daughter and then chastised herself for harbouring false hope.
In many ways, Lily felt more desperate than ever. Before her two new friend's revelations, she had got herself into the mindset of just taking each day as it came. Lily had Allie and the hospital to focus on and she'd almost successfully learnt to compartmentalise her thoughts to just deal with the

here and now. She hadn't yet said anything to Ethel. She had enough to worry about with James and Lily had a nagging feeling that something must be wrong, not having heard from him for so long.

She'd often thought how she would have reacted if she had found out that Bert wasn't her natural father. To say they hadn't always seen eye to eye was an understatement, but she knew that they had grown closer in the last year or so of his life for which she would forever be grateful for. Lily understood him even more in the light of the revelations that had followed his death. There were lots of missed opportunities to be more like a daughter to him which she would always regret, but she knew that she loved her dad. How could James ever say that about Henry when Bert had been his father in every other way that mattered?

Lily spent most of the morning at the hospital carrying out mundane tasks that needed little thought, and that suited her just fine. She felt as though her head was about to explode with unanswered questions and worries and there was no room for anything else.

"If you don't mind me saying so, my dear, you look a little under the weather this morning," Lizzy commented as she struggled past with a mountain of freshly washed snow-white sheets in her arms.

"For goodness sake, Lizzy, I'm fine. Why is everybody so interested in my state of health suddenly? Haven't you got more important things to worry about?" Lily immediately regretted being so sharp and felt herself flushing.

"Lizzy. I'm sorry," she apologised. Lizzy remained her greatest friend and Lily was ashamed for taking her frustrations out on her. Lizzy unceremoniously dumped the bundle she was labouring with on the bed beside her.

"Remember, my dear, I have got broad shoulders. It's all water off a duck's back to me and what are friends for if not to shout at when you're having a bad day. We all have them." Lily smiled gratefully at her friend.

"I'll tell you, Lizzy, but I'm not quite ready yet. I need time to think it through for myself first." Lizzy gave Lily a brief hug.

"Child, I'm here when you need me but don't leave it too long and remember a problem shared is a problem halved and all that."

"Thank you, Lizzy. I don't deserve you."

"Few do, my dear. Few do, but most don't get a choice." Lily laughed and felt the weight momentarily lift away from her.

"That's so true, and I thank God for it. That's something that he has got right if nothing else."

"Now, now, Miss Armitage. Don't go giving up on him upstairs that easily. You never know he might come through yet."

"I think it's you that will be knocking on the pearly gates begging St Peter to let you in when the time comes if you carry on like this," Lily protested. Lizzy gave Lily a surreptitious wink.

"On that note, my dear, I'd better get these sheets to where they are needed. It might gain me some points to make up for my blasphemous past." Lizzy struggled to pick up her huge bundle again.

"No, you're right." Lily said, "There's no rest for the wicked though but let's try and catch up later. We don't seem to have spent five minutes together recently."

"You're too much in demand. That's your problem. When are you seeing Henry again anyway?" Lizzy shouted back from halfway down the room. Lily ran rapidly to her friend's side despite the no running rule in operation on the ward.

"Lizzy, please keep your voice down and what do you mean anyway?" Her meetings with Henry were something that she hadn't told anybody about. She knew Henry to be so different now but couldn't cope with the questions and raised eyebrows it would cause if it became common knowledge.

"He was here this morning. Asking for you. Helen was supposed to tell you but seeing as you've got a face like a goldfish out of water it looks as though she didn't. She's got a head like a sieve that girl." Lily could feel herself becoming hotter by the minute.

"Here! This morning?" She could feel her voice going up an octave as it always did when she was stressed.

"Mum didn't see him, did she?" God forbid if she had and what on earth was Henry thinking? Plainly, he could see the trouble it would cause.

"Calm down, Lily, please. He came in when Ethel was out in town with Allie. He probably watched until they were safely out of the way and your secret's safe with me,"

"It isn't a secret. He's simply a friend, but I just hadn't got around to mentioning meeting up with him again." Lily felt herself getting tied up in knots and felt guilty even though she hadn't really done anything wrong.

Lizzy sighed and looked Lily in the eyes.

"Look, Lily. I'm the last one to judge, but I do seriously think that you need to take the afternoon off. You look as though you're going to explode. Don't worry about Allie. You know she'll be looked after. Take some time for yourself." Lily would usually have set up some protest but felt that her friend might very well be right. If nothing else she had to try and get to Henry before he turned up at the hospital again. Her mother couldn't take anymore worry, and Lily knew what she had to do, but she just needed a little breathing space first.

Lily took deep breaths of the late afternoon fresh air. It was sunny today, but it was proving to be a wet June, and the river was flowing in full spate. Lily couldn't remember when she had started the habit of walking on its banks when she needed time to think. She did know that its ongoing perpetual course seemed to calm her. The river wasn't always the same. It changed with the weather and the seasons. It wasn't even dependable and sometimes wildly unpredictable, but it had become Lily's place, and she was grateful for its presence.

The afternoon was unseasonably chilly, but Lily didn't really notice apart from subconsciously wrapping her shawl a little tighter around her shoulders. It was hard to see ahead as she was walking with the sunlight directly in her eyes, but she didn't really need to see to know that the dim silhouette in the distance was him. Lily could have pretended to herself that it was a coincidence and that when she set out on her walk, that's what it was – merely a stroll to clear her head. She comforted herself with the thought that this was partially true, but of course she knew that it was likely that Henry would be there. Like her, the river gave him peace and walking its banks gave him the physical exercise he needed to further his chances of remaining well.

Henry raised his hand in a half greeting and then dropped it and began striding purposefully towards her. Lily felt her heart begin to beat faster and for some inexplicable reason, she felt momentarily afraid. Flashes of the alley came back to her, and she turned on her heel and began to rapidly walk the other direction back towards town. Lily willed herself not to turn back because she wasn't at all sure what she was going to say or do now she was faced with the immediate situation. Maybe Henry would think she hadn't seen him and drop back. He'd been to the hospital though looking for her. Lily knew that something had changed, and it was that more than anything that frightened her. She couldn't hope to outrun him and how ridiculous that would look anyway. She took a deep breath and turned to face him as he came up almost level with her.

"Lily! Wait! Didn't you see me? What's the matter? Are you late for something?" Henry's face was a picture of puzzlement and Lily couldn't blame him. She had been acting completely irrationally, and she could feel herself beginning to redden.

"I'm sorry Henry. It was the sun dazzling me I think, and then I realised I hadn't left instructions for Allie's feed." She could hear herself gabbling but seemed unable to stop.

"I'm sure she'll be alright, Lily. After all, it's not the first time family and friends have been left to look after her."

"What are you implying now, Henry? That I'm a neglectful mother!"

Even during her ire Lily couldn't fail to see the hurt on Henry's face and wondered what was wrong with her though deep down she knew.

"Lily, my dear. You've got it all wrong. I think you are a brave and wonderful mother to Allie. I just don't like to see you so busy with everybody else that you have no time for yourself. You run yourself ragged at that hospital."

"I'm just doing my duty like everyone has to in these horrible times. Is that so wrong?" Lily knew that she needed to keep some of her anger to prevent the tears that weren't very far away from falling.

Henry tentatively took her arm and guided her to the nearest bench pressing her down gently and then sitting beside her.

"Oh dear, this isn't how it was meant to go at all. I've never been very good at this sort of thing."

"At what sort of thing, Henry? I don't really know what we are doing here, and I don't know what you were doing at the hospital earlier. Suppose my mother had seen you?"

"Would that really have been so bad, Lily? Does she hate me so much still? I wouldn't blame her, but the man I am now would never have taken her away from her husband no matter what the circumstances. You do believe me, don't you, Lily?"

Lily could tell by Henry's fervent tone that he at least thought that he meant it.

"I don't think she thinks about you much at all anymore, Henry. It's all in the past." If Jamie never came home again, it indeed could be. Whatever was ahead though Lily knew this was the last thing she wanted to happen.

"It is Lily, and I'm glad everybody sees it that way because it's time to move on. I can't and shouldn't be punished for my sins forever."

Lily did agree with this. Few of us she reflected led a pure life in thought and deed, and she didn't believe a person should be judged purely on their mistakes. She almost smiled as she remembered her and Lizzie's conversation from earlier. If we were all judged by our past actions, Lily thought that the kingdom of heaven would be a very lonely place.

"You're right Henry, and you have been a good friend to me. I'm not that naïve girl you used to know anymore, and I'm not stupid enough to think that there is a knight on a white charger around every street corner."

"Maybe just one or two?" Henry smiled looking a little ashamed.

"Maybe," Lily replied smiling a little, "but we can't carry on like this Henry. It's got to stop."

"You're so right, Lily. It does."

Even though it was what Lily wanted or at least saw as the only path open to them, she was a little disappointed that Henry had given in without more of a fight. Whatever it was or wasn't between them they had spent many hours together since Henry's discharge from the Army. In some ways, she felt she'd opened up to Henry even more than Alex, especially about her grandmother's abuse of her father and how it still haunted her. She didn't really believe that herself or Allie could ever be capable of such an act but maybe her Granny Armitage in her earlier years had a softer side. She'd brushed over the subject with Alex, but he found it difficult to see the evil in anybody. His kind, gentle nature had been one of the reasons why Lily had been attracted to Alex in the first place, but at times it infuriated her. She felt that Henry understood far better the dark places people can travel to when they are pushed to the edge.

Lily dragged her thoughts back to the man standing in front of her. She would really miss their walks and talks but knew that she had been lucky not to have been branded a scarlet woman so far. Her friends and neighbours had been surprisingly understanding when Allie came into the world. Lizzy had admitted that women who had children out of wedlock in London were treated harshly. One young pregnant single woman she knew had moved to another town where nobody knew her to escape the stigmatism. Lily reasoned that northern women maybe had their heads screwed on a little tighter but even Derby women had their limits. It was her duty to focus on Allie and the work she was doing at the hospital and not be fraternising with single men on the riverbank.

"I'm so glad that you see it like that, Henry. It has to be for the best doesn't it?"

"Lily please stop talking for a few minutes and listen then if you want to walk away you can, and we'll never cross paths again." Lily resigned herself to another ten minutes. After all, perhaps she owed Henry that much. She felt sorry for him that it had come to this as she knew that since returning from the war, he hadn't made many friends. Being in and out of the hospital and battling a potentially terminal illness had made it a lonely time for him but he'd gained so much strength since she'd first set eyes on him again. She felt sure that he would pull through now.

"It can't come as a great shock to you when I tell you how important our meetings have become to me. When I saw you here on that first day, I was afraid of how you would react to me. I was so ashamed of my behaviour towards you and your mother, and I'll always have it on my conscience.

"Henry. Truly it doesn't matter anymore. We've talked about that. It wasn't you that day but your illness turning you into something you're not."

"Maybe, Lily, but it still doesn't make it right, but I can try and make it up to you as best as I can."

Lily couldn't help but feel confused. They'd already talked about the past, and she thought each of them had found a way to come to terms with it.

"What do you mean, Henry? It's been a long week. I'm tired, and I'm not really following you."

Henry took her hand, and Lily couldn't but help feel a rising panic.

"My dear. You must know how I feel. I'm in love with you Lily."

Lily felt as if everything around her had slowed right down and she was in the middle of a bad dream.

"Oh, nothing like before." Henry was quick to continue as he noticed the incredulity on her face. "If truth be told that was probably more lust than love and maybe a part of me thought that I'd had the mother and now there's the possibility I could have the daughter. Please don't look so shocked my love. I only say that to show you how much I have changed. I'm not that arrogant yet insecure fool who thought that any woman who looked his way was there for the taking. I really love you, Lily and wondered if you would do me the great honour of becoming my wife?"

Lily could feel the familiar yet unwelcome feeling of uncontrollable laughter bubbling up inside her. Mrs Poynton or Mrs Ingram! Now which slipped best off the tongue? Lily swallowed hard to quell the hysteria, rose from the bench and glanced briefly at Henry. Gathering up her bag and shawl she turned her back on him and began to walk steadily back to town without saying a word.

CHAPTER THIRTY-FOUR

Spring 1917

Lily didn't go back to the river again for many months and was grateful to Henry that he didn't try to track her down. It became a particularly difficult period. Lily felt in a complete quandary over so many things and couldn't seem to think back to a time when her life had been remotely settled. She knew that her mother and Lizzy were worried about her, but Ethel had her distractions, and Lizzy was so busy at the hospital that they let Lily be.

There had still been no news of James, and the initial euphoria of discovery that Alex might still be alive had dissipated with time and Lily was no closer to knowing whether he was alive or dead. Lily's days seemed to pass in a haze of routine, and she flung herself into caring for Allie and the soldiers in her care. If nothing else, they could all work to give the poor men, who had given so much for their country, some hope for the future.

Lily found herself increasingly drawn into the company of Charlie or maybe it was Charlie who was instigating their conversations. Either way Lily found herself sitting with him on a regular basis as she either tended to his wounds or just enjoyed his company in one of her few tea breaks from the drudgery of hospital routine. Lily felt as though he was the only one who could really make her understand what Alex might be going through.

Yet as she listened to his stories from the Front Lily again began to lose hope. Even if Alex were in one of the camps how could he possibly be in any fit condition to survive its rigours? She again began to realise that she might very well have to face the idea that he was no longer in this world.
In the dead of night when the silence threatened to deafen her, she even thought about accepting Henry's proposal. Allie needed a father so why not keep it in the family? Ethel remained adamant that Henry wasn't going to find out that he had a son, but Lily was doubtful that it could stay a secret for always.
The year dragged inexorably from one grey day to another. Even Allie seemed to pick up on the melancholy mood in the house and became more restless often waking in the middle of the night and refusing to be lulled back into sleep. Ethel looked like a shadow of her former self and admitted that she thought it unlikely James was going to turn up alive. Lily tried to be positive but couldn't hide the emptiness in her eyes. Lizzy worried that both had reached the end of the incredible strength they had shown throughout the whole conflict.
The only time Ethel brightened slightly was when Roy popped round to see how they were doing. Lily no longer saw him as a threat. She saw that he was a good man and how could anyone threaten a dead man. Lily felt that she was becoming harder and some days felt utterly devoid of emotion. Maybe this was how Granny Armitage had felt when she sidled along the landing to her son's room in the dead of night. After all naughty children needed to be taught a lesson.
At times Lily's thoughts became so jumbled that Henry's voice and Alex's face seemed to become one person though she wasn't sure what they were asking her to do. Lily now knew that this war wasn't going to end. This was her

"forever." It wasn't so bad. She wasn't in any pain but just wished that the voices in her head would stop. They annoyed her because she could never hear what they were saying, and she hated people who kept secrets.

"Thank goodness. At last, she's settled." Ethel glanced across at Lizzy who for the last two nights had stayed with her while Lily seemingly drifted in and out of conscious thought. The two women had become fast friends and gave extra strength to each other.

"Don't worry." Lizzy gently patted Ethel's left hand. "The doctor said that she's exhausted and this sleeping is just what she needs."

"I feel so bad though, Lizzy. I'm her mother. I saw her breaking down in front of my eyes but couldn't find the words to comfort her."

The two women sat quietly. They were comfortable in each other's company and didn't feel the need to fill every waking moment with incessant chatter. Lily had told Lizzy almost everything a few days after leaving Henry permanently stranded on the riverbank. With the onset of Lily's illness, Lizzy had confided in Ethel and had been amazed at the magnanimity of Ethel's reaction. Lizzy loved Lily but at that moment realised that in the usual way of things a mother's love for her child was all-encompassing. Lizzy felt a little sad as she understood that it was now highly improbable that it was a love that she would experience. That night she had got down on her hands and knees and prayed a little uncomfortably to a God that she wasn't sure existed. It wasn't for herself she prayed or even for Lily but for the woman she had finally left earlier that evening. A fierce lioness defending her cubs to the bitter end.

A week later in early March, Spring decided to make a brief appearance. Lily though still weak was sitting in a faded armchair across from where her dad used to sit by the hearth. Ethel smiled across at her as she busied herself making a meat and potato pie though it was mostly potato if the truth be told. Though Lily still looked tired, there was colour in her cheeks, and she smiled back at her mum. Lily knew that she'd been ill but couldn't remember much about it. Just a memory of distorted images and whispers that didn't seem to make any sense. A knock at the door brought her quickly back to the present as her mother wiped her hands on her apron and went to answer it.

"Now who can that be? If it's Roy, he can come back later when I haven't got flour on my hands, and I'm not sweating like a pig." Lily vaguely remembered a conversation from many moons ago between her mum and dad about pigs not having the ability to sweat and laughed softly. How sweet and straightforward their life really had been then if they could all have only appreciated it.

Lily really hoped that this wasn't more visitors. They did mean well though Lily suspected that some of them came more out of curiosity than kindness. She could imagine the talk there would have been on the streets.

"Have you heard about the Armitage girl? She's not very well you know?"

"Gone mad so I believe."

"Well it runs in the family, so they say."

Lizzy had regaled some of the stories that were being bandied around on the street in her usual witty, sarcastic tone and had made them all cry with laughter. Too much water had gone under the bridge for any of them to care excessively anymore what anyone else thought. Lizzy was the only person Lily really welcomed now but knew that it wouldn't be her as she had gone back to London for a few days to tie up some loose ends concerning her property down there. Lily was still not sure why Lizzy had suddenly decided to sell up and come back to Derby. She suspected that it was more than her just missing the people and the place, but she knew Lizzy would tell her when she was ready.

So, both herself and Ethel were surprised to see their friend sweep into the little kitchen both breathless and hatless. If nothing else Lizzy liked to keep up appearances and it was the fact that she was hatless that worried Lily more than anything else. Lily had not seen her friend so agitated for a long time. Her first thought was that Lizzy had been attacked, but there was no sign of any physical injury. Ethel closed the door to keep the cold out and looked as confused as Lily felt. Lizzy gradually registered their concern and seemed to calm down a little.

"I'm so sorry my dears for barging in like a wailing banshee. I can see that you both think that I have lost my mind completely and you could indeed be right, but I needed to come and speak with you both straightaway." Lily felt a mixture of intrigue and alarm as to what had possessed Lizzy to come rushing back from London post-haste.

"I'll get you a brew, Lizzy." Ethel fell back on her natural resource in times of uncertainty or crisis.

"Oh yes, Ethel. I'd love one in a bit, but I need you to come and sit down with Lily while I tell you something."

Ethel looked a little apprehensive but dragged one of the wooden chairs from beneath the table and made Lizzy sit down while she took a seat opposite. Lizzy seemed to gather herself before she spoke.

"Now I don't want you to get your hopes up only to have them dashed down again, but I'm hoping there's going to be some good news for both of you down in London. I'm almost afraid to speak the words in case I'm wrong and I thought about keeping it to myself for now, but I just can't keep something like this from either of you."

Lily thought that Lizzy looked quite nauseous but at the same time flushed with an almost maniacal look of excitement. She sincerely hoped that her friend wasn't going to be another casualty of a fragile mental state. Her poor mother had put up with enough. Ethel took Lizzy's hands between hers and Lily saw that both women were trembling as they considered each other's eyes.

"Tell us, Lizzy. Just say the words." At that moment Lily almost felt as if she had been forgotten. The silence seemed to go on forever though it couldn't have been more than a few seconds.

"It's James, Ethel my dear. I think it's very probable that he's alive and I know where he is." Lily felt like a child might feel on Christmas Day when they'd been willing Father Christmas to bring them that new bike, they'd seen in Kennedy's window a few weeks ago. They look at the package before them. It looks suspiciously like a bike, but they know their parents aren't very well off and they don't really expect it. They tear the wrapping away with trembling fingers, and it's not until they can see it, they can believe. Lily didn't feel euphoric but scared, and Ethel had never looked so pale. Even when they had learnt of Bert's death, Lily wasn't sure that she had looked as white as she did now. They had waited so long for news of either of their men that when it came, they weren't sure what to do with it.

"I know this has been a shock" Lizzy continued." What a stupid thing to say. Of course, it's been a shock, but I couldn't keep it to myself until I was entirely sure. For one thing, they won't let me in as I'm not family, so I had to ask around before I was confident enough to face you two."

"Wouldn't let you in where Lizzy? Just calm down and then maybe you'd better start from the beginning." Lily felt some strength returning to her bones as she took charge of the situation. Lizzy took a deep breath and continued.

"Well last night after I'd got into London, I had to walk along Harrow Road…"

"What on earth were you doing there?" Lily was horrified at the danger her friend put herself into from time to time. "It's supposed to be infected with more venereal disease than any other district in London isn't it?"

"The things you do know my dear never ceases to surprise me." Lily couldn't help but smile as she saw the friend she knew gradually returning.

"Oh, Charles and I talk about all sorts of things. You could say he's a man of experience." Lily lifted an eyebrow, and Lizzy laughed out loud which seemed to jolt Ethel back to some awareness of what was going on around her.

"Suffice it to say that I wasn't on my own but walking with one of the junior doctors who was on his way to visit the patients at the Paddington Military Hospital. Philip and I got to know a variety of people in the time we were down there, and I wanted to visit the hospital to see if I could get any insights into the best way to go about things for our soldiers. It's a terrible place really, Lily. It was a workhouse, and the injured men have to clamber up and down inconvenient and narrow staircases to get anywhere but the commitment of the doctors and nurses is second to none."

"James is there isn't he, Lizzy?" Ethel's voice made Lily jump. She had almost forgotten her mum was there, so intent had she been on hanging on to Lizzy's every word.

"I think he is, my dear. I really think he is, but they wouldn't let me see him. Something about not being a relative and the soldiers who have recently been brought in are kept away from virtually anybody."

"How do you know it's him then, Lizzy?" Lily was trying to maintain a level head, but her heart was racing.

"My young gentleman friend told me they'd recently had a new admission who had really lifted both the patients and the staff with his humour and positivity. Talk got around to his family, and he told this doctor that he came from Derby and that he had a sister called Lily and that he had not so long ago fallen out with his mum. Sound familiar?"

"Why haven't they contacted us though? I don't understand." Ethel sounded as vulnerable as Lily had ever heard her.

"Well, for one thing, my dear he hasn't been there that long, and all these things take time. The machinations of war are often slow to unfold. The other reason is that he said he didn't want anyone to contact his family and James has got the right to say that, especially after what he must have been through."

"It's my fault. I should never have told my poor boy about his father." Lizzy looked more than puzzled, and Lily realised that was one of the few things she hadn't told her friend not thinking it was her place to do so.

"I'm not completely sure it's that mum," Lily tried to console Ethel. "He's not one to normally hold a grudge for long, even one as big as this."

"Well I must admit I'm a bit lost but no matter, "Lizzy continued, "but one thing you need to know and I'm so sorry I have to be the one to do it, but all the soldiers who enter Paddington do so because they have lost a limb or limbs."

"We have to get to him, Lily. We have to get to my boy." Lily opened her arms to her mother who came to them as though she were the child. Lily held her as tightly as her slowly returning strength would allow. As Ethel knelt with her head in Lily's lap both of their bodies rocked back and forth as they were wracked with silent sobs while their friend sat beside them with tears unashamedly running unchecked down her face.

CHAPTER THIRTY-FIVE

April 1917

In any other circumstance, Lily would have enjoyed the trip to London. She had only been once before with Henry and had found it to be a thoroughly exciting city. As it was, Lily still felt weak and tired, and the passing scenery was a blur. She thanked the Lord that Lizzy was at her side, capable and commanding as always.
After the initial euphoria of James almost definitely being alive, both Lily and Ethel had been unsure of how to proceed. Ethel's first instinct had been to rush down to London straightaway and demand to see her son. By then Lizzy had been told of James's parentage taking it all in her stride.
When the dust had settled, Lizzy had reminded them of James's wish to see nobody from the family.
"He's hurting, Ethel." Lizzy spoke to her new-found friend one night after Lily had turned in." His whole life has been thrown into turmoil, and it's going to take some time. He's now got to heal physically as well as mentally."
"Don't you think that I don't know that, Lizzy? I know it's all my fault and I feel such shame."
"But then if it hadn't have happened, my dear, James would never have existed. You wouldn't have had a wonderful son and Lily a devoted brother."
Ethel had pushed the hair out of her eyes. She was just so tired, but she also knew that the experiences of the last few

years had made her stronger and with that strength had come a more pragmatic way of dealing with problems.

"It will have to be Lily that goes, won't it? I don't want to ask it of her, but he's more likely to agree to see his sister than me. He must be so angry at me, Lizzy."

Lizzy could have denied it, but the war and this family had survived too many lies already.

"Maybe he is, but he's in pain, and he eventually needs to come home and maybe Lily is our best chance at bringing him back."

As Lily watched the scenery rushing past without really seeing it at all she remained afraid that James wouldn't agree to see her. Both shared a stubborn streak, and she knew that in the past they had both cut off their nose to spite their face. Lizzy glanced across at her friend every now and again but sensed that this was a time to be quiet and she had plenty to occupy her thoughts as well. So, lost in their own worlds they both were that they seemed surprised to soon be standing where Lizzy had stood just a few short days ago. The whole area felt oppressive to Lily. She didn't see how it could possibly promote any sense of wellbeing among the convalescing partially disabled young men who frequented its environs. Their own little hospital on the edge of Derby with its far-reaching views over the surrounding fields seemed a far more appropriate place to set men on the road to recovery.

As they approached the hospital buildings, it all appeared very grey and imposing. Lily's heart sank even further. She wasn't sure how they were going to get into the place let alone get to see her brother. She had made the rare mistake though of forgetting Lizzy's influence. It was clear before they even got to the building that Lizzy was a familiar figure to the men on the street with an occasional greeting here and an odd nod there. Not for the first time and it wouldn't be the last Lily wondered precisely what Lizzy and Philip's business had been in London. Though Lily hadn't really realised it until after his death Philip had been a very wealthy man.

Without again really registering how they had got there Lily found herself in a small reception area. She still felt as though she was in a dream and events were happening to her with little input from herself. A formidable looking lady, who could have been Lizzy's twin, sat behind a massive oak desk that took up most of the space in the tiny area. For a moment Lily was taken back to her first day at Crown Derby and her first encounter with the indomitable Miss Hardcastle. Lizzy, however, seemed entirely comfortable with the receptionist and it wasn't long before a relatively young attractive but tired looking gentleman came to speak with them. He straightaway took Lizzy's hands in his and gave them both a kind look.

"It's good to see you again Miss Hardcastle. You're always very welcome especially when you bring along such a charming young companion as well." Lily couldn't help but smile back. Even though she felt as though she could hardly breathe for anxiety the young doctor had a natural warmth about him that immediately made her feel a little better.

"Lily let me introduce you to Dr Bennett. He's been the one principally in charge of James's care though of course with me not being a direct family member I haven't been privy to what care is needed and…"

Dr Bennett looked a little flustered at Lizzy's little outburst, and Lily smiled sympathetically at him.

"You know that I would have told you if I could Miss Hardcastle, but rules are rules."

"Rules are meant to be broken when they don't make sense, but I apologise. You have to understand how frustrating this has been for us all."

"Of course. No apology needed and please call me Andrew. Apart from a few rules that I'm afraid do make sense to me there are few formalities here, and we all muck in together and do what we can."

"Sounds familiar." Lily directed her remark at Lizzy and Andrew laughed. He was enjoying himself immensely in the presence of two such obviously intelligent ladies who were certainly not afraid to voice an opinion. He just wished that he had better news for the people who ended up on his doorstep though maybe knowing their loved one was at least alive was good news enough.

"To get to the point which I'm sure both of you ladies would appreciate rather than going all around the houses to get to the same result is that James won't see you. He's made it quite adamant and much as I think he might be wrong, especially in this instance, I have to remain loyal to my patient."

Lily felt overwhelmed with despair and tiredness though Lizzy took it all on the chin.

"I told you, my dear. James needs time and maybe we shouldn't have come rushing down the country at the drop of a hat. He did make his wishes clear beforehand. We can't blame James that we ignored them. Lily could feel her lip tremble. She was much recovered but still far from well, and she'd really thought that if they'd literally turned up on his doorstep, James would change his mind.

"Maybe if you find some accommodation and give him a few days then he might come around. He's been through a lot, and you could always do a bit of sightseeing." Andrew ventured.

"I agree, "Lizzy said, "but I don't think that Lily feels that she can leave her mother or daughter for so long though I'd be happy to hold the fort."

"I don't expect you to do that. Thank you, Dr Bennett, Andrew. There's nothing more that you can do but thank you very much for seeing us at such short notice."

"The pleasure was all mine. I assure you, and I very much hope that we will see you again soon. Now if you excuse me, I will have to get back to the fray."

As they watched him rapidly recede into the distance, Lizzy gave Lily that distinctive look. The look that only close friends would recognise and which said," I know you're up to something."

"Well, Miss Armitage I know that you wouldn't have given up without a fight. So, what's the plan and is it legal?" Lily fixed Lizzy with her startling blue eyes, and Lizzy could see the light returning to them.

"I'm not going back to Mum without seeing James, but I'll need your help to do it."

"Whatever you need, my dear, I'm at your service."

Thirty minutes later Lily stood before her friend dressed in full nursing regalia. Maybe it would be wise to draw a veil over how this was accomplished. Suffice it to say it involved a member of the nursing staff who Lizzy knew and who would turn a blind eye for a small remuneration of course. A younger Lily and indeed Lizzy may have raised some moral objections to this, but war and personal tragedy had changed both. The young nurse in question had a family of three to feed with no guarantee that her husband would return from the war. Lizzy had enough money to hire the use of her uniform for an hour so that her friend could see her brother. It was a win-win situation all around, and none of them could see any harm in that. Nurse Collins was on her way home anyway, and Lily wasn't going to start performing complicated surgical procedures. The small matter of impersonation they tried to put to the back of their mind.

Lily's heart was beating nineteen to the dozen, but she felt more alive than she had done for a long time. If the situation hadn't been so serious, she would have laughed out loud at their audacity. Now it was all about timing. She heard the chatter as a group of nurses headed their way. Lily waited until they had almost passed, pretending to tie her lace, and at the last minute, she tagged onto the group who were hopefully making their way to the wards. Lily reasoned that in a hospital that could hold up to 300 men at a time the chances were that not all the nurses would know each other by sight. If the worst came to the worst, she could always say she was new.

Luckily, nobody seemed to find anything amiss as the group sailed along the icy cold corridors and traversed the narrow stairs as if it was second nature. Lily had listened to Lizzy's tales of the complexity and impracticality of the building for its present purpose, and she had to agree. Despite the difficulties though or perhaps because of them, there was little sign of depression or downheartedness. Quite a few jokes, some of them quite crude, were directed towards the nurses as they passed but they seemed to take it in good part with a few giving as good as they could get.

As they passed through the wards, Lily was shocked at the severity of some of the injuries she saw. She wondered how some of the men could still be alive never mind yelling lewd comments to the nurses. She did know though, mainly from talking to Charlie, that amputating these soldier's limbs had probably saved their lives by preventing infection from setting in and poisoning the rest of their bodies.

Lily anxiously scanned the rows of beds as they went along. She was not sure of their destination or what she would do once she got there. Maybe she should peel away from the group like one or two of the others already had done but then where she would go? She began to feel hot, and her legs were shaking so badly she thought they would give way at any minute. There could be serious trouble ahead if she was discovered and she wasn't at all sure where Lizzy had ended up.

Lily heard him before she saw him. James had always had a rich baritone laugh out of all proportion to his slim athletic frame. It didn't surprise her that there was quite a group gathered around the bed where he lay half propped up by a mountain of white pillows as he'd always had a natural way with people It was warm in the ward which surprised Lily and his covers were thrown back. Lily sighed with relief as she saw both his legs sticking out of a very unfashionable pair of shorts. She stood rooted to the spot as she gazed upon the brother Lily had doubted, she'd ever see again. He looked both older and thinner but surprisingly healthy considering what he'd been through. Being regularly exposed to the elements had given him a weather-beaten look that suited him, and she wasn't surprised he had a group of nurses around him like bees around a honeypot.

It wasn't until one of his entourage moved slightly to one side that Lily saw what she had mentally been preparing herself for, ever since Lizzy had told them he was alive. James's right arm ended in a stump just above his elbow. It looked incongruous sticking out from the short-sleeved pyjama jacket that he was wearing and seemed to be the uniform of most of the patients there. Lily wasn't horrified by the injury. Charlie hadn't been the only one of their patients to have lost a limb in action. She was horrified though that this had happened to her little brother. Horrified that the world seemed to have lost its way and was sending young, intelligent men, the cream of the crop out to be used as fodder for a war that many people were still confused as to why it had all started.

Lily must have given an involuntary cry as the ward fell silent and several pairs of eyes turned her way. James looked puzzled and then confused. Lily swallowed hard to keep her tears at bay as recognition slowly dawned on James's face. "My God, Sis! Have you changed careers or what?" The people around the bedside dissipated. They sensed that something important was happening and that they weren't really welcome anymore. James held out his left hand to his sister and Lily rushed to his side. He brought his arm around her pulling her down on the bed beside him, and she buried her head in his shoulder. The trembling of her body mixed with his and when they eventually pulled apart tears were glistening in both their eyes.

Their reunion was slightly marred by Matron menacingly charging along the ward with Lizzy hot on her heels. Lily was sure she was going to be thrown into prison for stealing someone's identity, but Lizzy appeared to say something to Matron who seemed to laugh as they both disappeared into a side room. James's face was a picture of perplexity and Lily thought he wouldn't have looked more shocked if he had seen David Lloyd George walking towards them.

The two siblings turned to each other, and their tears turned into tears of laughter, and their bodies shook until they both ached even more. After they had calmed slightly, Lily smiled at her brother and for the first time in so long felt pure joy. The rest of the ward looked at them with sympathy as if they were a little crazy. Perhaps they were, but in a world, that seemed to have temporarily lost its sanity they fitted in just fine.

EPILOGUE

December 24th, 1918.

The day Lily had found her brother again now seemed like a distant memory. It had taken many months of rehabilitation before James was ready to go home. In all that time he had still refused to see Ethel but when he appeared at the door, a week before Christmas 1917, any barriers that remained dissolved at the sight of the mother he had not seen for over a year. Lily had devoted herself to caring for James and Allie, and in November 1918 the nation rejoiced as hostilities ended and the world was again at peace.
It was about half an hour before sunset as Lily closed the door on Ethel and James and emerged onto Peel Street. The two of them still had a lot to work through, but she was confident that they would get there. It wouldn't hurt to leave them in each other's company for an hour. As another Christmas approached, Lily accepted that Alex was dead, and Henry seemed to have disappeared into thin air.
Lily wished him well wherever he was.
Her steps again took her to St Peter's churchyard. Lily found it almost unbelievable that it had been nearly eighteen years since she had sneaked into Granny Armitage's funeral and she didn't understand what drove her to be here again. She was glad she hadn't known her Grandma Armitage, but it saddened Lily when she thought about her grandad. Her mum had always professed that Lily had a lot in common with him yet as she stood in front of his grave all she now

felt was a disappointment and a nagging feel of regret that he would never be able to provide her with any answers. When Lily had stood here before she had been an idealistic young girl desperate to spread her wings and escape her family. Her world had been full of absolutes, but now she realised it consisted of muddy shades of grey with the occasional fleeting rainbow thrown in. Lily held Allie's hand more tightly as it began to rain. It was her duty to give her daughter aspirations in life. By hook or by crook she would open Allie's eyes to the beauty of the world and veer her away from the ugliness and inhumanity that they had just witnessed.

Lily couldn't help feeling angry towards Grandad Jack and struggled with the idea that he hadn't known what evil was perpetrated under his roof. Lily still often woke up at night drenched with sweat, sure that she could hear a little boy's whimpers of humiliation and pain cutting through the night. She turned away from the grave not sure that she would come here again.

"Happy Christmas, Dad," she whispered as she made her way back towards the lych-gate anxious to now be home before the darkness closed in completely. The well-dressed man stood concealed by the trunks of the massive oaks that had stood, across from the elms, like sentinels in the churchyard for centuries. He watched as Lily was swallowed up by the murky evening. He had been keeping Lily in his sight for a while and one day the time would be right to reveal himself, but it wasn't this night. The man turned up his jacket collar against the increasing drizzle and headed in the opposite direction, away from Lilly and Allie. He would see them again soon enough.

Printed in Poland
by Amazon Fulfillment
Poland Sp. z o.o., Wrocław